'Wh... for

themsel... ...att.' CHARLIE HIGSON

'One of those grab 'em by the throat thrillers

that takes off on the first page.' **EOIN COLFER**

'A riveting read – fast-paced from the off and

with breathless action. A perfect haven for young readers!'

CHRIS BRADFORD, AUTHOR OF *YOUNG SAMURAI*

'From the explosive beginning to the heart-stopping end,

The Haven is a thrilling, gripping adventure. Simon Lelic has

created a vivid underworld and a great hero faced by a truly

twisted villain.' **SHANE HEGARTY, AUTHOR OF *DARKMOUTH***

'An action-packed book, rammed full of

adventure and danger. I loved reading this book.'

BELLA RIX-CLANCY, AGE 11, LOVEREADING4KIDS

'*The Haven* is exciting, captivating and unpredictable.

I loved it!' **MADELEINE, AGE 12**

'Lots of unexpected twists, interesting characters

and a thrilling plot. I would definitely recommend this book.'

CHARLIE, AGE 13

'Adventurous, and thrilling.'

HARSH BUDHDEO, AGE 11, LOVEREADING4KIDS

By Simon Lelic:

The Haven

The Haven: Revolution

The Haven: Deadfall

And for adult readers:

The Liar's Room

The House

The Child Who

The Facility

Rupture

THE HAVEN
REVOLUTION

SIMON LELIC

HODDER CHILDREN'S BOOKS

First published in Great Britain in 2019 by Hodder and Stoughton

1 3 5 7 9 10 8 6 4 2

A CIP catalogue record for this book is available from the British Library.

ISBN 978 1 444 94762 5

Typeset in Adobe Garamond by Hewer Text UK Ltd, Edinburgh
Printed and bound in Great Britain by Clays Ltd, Elcograf S.p.A

The paper and board used in this book are made from wood from responsible sources.

MIX
Paper from responsible sources
FSC® C104740

Hodder Children's Books
An imprint of
Hachette Children's Group
Part of Hodder and Stoughton
Carmelite House
50 Victoria Embankment
London EC4Y 0DZ

An Hachette UK Company
www.hachette.co.uk

www.hachettechildrens.co.uk

FOR THE COUSINS:

ELKA, MILO, JAY, HENRY, HARI AND LORNE

PROLOGUE

Errol was already deep into the woods when he heard the monster.

He'd heard rumours of its existence before, of course. Everyone had. It was almost the first thing you learned about when you came to Forest Mount. Most kids pretended not to believe in it (*A monster in the woods? That's kids' stuff, made up by the teachers to scare us into doing what they say*) but Errol knew that everyone did really. He could tell from the way even the older kids peeked out through the dorm windows at night, and jumped at every creaking floorboard and hooting owl.

And now there couldn't be any doubt. Out here, in the dark, all alone, Errol could *feel* that the monster was real. And those were footsteps he'd heard, he was certain. Not human ones, though. Rather, the soft, creeping steps of something that had made the woods its home.

He hurried on, the bobbing torch light at his feet betraying his panic. A tree limb grabbed his backpack and tried to wrench it from him, and after a brief tussle Errol gave it up. There was nothing of any value in the bag anyway. A change of clothes, some rolls stolen from breakfast: nothing worth slowing down for. Everything he treasured – the one thing he treasured, actually: a photograph of his long-lost sister – was in the front pocket of his jeans. If anyone tried to take *that* from him – a demon tree, the monster in the woods, even Colton Crowe, the head pupil and school bully – Errol would have fought back with all the energy he had.

For a moment the thought of his sister gave him courage, and Errol pressed on through the undergrowth with renewed resolve. He would escape. He *would*. And he would find his sister at the place she called the Haven. For days Errol had been planning this, and there was no way he was going to allow himself to fail. Not when he was so close.

In fact he could see it. Could he? The edge of the woods. The shadow of the wall: the final boundary between him and freedom. It was barely twenty, thirty metres ahead.

There was a growl.

Errol stumbled in his fear, almost falling. And then he heard it again. A mean, deep-throated rumble.

He spun, and immediately collided with a tree – one he would have sworn hadn't been there before. The torch he was clutching slipped from his grip. It hit something hard on the forest floor and immediately the beam went out. The only light now came from the moon high above the canopy, which shone down on Errol like a sentry's spotlight.

He started to run.

The school was to his right – even in the dark its looming walls were impossible to miss – and Errol veered until it was once again at his heels.

A snap behind him. Loud. Swiftly followed by another. Whatever was chasing him was big, and it was *fast*.

Suddenly there came another noise off to one side. Rather than the monster this time, it sounded like—

'Quick. We're losing him.'

'Don't worry. He's not getting away. Not if I can help it.'

Prefects.

And unless Errol was imagining it, that second voice belonged to Colton Crowe.

Now the choice was to be eaten by the monster or hauled back to school, no doubt straight to Professor Strain's office. Errol didn't know which would be worse.

His instinct was to stop running, to tuck in tight behind a tree, but with the monster close by he didn't dare. Instead he picked up his pace, hoping the prefects would simply pass him by – but he failed to spot a tree root in the gloom, and fell with an *oof* to the mulchy floor.

'There!'

A torch beam flicked on and lasered through the trees directly towards him. Behind it, Errol knew, was Crowe. He couldn't see him past the dazzling light, but he could picture him: his jutting chin, his silver eyes, his swept-back hair, black as the bird that gave him his family name.

'Get him!'

The prefects began barrelling towards him, heedless now of how much noise they made. And from Errol's opposite flank, something else was closing on him too – something determined not to be cheated of its prey.

He scrambled upright, and started sprinting for the gap that was narrowing in front of him.

'There's no use running! Where else have you got to go?'

The sound of Crowe's voice was bad enough, but from the other side Errol heard something worse. That growl again: closer, closing . . .

The tree line. It was right ahead. And the wall was barely twenty steps beyond it.

Errol broke through the final row of trees and found himself sprinting through the moonlight across open ground. It was the final stretch, the last few metres until safety.

Six steps . . .

Five . . .

Four . . .

'Got you!' came a voice behind him, as something grazed his left shoulder. A hand? A claw?

Errol leapt. It was all he could do. And as he tumbled he heard the sound of laughter, and the monster from the woods gnashing its jaws.

1 KING PJ

The blow caught Ollie Turner on the side of his head before he even saw it coming. It was just a tap, enough to push Ollie off balance, but not to knock him out. The girl was toying with him, he realised. All his training, all his hard work, and Ollie was still hopelessly outclassed. The fight would be over before it had really begun.

Chin up, Ollie told himself. *Hands long. And stay on the balls of your feet, just like Song taught you. This isn't a training exercise any more. This is* real.

He danced to his right, dodging another kick to his temple. He lunged with his own leg, attempting a front kick, but found his foot prodding the air. Before he knew it Ollie was staring at the ceiling. He hadn't had a chance to snap his leg away before the girl had caught hold of his ankle and toppled him backwards.

As he landed the breath went out of him, and Ollie was tempted to lie where he'd fallen. At least then it would be over, his humiliation complete.

But if there was one lesson Song hadn't needed to teach him, it was to never give up. That was something Nancy, Ollie's guardian, had instilled in him since he was small. And now that Nancy was gone – murdered by Maddy Sikes, just like Ollie's parents – he was more determined than ever not to let her down.

As the girl moved to pin him, Ollie rolled. In one swift movement he was back on his feet – staggering, but with the advantage of having taken the girl by surprise. He kicked again, and though the girl attempted to block, this time the ball of his foot found its target.

'*Yame!*' called Song, issuing the Japanese instruction to stop. For someone who was ordinarily so quiet, in the dojo she was surprisingly assertive.

Ollie retreated to his end of the mat. His opponent – a nine-year-old brown belt called Vanessa – moved to hers. They bowed, and the final part of Ollie's first karate grading came to an end.

'Thank you, Vanessa,' said Song, moving towards them, 'for volunteering to teach Ollie a lesson. And, for not putting him on his backside in the first ten seconds. I know you could have if you'd wanted to.'

The brown belt blushed and bowed again.

'As for you, Ollie,' Song went on, 'your guard was hopelessly open, and you telegraphed every single kick. How many times have I told you to disguise your movements? Feint first, *then* strike.'

'I know, I—'

'And control your breathing! I could hear you panting from the other end of the dojo. Even if you're tired, you mustn't *show* you are.'

Ollie dropped his head. So much for earning his first belt. Having only started karate lessons a couple of months ago, shortly after joining the Haven, Ollie was still a white belt, but he'd hoped to graduate to orange.

'I failed,' he said to Song. 'Didn't I?'

Around Song's middle was a fraying black belt, worn in training for so many years it was almost white again. At the Haven it was kids who taught kids – no adults were allowed, other than Aunt Fay, the Haven's founder – and, as well as being the Haven's maths whizz, Song was the resident karate instructor. Like Ollie, she was one of the handful of kids that made up the Haven's investigations team, the core group that ran the organisation and undertook the most dangerous missions. The Haven was a sanctuary for kids in trouble, and often in order to get those kids to safety, Ollie and the others were forced to put their own lives on the line.

Song looked at Ollie in obvious disappointment. And then she smiled.

'I didn't say you failed, Ollie. All I said was you could have done better.' Her hands appeared from behind her back. 'Here.'

To Ollie's amazement, Song bowed, and held out a neatly folded orange belt.

'But . . . I lost. You said it yourself, Vanessa was kicking my butt.'

'Vanessa will *always* be able to kick your butt, Ollie. I never expected you to beat her. But what you demonstrated when you were sparring was your attitude. If you'd stayed on the ground when Vanessa put you there, you really *would* have failed. Instead you got to your feet and even managed to score a point.'

Ollie looked across and saw Vanessa smiling at him. This time Ollie was the one to blush.

There was applause from the other students in the dojo, and Ollie allowed Song to help him tie his new belt. He knew it shouldn't have been a big deal. It was only an orange belt, after all, and he was a long way from being even half as good as the other students in the class. Even so, it felt like an achievement, and Ollie couldn't stifle a flush of pride. He knew Nancy would have been proud of him, too.

'Ollie?'

The applause dwindled, and all eyes in the dojo turned to the doorway. Standing at the threshold was Sol, Ollie's closest friend. Sol was on the investigations team, too, and he more than anyone had helped Ollie to feel like the Haven was where he truly belonged.

'Sorry to interrupt,' Sol said. 'But you said to come and find you when there was any news.'

'Is it Flea?' said Ollie. 'Is he back?'

Sol nodded. 'He is. They all are. And Flea's hurt.'

It was odd. Ollie had spent far longer in their temporary home underground than he had in the previous Haven before it had been destroyed, but even so he couldn't help missing the old building. It had been a wreck, too dangerous in parts for the Haven kids to use, yet it had also felt immediately like home. It had been a library once, and Ollie recalled the smell of books he'd noticed the very first time he'd been led through the Haven's doors.

In contrast, the abandoned London Underground station that was now their base only smelt of damp. There was no triple-height entrance hall like there had been in the old building, with its grand central staircase and wood-lined mezzanines. Instead, there was just a network of musty storerooms and disused tunnels – some larger, some smaller, but all low ceilinged and covered with dirty, crumbling tiles.

The main hall, as they called it, was the biggest space they had down here. It had once housed the station's escalators, but these had been sealed off when the station had been closed, meaning the area was effectively cut in two. At a push, every one of the Haven's 146 children could gather there, but really they needed a room twice as large.

Elsewhere, the corridors that had once led to the station's platforms had been turned into dormitories. There were some bunks – the ghost station had been equipped as an emergency shelter, and they'd also managed to scavenge a fair amount of supplies from the old Haven after the fire that had destroyed it had been put out – but mostly the kids slept on blankets on the floors. They had plenty of food, and a bit of cash in reserve after the sale of the watch Ollie had snatched from Maddy Sikes's wrist just before she'd met her end, but space was so tight, Ollie had frequently woken up with a neighbour's foot on his pillow – and, once, with Sol's toe wedged up his nostril.

'What happened?' Ollie asked his friend as they walked from their makeshift dojo towards the area that had been set aside as the infirmary. 'Is Flea hurt badly?'

'Badly enough,' said Sol, 'but he'll survive. As for what happened, he wouldn't tell us. Said he wanted to wait for you. Save himself explaining everything twice.' Sol glanced at Ollie with a glint. 'What he actually said was, he'd wait for King PJ to grace him with his presence.'

There was a glitch in Ollie's movements. 'King PJ?'

'I actually thought it had a nice ring to it,' said Sol, smiling.

Ollie gave half a smile back. Flea couldn't have been that seriously injured if he'd managed to summon the energy to find a new way of insulting Ollie – which, since Ollie had taken over as the Haven's leader, seemed to have become Flea's mission in life. In fact, it had been his mission virtually since the moment he and Ollie had met.

'What about the others? Was anyone else hurt?'

'Flea's goons, you mean?' said Sol.

Ollie had insisted on a vote before agreeing to take over from Dodge, the Haven's previous leader, and though more than eighty kids had cast their ballot in Ollie's favour, that left around sixty who'd favoured Flea, the only other person to put himself forward for the post.

'You shouldn't call them that,' said Ollie. 'We're all on the same side, remember?'

'Huh,' said Sol. 'Tell that to Flea and his cronies.'

Ollie frowned, but didn't argue. He knew Sol took Flea's objection to Ollie being in charge even more personally than Ollie did. Ollie himself tried not to let it bother him. Apart from anything, he secretly felt Flea and the others had a point. They were stuck down here in the abandoned Underground station, for example, and Ollie didn't have a clue how to get them out, to a place more like their former home. And though the Haven's mission was to help kids in trouble, to offer them shelter if they needed it, there'd been no missions lately, no new arrivals. The truth was, all they'd done over the past few months was get by.

'Hi, Ollie,' chimed a pair of voices, and Ollie blinked and raised his head.

'Hey, Leo. Hey, Mia.'

Both of the kids they'd passed were firmly in Ollie's corner, and Ollie took some heart from the enthusiastic way they'd greeted him. But a few paces on, he and Sol came across another group of kids in one of the narrow tunnels, and they all deliberately turned their backs. Ollie couldn't hear what they were saying to one another, but from the sharp smiles and snide whispers, he reckoned he could have made a fair guess.

He recalled walking the Haven's halls for the first time with Dodge, how the other kids had greeted Dodge like a hero. Ollie didn't want that – he reckoned those who'd voted for him had an over-inflated idea of what he was capable of already – but he hated the idea of people at the Haven taking sides. If things didn't improve, Ollie knew, there was a very real danger that the entire community would split right down the middle.

'Don't let it bother you, Ollie,' said Sol. 'They'll come round. Even Flea will eventually. You just have to give them time.'

Ollie wasn't convinced, though he did his best not to show it.

'Besides,' Sol went on, smiling grimly, 'after we hear what Flea's got to say, I reckon we'll have bigger things to worry about.'

2 BITTER RIVALS

'Nice PJs, PJ.'

It was the first thing Flea said to him as Ollie approached the bed where he lay. 'PJ' had been Flea's nickname for him since the day they'd first encountered each other in the sewers, when Ollie had been wearing his old dinosaur pyjamas. It was something Flea never intended to allow Ollie to live down, and the sight of Ollie in his karate suit was obviously too much of an open goal for him to resist.

'And I see Song gave you a sympathy belt,' Flea went on. 'Shame orange isn't really your colour.'

'It's good to see you safe, Flea,' Ollie answered. 'I'm glad you're still in one piece.'

'Yeah, well,' Flea said. 'Some of us already know how to handle ourselves. We don't need to take self-defence lessons from a girl.'

'Watch it, Flea,' said Jack, who was seated in her wheelchair at Flea's bedside. Jack was one of the smartest people Ollie had ever met – she was the brains of the investigations team, and its ICT expert – and Ollie knew from experience that she was also every bit as fierce as Song was. Jack's temper matched her short, spiky hair, which was almost the same colour as Ollie's new belt. 'You wouldn't be saying that if Song were here,' Jack went on. 'And if you weren't lying there bleeding, I'd teach you a few lessons myself.'

'Just ignore my thick-headed brother, Ollie,' said a voice, and Ollie turned to see Lily at the foot of Flea's bed. Including Ollie and Sol, there were almost a dozen people crowded around Flea's bunk, most of whom counted themselves among Flea's supporters. And it was clear what they thought of Ollie from the way they'd sniggered at Flea's jokes.

'Well done on passing your grading, by the way,' Lily said. 'You should be very proud.'

Ollie nodded his thanks, but when he met Lily's soft brown eyes, she looked away. Lily had always been nice to Ollie, ever since that day in the sewers. But just lately she'd taken to acting strangely around him – always finding some excuse to avoid talking to him, or for leaving the room just as Ollie arrived – and he had no idea why. Nothing had changed as far as he was concerned. Well, there was the whole Dodge thing. And Ollie's election as the Haven's leader. And the lot of them being forced to live underground, in rooms that smelt of old trainers and breathing air that tasted of soot.

But other than *those* things, nothing had changed, certainly not between him and Lily. He wondered whether she was mad at him, or, like so many others around here, just disappointed.

A racking cough behind him made Ollie turn. For the first time he noticed how busy the infirmary was, and not just because of Flea. All of the other beds were taken, by younger kids mostly. Ollie couldn't see anything obvious that was wrong with them, but the cough he'd heard from the girl behind him had sounded like a train derailing into gravel.

Jack appeared at Ollie's side. 'It sounds worse than it is,' she said. 'So Galen tells me.'

Galen was the closest the Haven had to a doctor, and Ollie could see her tending one of her patients near the entrance to the arch-shaped anteroom. She was sixteen years old, the maximum age for kids at the Haven, and she'd been teaching herself medicine since she'd first arrived at the age of eleven.

'What's wrong with her?' Ollie asked Jack, wincing as the little girl coughed again.

'Croup,' said Jack. 'Other than Flea, all the kids in here have got respiratory issues of one kind or another. Asthma is the biggest one. It's the air down here, Galen reckons. It's messing with people's lungs.' She leant a fraction closer, lowering her voice. 'We need to get out of here, Ollie. And soon.'

Flea had been listening in. 'Too right we need to get out of this rat hole,' he said. 'If you want my opinion, we should never have left the old building in the first place.'

There were nods of agreement from his admirers.

Ollie couldn't disguise his incredulity. 'What do you mean? It was on *fire*. We didn't exactly have a choice.'

'There's always a choice, PJ. The way there's a choice between who takes command of this sinking ship.'

'People already *made* that choice, Fleabag,' said Sol. 'They elected Ollie.'

'They did,' Flea conceded. 'But that was back when everyone was under the impression that PJ here had somehow saved the city. Who would they elect if they were asked to vote now, I wonder?'

Ollie felt an uncomfortable flush. He glanced about him, and saw Lily look awkwardly at her feet.

'If it had been up to me,' said Flea, raising his voice so everyone could hear, 'there's no way we would have let the old Haven burn. We would have stayed and put the fire out, not run away like frightened animals.'

Sol spoke over the chorus of approval. 'You were there when the fire broke out,' he said to Flea. 'I didn't see you reaching for a bucket.'

'It just so happened I was a trifle busy,' Flea retorted. 'Someone had to stop Maddy Sikes.'

'That was Ollie! All you did was follow his lead!'

'How do you know, Sol? Were you there? Were *any* of you there, other than Lily?' Flea cast his eyes around the group, and then back at Sol. 'You can believe whatever fairy tale you want. The truth is, *I* was the one who broke us into the airport. I got us aboard that plane. And I was the one who distracted Maddy Sikes so we could recover the detonator.'

Sol huffed. 'So Ollie could, you mean. From what I heard, Flea, you spent most of the time asleep in one of the seats.'

'I wasn't *asleep*, I was *unconscious*! Briefly. I'd like to see you take a blow like the one I did and still recover in time to rescue the pilot.'

'One of the bad guys, you mean?' Sol countered. 'Great work, Flea. And anyway it was only thanks to Ollie that you—'

'*Enough.*' Lily was almost on the brink of tears. 'Ollie and Flea *both* helped stop Maddy Sikes. OK? We all did. Dodge included.'

There was an uncomfortable silence. It had become an unspoken rule at the Haven not to mention Dodge's name; mainly, Ollie suspected, because none of them were quite sure how to remember him.

'How about you tell us what happened, Flea?' Ollie said. 'How did you get hurt? I thought it was supposed to be a reconnaissance mission?'

Flea appeared reluctant to change the subject. It was an argument he wanted to have, clearly, and it was obvious he felt as if he was winning. But when he noted his twin sister's reaction, he bit down on whatever he'd been about to say.

'It was,' he grumbled instead. 'But I guess some people take exception to being watched.'

Jack had been following the argument mutely, but now that attention had returned to the matter in hand, she leant forwards in her chair.

'What did you find out, Flea? What did you see?'

Flea turned to Jack and winced an apology. Jack was the one member of the investigations team – which comprised Ollie, Sol, Lily, Flea, Jack and Song, as well as Erik, the group's languages expert – who Flea only ever treated with respect. Mainly, Ollie knew, because he was afraid of her, although today he would also have been aware how desperate Jack was for good news. It was because of Jack that Flea and the others had embarked on the mission in the first place. Or, more accurately, because of the younger brother Ollie hadn't known Jack had.

Jack hadn't seen her brother Errol for six years. They'd been separated when they were young. Shortly after their mother had died, in fact, and their stepfather, Rufus, had decided that two kids were more than he could cope with, particularly when one of them was in a wheelchair. He'd put Jack into care, and then enrolled her brother into boarding school. But throughout everything that had happened to them since, Jack and Errol had stayed in touch. They'd emailed each other almost daily – until, just over a fortnight ago, and shortly after Errol had started at

Forest Mount, a private school in leafy north London, her brother's emails had suddenly stopped. Worse, he'd been talking in the weeks before about strange things that had been happening at the school. Ollie didn't know all the details, but he'd seen how worried Jack had become. Flea had volunteered to check things out, and had clearly found more than he'd bargained for.

'There was no sign of your brother,' said Flea, in answer to Jack's question. 'But we didn't get within fifty metres of the school before someone chased us off. They had spotlights, truncheons, guard dogs. And . . . something else.'

'What do you mean, *something else*?' said Lily.

'I . . . It doesn't matter.'

For the first time when Ollie met Flea's eye, Flea was the one to look away.

'The point is,' Flea went on, 'the place was more heavily guarded than Buckingham Palace. It was right on the top of a hill, like a medieval castle or something. On one side the hill falls away, so steeply it's basically a cliff. There's a single road leading up from the gates, but everywhere else is just forest. That's where they spotted us, when we were trying to squeeze through the brambles. And that's where we heard . . .' Once again Flea stopped himself. 'What I mean is, that's where I got hurt. If I didn't know better, I'd swear one of those tree roots reached up and grabbed my leg.'

Flea looked down and hoisted his T-shirt, revealing a blood-soaked bandage just below his ribcage.

'I tripped and landed badly. On a branch or something, I guess. It stuck in my middle like a spear.'

Flea lowered his T-shirt, and Ollie winced.

'So I was right,' said Jack, her normally stolid voice shaken. '*Errol* was right. There's something going on at that school. Something they don't want the rest of the world to see. But maybe Errol *did* see it. Maybe that's why he's disappeared. Maybe they've . . . hurt him, or . . .'

Jack looked around desperately, and Ollie was shocked to see her so upset.

Lily took Jack's hand. 'We don't know that,' she consoled her. 'Maybe Errol's just been busy. With revision or something. Or the Internet is down at the school.'

'Come off it, sis,' said Flea, voicing the scepticism they were all feeling. Flea was brave and he was strong, but one thing he didn't do was tact. 'The kid's been in touch with his sister almost every day for, what? Six years?'

He looked at Jack, who nodded her affirmation with a pale face.

'And then he starts at this new school and a couple of months later just falls off the grid? A school that's protected by guards, by the way, and has . . . *defences* all around its grounds?'

He shook his head dismissively.

'I hate to say it, Jack, but there's not a doubt in my mind that you're right. There's something going on. Errol's in trouble, which means other kids are probably in trouble, too. The only question is . . .' And here Flea fixed his eyes on Ollie. 'What does our fearless leader intend to do about it?'

3 SCHOOL SUCKS

'Look,' said Jack. 'See for yourselves.'

The entire investigations team had assembled. Song had joined them from the dojo, and Erik had been waiting in the new control room. Erik was slim, fair-haired and wore round, frameless glasses. He was as loyal to Ollie as Sol was, being convinced that he owed Ollie his life.

When Jack pointed to the screen on her laptop, Ollie and the others gathered round, although really they were squashed in tight already. One of the biggest losses to the investigations team when the old Haven had burnt down was the area they'd used as a control room then. It had been the Haven's nerve centre, the place from which Ollie and the others had assembled to co-ordinate operations. In terms of the equipment they needed, they'd salvaged what they could: the sewer maps, some charred furniture, plus the smoke-damaged remains of several computers that Jack had managed to resurrect. But, as in the rest of the Haven, the thing they missed most was the *space*.

Their control room now was the old station master's office. Which sounded grand, but in reality was little bigger than a caretaker's cupboard. There was no room for any of that furniture they'd scavenged, just a small square table on which they'd positioned a battered laptop.

Jack sat in the middle of the group, her fingers dancing across the keyboard. Song, Erik and Sol were to her left; the rest of the investigations team to her right. Ollie was crushed uncomfortably against Flea, who was protecting his wound on one side and jabbing Ollie with his elbow on the other. Ollie would have moved away, but that would have meant shifting closer to Lily. Somehow it was less uncomfortable putting up with Flea's elbow than it would have been pressed against his sister.

'Here,' said Jack, finding what she was searching for. 'He joined the school in May, so this is one of the first emails he sent me.'

Sent: Mon 28/05, 01.35

From: erroltheeagle@lightning-mail.co.uk

To: jack14@cryptomail.com

Subject: Re: school sucks

Hi Jack,

It's true what I told you before. I hate this place. And it's nothing to do with what you said, with adjusting or whatever to a new environment. I know it's always horrible when you're made to go to a new school. Since Mum died I've been sent to enough of them. Being the new kid, not having any friends, not knowing what's cool and what just makes you look like an idiot without you even realising – I hate all that stuff, too. But with Forest Mount it's more than that. It's *worse* than that.

There's the building itself, for a start. It's old. Like, *really* old. And it's *creepy*, like some haunted museum or something.

The woods don't help. They're right outside. And some kids say—

It doesn't matter what they say. It's scary enough here without believing their stupid stories.

And Professor Strain. Did I tell you about Professor Strain? He's the headmaster, but really he's like some evil dictator. I've only spoken to him once, but once was enough, believe me. He made me come to his office. He makes all the new kids go to his office, particularly if they start in the middle of term, like I did. He's tall and he looks a bit like Grand Moff Tarkin out of *Star Wars*. I tried to pretend I was Han Solo, all cool and calm like when Greedo points his blaster at him in the Cantina, but it didn't help. He still made me feel like Rebel scum.

The worst thing, though. The *very* worst thing, I mean, is Colton Crowe. He's the head pupil. Which means he should be nice, right?

Wrong.

Times about a gazillion.

Crowe's in charge of the prefects, who are sort of like his private army. The school uniform here is black and white, but the prefects wear black shirts, black blazers, black trousers, black everything. And they are – they're like an army, not like prefects at all. They had prefects at St Hilda's, where I was before, but at St Hilda's all they were was a bit bossy. Here they're *mean*. It's like they take secret torture lessons or something. How to twist a finger as far as it will go without snapping. Where to jab someone with your thumb so it makes them scream but doesn't leave a bruise. And everyone's loaded, with rich mummies and daddies. Like Colton Crowe. Crowe's dad is a knight or something, and everyone else's parents are important, too. They've all got titles and land and *money* basically, and

Someone's coming.

Sorry – I've got to go. I shouldn't be down here at this time of night. The computer lab's off limits after six. The whole entire downstairs is.

I miss you, Jack. I wish you were here. Or, even better, I wish I was where you are.

Love,
E

'Why does he call himself Errol the Eagle?' asked Sol.

Jack gave a sort of shrug. 'He's only eleven. And he's into nature. When we were young he used to collect dead stuff. Like dead butterflies, dead flies, a dead shrew he found once when he went out walking. I always thought it was gross, but Errol insisted it was science. He wanted to be a naturalist.'

'A naturalist?' Sol echoed. 'You mean he wanted to run around naked?'

'That's a naturist, dummy,' said Lily. 'A naturalist is someone who studies nature.'

There were titters around the room at Sol's expense, but Ollie kept his eyes on Jack. Not once did she come close to smiling. She wore the same expression of concern she'd carried with her from the infirmary. It was unnerving seeing her so upset. Jack was their rock, ordinarily. The closest they had to a grown-up, other than Aunt Fay. Which meant sometimes Jack lacked a sense of humour, but never to the extent she was displaying now. More than worried, Ollie realised, Jack was genuinely afraid.

'Here,' she said, scrolling through her inbox. 'This is from a few weeks later.'

Sent: Thu 14/06, 03.50

From: erroltheeagle@lightning-mail.co.uk

To: jack14@cryptomail.com

Subject: Re: school sucks

It's even worse than I thought. There's something going on here, I swear it. Something bad.

Me and my friend George, we were late for history, so we decided to take a shortcut through the East Wing. Which is allowed, it's not off limits, but pupils tend to avoid it because Professor Strain's office is right in the middle of the main corridor.

At first George refused to come with me, but I was like, you've got a choice, George. Run the risk of bumping into Professor Strain, or get put in detention for *definite* because you were late for class. Which you'll probably have to spend with Professor Strain *anyway*.

So we take the shortcut, obviously, but we're not even halfway down the corridor when we hear voices. And George immediately panics. 'It's Strain,' he goes, 'he's coming!' Which to be fair is what I'm thinking, too.

But when the voices get closer I realise it's worse than that. It's not Strain. It's Crowe. And we're two year-sevens all alone where nobody else can see us, meaning Crowe's going to think it's Christmas. Plus, by the sound of it he's got at least two other prefects for company. Which means not only are we outsized, we're also outnumbered. Although, with Crowe, you sort of feel outnumbered even when it's one on one.

'In here,' I tell George. 'Quick!' And I pull him into the nearest doorway. It's a classroom, and thankfully it's not being used, so we're able to hide behind the door with just our eyes poking above the glass.

'You've made the right decision,' Crowe's going, when he appears. 'With the information you've given us, your parents will have no choice but to fall in line. Welcome to the revolution, gentlemen.'

They stop in front of a wall, just along the corridor from Strain's office. And it's just a wall, I'm thinking. It's covered in dark wood panelling, but that's not unusual at Forest Mount. But then I see Crowe press something on one of the wooden panels. And guess what happens? The panel slides away, and behind it there's a secret door!

George and me look at each other, wide-eyed.

'A hidden passageway,' George goes. 'I bet that leads down to the dungeons.'

'The *what*?' I say.

'The dungeons. From the olden days. Apparently there's a whole two floors below the school that nobody even knows about. They used to keep prisoners down there and torture them.'

I don't say anything. It's the first I've heard about there being *dungeons* at Forest Mount, but to be honest it doesn't exactly surprise me.

'Remember,' says Crowe, his hand on one of the prefects' chests, stopping them from going through the doorway. 'Not a word about what you're about to see. To *anyone*. Is that clear?'

The prefects nod, the way I've seen muggles nod when they've been cornered by Crowe and he's got their arms all twisted behind their backs and he's asking them if they understand who's boss.

'And do exactly as you're told,' Crowe instructs. 'Remember, if everything goes according to plan, then one day very soon you'll be—'

But I don't hear any more, because as soon as he leads the others through the door, his words are drowned out by this wailing sound. I only hear it for an instant, and it cuts off the moment the secret door slides closed behind him. But what I realise, when I think back, is that the sound I heard? The wailing sound? It was a *scream*.

We don't hang around after that. George is up and running so fast, I

The email vanished, and Ollie was left staring at Jack's inbox. She'd started scrolling to bring up another message.

'Look at this one,' she said. 'This was from barely a week later.'

Sent: Wed 20/06, 23.47

From: erroltheeagle@lightning-mail.co.uk

To: jack14@cryptomail.com

Subject: Re: school sucks

George is gone, Jack! They've taken him!

One day he was sitting next to me in class, the next there was just an empty chair.

At first I figured he was ill or something, but when I looked he wasn't in the dorm. And I checked the nurse's station, the canteen, the common room – *everywhere*. So then I figured he must have gone home, like maybe there'd been a family emergency. So I asked the secretary, Ms Brownlow, but she hadn't seen him either. Nobody has!

Which is how I know.

They've *done* something to him.

They *must* have.

What I think is, somehow they found out about what we saw. Maybe . . . maybe George said something to someone, and somebody overheard him who shouldn't have.

And I know you think I'm imagining things, Jack, but

'That's what I said to him,' Jack said, pausing as she scrolled through Errol's email. 'That he was probably just imagining things. I thought he was exaggerating, you see. He was *always* exaggerating when we were little. Always making things up.'

She used a palm to wipe away a tear.

'They get shorter after that,' she said, getting back to the emails. 'This one's from the beginning of July.'

She brought up another message and highlighted a section of text.

more bad news. The worst. I've been trying to keep my head down, as you said. Just to get through to the summer holidays. But they told me this morning.

I'm staying.

The WHOLE summer.

Rufus is off on some business trip, apparently. And I know what you'd say. You'd say it was just an excuse, that really he's not going anywhere, that he wants rid of me the way he got rid of you. But it's *not* that, I know it isn't. He *does* want me, the way he wishes he could have kept you. He's explained it to me. How he only gave you up so you'd get better care. And I know you don't believe him, Jack, but I *do*. I have to.

And the point is, if it were any other school I wouldn't even mind. The only good thing is that it gives me an opportunity to poke about a bit, to try to find out what's really

'He's never got it,' said Jack, clicking away. 'About Rufus, I mean. Our stepdad. He genuinely thinks Rufus is one of the good guys, that he only sends Errol to boarding school for the sake of his education.' She shook her head. 'We used to argue about it all the time. Like, why would he need to send me away for better care, when he could have afforded all the extra help he wanted? Particularly with all my mum's money, too. She was rich as well, you know,' she added. 'If you ask me, that's the reason Rufus married her in the first place. He didn't *need* her money. He had plenty of his own. But with money, for some people, it's like the more they have, the more they want. You know?'

Ollie did know. For one thing, it described Maddy Sikes perfectly.

'But I could never convince Errol,' Jack went on. 'In the end I gave up trying to. After our mum died, and after I left . . . I guess he just wanted to feel loved.'

This time Ollie dropped his eyes, and he sensed the others do the same. It was unusual for anyone at the Haven to talk so openly about their past. For most of the kids here, what had happened to them before they arrived was generally something they did their best to forget. And ordinarily, Jack was the most tight-lipped out of all of them.

'After that Errol didn't say anything for a while,' Jack continued, working her finger on the mouse wheel. 'Not about the school, anyway. So I figured he'd calmed down a bit, maybe realised he was just being paranoid. But then, a couple of weeks ago, he sent me *this*.'

4 MESSAGE ENDS

Sent: Fri 27/07, 15.45

From: erroltheeagle@lightning-mail.co.uk

To: jack14@cryptomail.com

Subject: Re: school sucks

I've got so much to tell you, Jack. You won't believe it when I do.

I've been watching them, just like I said I would. Crowe, Strain, the prefects. And it's true, what I said before. They're building an army. Not a normal army, though, with guns and tanks and stuff like that. Strain's army: it's an army of *spies*.

It all makes sense. Think about it! All the kids here are super rich, right? Their parents are the most powerful people in the country. There's this kid called Robert, for example, and his dad is the Metropolitan Police Commissioner. And Brooklyn. Her parents run this, like, media empire or something. They basically *own* television. And the rest of the kids' parents are all Lord this or Lady that, and half of them are in the actual government. The Cupboard or whatever it's called. Not the Cupboard. The Cabinet.

So what's happening is, Strain's using Crowe to recruit them, and then he's getting all the kids to spy on their parents. And Strain, he's collecting all the information for . . . for . . . I don't know what for exactly, but it can't be anything good. I've seen Crowe writing it all down in this little black notebook he carries. He only gets it out when he thinks no one's looking, or when one of his spies is giving him information.

And the worst thing is, the kids who don't agree, who refuse to act as spies – Crowe tortures them. Down in the dungeons. That was that scream I heard, I'm sure of it! And I bet all the information he gets down there goes in his notebook, too, and he feeds it all back to Professor Strain. And maybe Strain's blackmailing people, getting them to give him money. Or . . . or something else. Something *worse*.

But I've said too much.

I can't take the chance writing anything more down here.

I'm using an encrypted server, just like you said I should, but they could still be reading this. They could have hidden cameras in the computer lab. Or even in the computers themselves. Didn't you say hackers could sometimes use webcams to see *out*?

And microphones. I bet they have microphones. I get so worried I might say something in my sleep that most of the time I try to stay awake.

But it will be over soon. For me, anyway.

I'll see you soon, Jack. I promise. I love you. Always.
E

'It was the very last time I heard from him,' said Jack, wiping a tear from her eye. 'And I know what you're going to say. You're going to say I was right to call him paranoid.'

Sol waggled his head, like he agreed, but was reluctant to admit it. 'An army of spies?' he said. 'Torture? You have to admit it sounds a bit far-fetched.'

'People would have found out,' put in Lily. 'Wouldn't they? They couldn't just go locking pupils up and get away with it. What about the parents? They'd be asking questions as soon as they failed to hear from their kids. There'd be uproar.'

'That's exactly what I thought,' said Jack. 'But since Errol went missing I've been reading up on the school, and he's right about the type of kids who go there. It's the most prestigious school in the country. And guess what? According to the newspapers, three pupils have supposedly run away from Forest Mount in the past three months.'

'Which means they didn't like the school,' said Sol. 'It doesn't mean they're locked in a dungeon.'

'Except not one of them has ever turned up,' countered Jack. 'They're all still missing. Their parents don't know where they are. No one does. And look what else I found. This was posted online only this *morning*.'

She produced a print-out taken from the BBC website. It was a news story, and Ollie and the others had to squeeze in tighter to be able to read it.

Tragedy strikes prestigious north London boarding school

A student's body has been recovered from a lake within the grounds of Forest Mount Private School.

The boy has been named locally as George Williams, 11, and police say all signs indicate the boy got lost while walking in the campus woods, and became entangled with weeds when he stumbled into the water.

'It seems this was a tragic accident,' said senior investigating officer, Detective Inspector Garrie Dalton. 'Our thoughts at this time are with George's family, and all of his friends at Forest Mount.'

An official statement from Professor Isaiah Strain, the headmaster of the school, is expected shortly.

'George Williams?' said Ollie. 'As in, your brother's friend?'

'Exactly,' said Jack. 'He sees what Errol sees, maybe tells someone about it he shouldn't have, then a couple of weeks later he turns up dead.'

There was silence for a moment as they considered the implications.

'I've read the headmaster's statement, too,' Jack went on. 'And it's basically a lot of empty words. He just repeats what the police said, that George's death was a tragedy, that students are warned to be careful around the lake. What I think is, the kids who don't go along with whatever Strain and Crowe are doing get *dealt with* somehow. They either end up "missing", like those other three kids, or they end up suffering some terrible "accident". Like poor George.'

'What about the rest of the kids, though?' said Erik. 'The ones who are supposedly in league with Professor Strain? Why would they agree to spy on their parents?'

'Maybe Strain's bribing them with something,' said Sol, who was clearly coming round to Jack's way of thinking. 'Like, with the money he's making, just as Errol said.'

'Or *frightening* them with something,' suggested Lily.

'It would have to be something pretty scary,' said Erik, doubtfully. 'To get them to betray their parents.'

Flea cleared his throat. 'Promise you won't laugh when I tell you this,' he ventured. 'But what I said before, about . . . defences. When I was talking about being chased in the woods?' He focused on Lily as he spoke. 'Well, there was something out there. Something *big*. Like a . . . a wild beast or something. We didn't see it, but we – *I* – heard it growl. And I can tell you, it's not a sound I ever want to hear again.'

Ollie shared a look with Sol. They knew full well that Flea wouldn't have admitted that he'd been afraid if he hadn't been genuinely spooked. And it took a *lot* to scare Flea.

'Errol mentioned Crowe saying something about a "revolution",' said Song. 'What did that mean, do you think?'

'That puzzled me as well,' said Jack. 'And the truth is, I don't know what it meant. But I've been reading up on Professor

Strain, and guess what he did before he started at Forest Mount?'

'With a name like that, my guess is he was a bad guy in a comic book,' said Sol. 'Either that or some kind of mad scientist.'

'More like a cross between the two,' said Jack. 'He had his own political party. It didn't last long. Strain's policies were considered too extreme. He wanted to close down the NHS, for example, and use the money to quadruple the size of the police force. And he said persistent petty criminals should be given the death penalty. Oh, and he wanted to block off the Channel Tunnel.'

'What?' said Erik. 'Why?'

'He said it was a "drainpipe of effluence",' Jack quoted.

'Effluence?' said Sol. 'Does that mean what I think it means?'

'Probably not,' said Lily, and the others laughed. 'But it sounds as if he wanted to stop people who weren't born here from coming into this country. Right, Jack?'

'Right. He wanted immigration cut down to zero.'

'Well, that would have ruled out my parents,' said Sol.

'Mine too,' said Erik.

'Mine three,' added Song.

'If you go back far enough down the generations, it would have ruled out most of our ancestors,' said Jack. 'And Strain didn't want to stop there. His main goal was the overthrow of the entire political system. In the interview I read, he said something about how this country needed to "abandon its experiment with democracy".'

'Get rid of democracy?' said Erik. 'And replace it with what?'

'With a leader who "didn't have to go begging to the people every time he wanted to get something done",' said Jack.

'"He",' muttered Lily. 'That kind of figures.'

'And get this,' Jack went on. 'Strain admitted his role model was Joseph Stalin.'

'Joseph Stalin?' said Sol. 'Doesn't he play for Liverpool?'

Lily rolled her eyes. 'Stalin was a Russian dictator, you idiot. He killed, like, thousands of people.'

'Millions, actually,' said Jack. 'Twenty-five million, according to some historians. He was one of the most brutal dictators the world has ever seen, as evil as Adolf Hitler.'

'So . . . what?' said Song. 'You think all that has something to do with what's going on at Forest Mount? Like, Strain wants to be a dictator *here*? His political party fails, so he comes up with some other way to take over the country.'

'But that could never happen,' said Erik. 'Could it?'

Jack shook her head. 'I don't know. I don't know what it is they're hiding, or what Strain is planning. All I really want to know is what's happened to my brother.'

Ollie had been following the discussion mutely, trying to take it all in.

'The last line of Errol's email,' he said. '*I'll see you soon*. It sounds as if he was planning to run away.'

'Exactly,' said Jack, snapping the laptop screen shut. 'And if he ran, and got away, why hasn't he been in touch?'

No one answered, and Jack shook her head desperately.

'Something's happened to him, I'm sure of it,' she said, wiping away another tear. 'The same thing that happened to those missing kids. Or George even. Or . . . or something worse.'

5 OLLIE OUT

The others were looking at Ollie expectantly. Flea's expression, meanwhile, was a challenge. *Well?* it said. *What have you got, PJ?*

Ollie placed a hand on Jack's shoulder. 'Errol's alive, Jack. I'm sure of it.'

Jack clearly wanted to believe him, but Ollie could see she feared the worst. 'You can't know that,' she said. 'I wish you could, but you *can't*.'

'Think about it,' Ollie insisted. 'Think about how another "accident" would look, so soon after what happened to Errol's friend. Whatever's going on at Forest Mount, they're obviously desperate to keep it secret. Which means there's no way they could take the risk. Right?'

A flicker of hope showed in Jack's eyes. She nodded at Ollie gratefully. 'Right,' she said, tentatively.

'So that's our starting point. Agreed?' Ollie looked around the room. 'We work from the premise that Errol is being held somewhere on the grounds of the school, which means it's our job to rescue him.'

'And how do you propose to do that exactly?' said Flea.

'Talk me through it,' Ollie said to him. 'How did you approach the school last time?'

'What do you mean, *how did we approach the school*? We walked up to it. On our feet.'

'But how did you get inside the grounds?'

'It's like I said, on the north side there's basically a cliff, so the only way in or out is from the south. We tried blagging our way in at the main gate, but the security guards there chased us away. So we went around the corner and scaled the wall – which wasn't easy, I can tell you. But we figured once we were over it would be easy. I mean, it's only a school, right? We weren't expecting the sentries, the dogs, the . . . woods. It's like a fortress that doesn't *look* like a fortress.'

Ollie thought for a moment.

'Where are the maps?' he said, casting round.

Sol moved quickly to the pile of rolled charts in the corner. Jack cleared the laptop from the table.

'There aren't any tunnels leading in if that's what you're thinking, PJ,' said Flea, crossing his arms against the sudden bustle around him. 'Don't you think I would have gone that way if there were? The school isn't connected to the sewer. It's probably got its own cesspit. And the nearest Tube line runs past the base of the hill. *Outside* the grounds.'

The maze of tunnels below the streets of London – the sewers, the Underground lines, old ventilation shafts – were how the

Haven kids usually got around the city without being seen. Even though they were an organisation dedicated solely to helping kids in need, they had enemies everywhere: London's street gangs, who resented the Haven for 'stealing' their foot soldiers; the authorities, who didn't know the Haven existed, and would have closed it down in the time it took to squiggle a signature. Plus, of course, all the people they'd crossed in the past. Maddy Sikes may have been dead, yet there were other powerful individuals who would have taken no greater pleasure than in seeing the Haven fall to ruins. And not just whatever building happened to be their base at the time. Rather, the very idea itself.

When Sol returned with a stack of rolled parchments across his arms, Ollie rifled until he found the one he was looking for. It didn't take him long. He'd spent hours studying the maps in the weeks they'd been living in the ghost station.

'Forest Mount,' he said to Jack as he spread one of the maps on the table. 'Has it always been a school?'

Unusually for Jack, she appeared a step behind what Ollie was thinking. 'For the past one hundred and fifty years it has been. It's about the most expensive in the country. That's the only reason our stepfather sent Errol there: so he could brag to all his stuck-up mates. That fact it was also a boarding school, meaning he never had to *see* Errol, was just a bonus.'

'But before that,' Ollie persisted. 'What was it – some kind of manor house or something?'

Jack frowned, still not seeing where this was going. 'I guess.'

Ollie peered down at the map, which showed London as it was in the eighteenth century. 'It was. Look.' He pointed to a patch of green to the north of the city, not far from the spot where Alexandra Palace now stood. 'It was called Forest Hall back in those days. The woods were just a part of its estate, as were all these outbuildings here.' He drew a circle with his finger around a clutch of buildings at the southern base of the hill.

'All that land was part of the same estate?' said Song. She was cross-referencing with Google Maps on her phone. 'It's twice the size of the school grounds now.'

'Exactly,' said Ollie, looking up. He felt a flutter of excitement. It almost compensated for the look of ridicule he was getting from Flea.

'Enough of the history lesson, PJ. How does any of this help us find Jack's brother?'

Ollie pointed to the outbuildings again. 'In the old days these buildings were inside the school's grounds. Now they're outside.'

'So?'

'So,' Ollie persisted, 'I remember Nancy telling me once how there's usually a whole network of underground passages between the buildings on old country estates. It was how the servants got around, where people hid to avoid religious persecution, that sort of thing.'

'You mean . . .' said Jack, catching up now.

'I mean, if we can get into the basement of one of these buildings, we'll most likely be able to find an underground passageway leading directly to the school. Or if not all the way to the school, at least past the current boundary wall.'

'Past the outer defences, you mean,' said Sol, grinning. He turned his triumphant look on Flea.

'Wait a minute,' said Flea, holding up his hands. 'Don't you think they might have thought of that? Even if there *are* tunnels, they're almost certainly being guarded too.'

'Maybe,' agreed Ollie. 'Maybe not. It's more likely they'll have security cameras set up, the way we do in the tunnels around the Haven. And Jack can handle those – right, Jack?'

For the first time in a long while, Jack grinned. 'You bet I can.'

'But . . . it might not just be cameras,' Flea pressed, clearly determined to find a flaw in Ollie's plan. 'They might have sealed the tunnels off.'

Ollie shook his head. 'They would only have been able to do so at the school end. And, like I say, all we need to do is get beyond the outer wall without being seen. After that . . . Well. After that we'll just have to improvise.'

'But we can't just go breaking into someone's house,' said Erik. 'Can we?'

'We wouldn't need to,' answered Ollie, bending over the map again. 'It's unlikely the former outbuildings would have been used as homes. They're more likely to be museums or council buildings or—'

'Or a church,' said Lily decisively, her fingertip landing on the map. Ollie looked where she was pointing, and saw one of the outbuildings was marked with a cross.

'The old chapel,' he said, smiling, and for once when he looked at Lily, she smiled back. 'So that's it,' Ollie announced, standing straighter. 'That's how we get inside. Flea already tried the front entrance. Now let's try the back. All we have to do is—'

He was interrupted by someone hammering on the control room door.

As one, the investigations team turned. Erik was nearest, and he yanked the door open.

It was Leo, the young lad Ollie had passed earlier in the corridor. Leo had been Dodge's biggest fan – once stopping him in the corridor in Ollie's presence and asking for his autograph – but in the rivalry between Ollie and Flea, Leo had transferred his allegiance to Ollie.

'Erik,' he panted. 'Ollie. All of you. You need to come. *Quickly.*'

Ollie felt his stomach flip. Since the old building had been attacked – set on fire by a vengeful street gang, at Maddy Sikes's provocation – he'd lived in fear of something similar happening again. The Haven's new location was a secret, fiercely guarded by everyone within its walls, but they'd felt just as secure in the old building. If someone found them, and started a fire somewhere in the ghost station, the result would be cataclysmic. They could all very easily be trapped down here, together with the smoke and the flames.

It was another reason they needed a new home. Somewhere more readily protected. And, if they *couldn't* protect it, somewhere from which they could easily escape.

Ollie was first through the door. He heard the others at his back, as they all raced to keep up with Leo.

'What is it?' Ollie asked him as they ran. 'Are we under attack?'

But Leo was breathless from sprinting to come and find them all. 'The canteen . . .' he gasped. 'The walls . . .'

Ollie's frown deepened. He didn't have a clue what Leo was talking about.

But as they drew closer to the tunnel that housed the canteen, he began to get an idea. There was a disturbance of some kind, clearly. It didn't sound as if they were under attack, though. Rather, what it sounded like was a—

'*Fight!*'

Ollie came to a halt at the threshold to the canteen. He almost couldn't believe what he was seeing.

People had formed a human ring, and whatever scuffle had

developed was taking place at its centre. Some of the kids watching had their hands over their mouths, clearly shocked by what they were witnessing. Others – Flea's supporters for the most part, Ollie noted – were clapping their hands to an inflammatory beat, chanting to urge the combatants on.

'*Fight! Fight! Fight!*'

It was as though Ollie were back at St Jerome's again, caught up in one of the brawls that sometimes took place after school behind the bike sheds. But this was the *Haven*. Things like this weren't supposed to happen *here*.

'Hey,' said Ollie. '*Hey!*'

The onlookers parted to let him through, but the kids involved in the fight either didn't hear him or paid him no notice. It took Flea to wade into the middle of it all and physically prise the combatants apart.

'All right, you lot, *pack it in*!'

There were four people involved, Ollie saw. Two of them he recognised from Flea's bedside in the infirmary. They were the same two boys who'd accompanied Flea on the mission to Forest Mount. One was thickset and bull-like, with close cropped hair. The other was skinnier, with limbs that were all angles and bones.

Their opponents, standing side by side now, were smaller than them. They both had long, dark hair, which for a moment covered their faces.

'Keya?' Ollie said, not quite believing what he was seeing.

The shorter of the two figures turned towards him, swiping her tousled hair from her eyes. The second figure looked across, too, and her braids also fell away.

'Imani!'

Ollie stared, temporarily speechless. Keya and Imani had joined the Haven at about the same time Ollie had. Together with the members of the investigations team, they were his closest friends in the entire place.

One of Flea's goons made a move to rejoin the fight, and Flea shoved him back.

'What the hell's going on?' Ollie said, finding his voice. 'Why are you *fighting*?' He looked from Keya to Imani, but it was one of Flea's goons who answered.

'It was these street rats,' the boy snarled. He was a good head taller than Imani, a head and a neck taller than Keya, but of the four of them he seemed to have come off worst. He dabbed with his fingers at his bloody lip. 'They started it.'

'That's not true!' Keya answered, stepping forwards herself. Imani seemed to have come to her senses quickest, and she placed a hand on her friend's arm to hold her back. '*Cowards*,' Keya spat at Flea's goons. 'Say it to his face, I dare you!'

Both boys glanced in Ollie's direction.

'Say what to my face?' Ollie asked, a warmth building from his stomach.

But Flea's goons ignored him.

'I told you, we didn't write it,' the boy who hadn't spoken yet said to Keya. 'It must have been someone else.'

The goons looked at each other, and this time made no attempt to disguise their sneers. They stood a little straight too, emboldened by the realisation that, whatever happened now, they were protected from further physical reprisals. Ollie caught a glimpse in their demeanour of how they'd managed to provoke Keya and Imani. And his friends *must* have been provoked, Ollie was sure.

'In case you hadn't noticed,' Ollie said, stepping to face the two boys, 'we're *all* street rats here. Every one of us.' He stared until the boys looked down. 'More to the point,' he went on, 'we're all on the same side.' This time he turned his glare on Keya, who finally had the grace to look ashamed.

'Now someone,' Ollie said, '*please*: tell me what's going on. What were the four of you fighting about?'

There was a silence. Nobody in the circle met his eye. Keya and Imani appeared as reluctant to fill him in as anyone.

Eventually Ollie felt a tug on his sleeve. Sol was pointing towards the wall. 'Over there, Ollie.'

Ollie looked – and finally he understood. On the wall of the canteen, in metre-high letters, somebody had sent Ollie a message. 'OLLIE OUT!' the graffiti read.

For a moment, all Ollie could do was stand and stare. Behind him, somebody tittered.

Shame swelled in Ollie's cheeks. He couldn't turn around. Couldn't face the goons who'd spray-painted the message, if indeed it was really them; couldn't look at Keya and Imani, who'd defended him. He couldn't even face Sol, because he knew exactly how his friend would be looking at him: with a pity in his expression that was worse in a way than outright resentment.

After weeks of feeling as if he was failing, and thanks to two short words scrawled on a wall, Ollie's humiliation was complete.

'We rescue Jack's brother,' came a voice: Flea whispering in Ollie's ear. 'That's the priority. Assuming you can even pull that off.' His sneer carried on his breath. 'But when it's over, PJ, I reckon it's time you stepped down.'

6 GHOST SQUAD

Ollie welcomed the dimness of the tunnels. He kept the torch beam from his phone directed at the slippery walkway beneath his feet, so that the others wouldn't see his face if they caught up with him.

Not that there was much chance of that. Ollie had deliberately pulled ahead, leaving Song, Erik and Flea half a dozen steps behind him. They were on their way to Forest Mount, through the sewers as far as the tunnels would take them.

Sol and Lily had wanted to come as well, but Ollie had deliberately selected Erik and Song to go with him. Sol would have tried to cheer him up, and that would only have made Ollie feel worse. Similarly, he couldn't face being with Lily at the moment. Despite a brief thaw back in the control room, the coldness that had developed between them had only intensified since the fracas in the canteen.

At least Erik and Song could be trusted to focus on the mission, and not be distracted by *politics*. Jack should have been there, too. If anyone had the right to be on this mission, she did. But her mobility issues and her technical wizardry meant she generally served the investigations team better by supporting them from her computer.

As for Flea, in spite of his injury he had insisted on coming as well. He'd openly admitted he didn't want Ollie stealing the 'glory'. Ollie's instinct had been to order Flea to stay behind, to give his wound time to recover, but a small voice in his head told him that at least if Flea came along, he wouldn't be able to cause any trouble while Ollie was gone. And with things already so tense between them, he'd been wary of starting another argument.

So he'd relented – but listening to Flea's voice reverberating in the tunnel, he was already beginning to regret it.

'Do you know the first thing I'm going to do when I'm leader?' he was saying, to Song and Erik, it seemed, but loud enough that Ollie could hear. 'I'm going to change the name of the investigations team.'

Facing forwards, Ollie rolled his eyes. What to call the investigations team had been itching at Flea since Ollie had known him. Personally Ollie didn't much care what they called themselves. It was what they *did* that counted, surely.

'And I know exactly what we should call it,' Flea went on. 'Are you ready? You're going to love this, I promise you.'

'I seem to remember you saying the same thing about "Shadow Puppets",' answered Erik. 'And that went down like a submarine with air holes.'

'Yeah, well,' said Flea, momentarily bitter. 'That was your loss. Although, as it happens, this name's even cooler. Ready?' Rolling his 'r's with his tongue, he gave himself a drum roll. 'We're . . . the Ghost Squad.'

Silence.

'Well?' Flea pressed. 'What do you think?'

Ollie glanced over his shoulder, and saw Erik share a look with Song.

'It sounds like some crappy kids' cartoon,' said Song.

Flea huffed. He plodded on for a moment without speaking. 'The Avengers, then,' he said at last. 'How about the Avengers?'

Erik chuckled. 'I'm pretty sure that's already been taken, Flea.'

'I *know* it's been taken. But *those* Avengers aren't real. We *are*.'

'But what would we be avenging exactly?' put in Song.

'Just . . . the usual stuff,' said Flea. 'Injustice. Discrimination. Prejudice.'

'And bad takeaways?' suggested Erik. 'Could we avenge bad takeaways? Because my belly still aches from that curry Sol brought home from Brick Lane the other day.'

Song laughed. She didn't do so very often, which was a shame, Ollie thought. Her laugh reminded him of Aunt Fay's, light and pure like a little kid's.

The thought cheered Ollie briefly. But then, imagining how disappointed in him Aunt Fay must have been – just like Lily and all the others – his mood darkened.

'Be quiet,' he snapped across his shoulder. 'All of you. You know the rules down here.'

Ollie focused forwards, angry at himself now for having lost his temper. And he felt like he'd done a bad impersonation of Dodge, which just about summed up how he'd come to view his leadership more generally.

They climbed above ground using an access ladder when they got to Highgate. Autumn was approaching, and it was one of those dull, dreary days when it was hard to remember it ever having been summer. Rain hung in the gloomy streets like a mist, making it damper outside than it had been down in the sewer.

'There.'

It was Song who spotted the chapel first.

It stood among a clutch of stone buildings that were clearly much older than the Victorian terraces that had sprung up around them. One of the former outbuildings did indeed look as though it had been turned into a museum, just as Ollie had predicted. Another was a visitors' centre. But the chapel, from the look of it, had been allowed to fall into disrepair. At the entrance to the grounds there was a lichgate, but the gates themselves were secured with a metal chain.

'Let's see if there's a way in around the back,' said Ollie.

The cemetery was ringed by a wall made of flint, and curtained by overgrown conifers. They found a gap where the wall was lowest, and shoved their way through the undergrowth on the other side. Soon enough they found themselves standing among the chipped teeth tombstones.

With the outside world shielded from view, it was hard to believe they were still in London at all. But for the ever-present background hum of traffic, and the slightly grubby taste of the city air, they might have been in a sleepy country village. The only other building visible to them from the rear of the chapel was Forest Mount itself.

The school sat perched atop the tree-lined hill that gave it its name. With its conical spires and imposing stone facade, it looked like a castle in some dark and twisted fairy tale. The forest below it did nothing to dispel the impression. The canopy was a tangled blanket of decaying leaves, utterly impenetrable to the outside eye.

Ollie and the others paused for a moment to peer up at their ultimate destination.

'Count Dracula called,' said Erik. 'He says he wants his castle back.'

'It's like something out of *Beauty and the Beast*,' added Song.

At the mention of beasts, Ollie caught Flea looking distinctly uncomfortable.

‘It’s just a building,’ he grumbled, not entirely convincingly. ‘It could do with a lick of paint, that’s all.’

Ollie watched as Flea strode off towards the abandoned chapel, then gazed back up at the school.

‘Come on,’ he said to the others. ‘We need to find a way down into the crypt.’

‘Wait,’ said Erik. ‘What?’ He turned from the school to face the church. ‘Did you say *crypt*? As in *tomb*? For dead people?’

‘Where else did you expect to find the entrance to the tunnel?’ said Song, pulling Erik along.

‘Couldn’t we just . . . I don’t know . . .’ Erik replied, ‘make our own tunnel or something? This is a graveyard, isn’t it? There must be a shovel around here somewhere.’

Flea had already located a way into the building when they caught up with him. He stood beside a rotten wooden door that he’d apparently managed to prise open.

The others followed as he led them stealthily inside.

They passed through an old storage room, and then emerged through another doorway behind the altar. It was hard to see in the gloom, but the building was even smaller inside than Ollie had been expecting. When the chapel had been in use, there would have been space for twenty or thirty congregants at most. Now, most of the pews were missing, and those that remained appeared as rotten as the door that had led them in. With the dust and assorted debris, what the church most resembled was a building site. Ollie wondered for a moment whether it was even safe.

'Ollie. Over there.'

Ollie followed the beam of Song's torch. There was a stone staircase leading down tucked into a corner of one of the aisles. After pointing his own torch up to the ceiling, just to check it wasn't about to fall in on them, Ollie led the others across the nave.

As he was about to descend the first of the steps, he felt a hand on his arm holding him back.

'Are we sure about this?' hissed Erik, obviously even more spooked now than he had been in the graveyard. 'What if someone finds us here?'

Flea pushed his way between them. 'I'd be more worried about *never* being found, if I were you,' he said. 'Once we're down in that basement, the whole building could easily collapse in on us. And then we'd be trapped in here, just us and all the dead people.'

At this last comment, Flea turned the torch from his phone upwards, so that the beam illuminated only his face. He made a ghostly noise, which echoed around the cold stone walls as he spiralled down the stairwell into the darkness.

7 TUNNEL VISION

'Aren't you glad I came along, PJ?'

They'd found the crypt. It was at the bottom of the stone staircase. Ollie could just make out the tombs in the darkness. But they'd come as close as they could get. Blocking their way into the basement beneath the church was an iron gate, chained in place and secured with a rusted metal padlock.

Flea wasn't to be deterred, however. He stood frisking himself, until he located what he was looking for in one of the pockets of his combats: a battered leather pouch, which was filled with a variety of what looked at first glance like misshapen screwdrivers. It was his lock-picking kit, Ollie realised.

'Stand aside,' said Flea, even though there was nobody in his way. He frowned at the padlock, then selected one of the tools in his pouch. He fitted the crooked end into the keyhole and, listening carefully as he worked, wiggled it gently from side to side. There was a click, and Flea grinned, and suddenly the padlock burst open.

'*Voilà*,' Flea said, opening the gate. 'Who says I'm just a pretty face?' He bowed as he ushered Song and Erik through.

When Ollie tried to follow them, Flea stepped across his path and barged ahead of him. It was a typical Flea manoeuvre, and Ollie didn't know why he was surprised.

Catching up with the others in the crypt, Ollie heard Erik emit a low whistle. 'And I thought the graveyard was creepy,' he said.

Ollie would have had to admit that the crypt would have been the perfect setting for a horror movie. Even with their modified torch beams set to maximum, the light from their phones barely penetrated the darkness, which seemed thicker down here than it did in the sewers. The crypt's ceiling hung low, brushing the top of Ollie's head. A single tomb dominated the space, but there were other markers around the edge of the room that indicated more than one person had been buried here.

Ordinarily Ollie would have been fascinated by the sense of forgotten history. It must have been decades since anyone else was last down here. Right now, however, there was a job to be done.

'Look for a doorway,' Ollie instructed. 'Or an outline of one on the wall somewhere. Anything that might lead to a tunnel. The school is to the north, so chances are it would be—'

'Right here.'

When Ollie swung his torch, he saw Erik peering nervously at his feet.

Ollie edged closer. There was a hole in the ground, which seemed to swallow the light from Erik's phone. The only thing Ollie could see clearly was that the hole, like the door into the room, was blocked off by an iron grille. And this time there was no lock for Flea to pick. The bars had been cemented into the ground.

'Oh well,' Erik said, standing upright. 'Can't say we didn't try. Back upstairs then? Anyone fancy stopping for a hot chocolate on our way home? I think I saw a café on the corner.'

Ollie bent to get a closer look at the grille. He reached for one of the bars with his free hand, then tucked his phone into his pocket and gripped the iron railings with both. He pulled. The grille was loose where the concrete had crumbled, but there was no way Ollie was strong enough to wrench it free.

'Flea?' he called. 'I think this falls into your department.'

Flea sneered slightly as Ollie stepped aside. He pulled up his sleeves, then squatted over the grille and rolled his meaty fingers around a bar at each end. He took a breath, steadying himself. And when he heaved . . .

Nothing happened. The grille clung stubbornly in place.

Flea looked at Ollie without a trace of a sneer this time. His expression seemed to suggest Ollie had tricked him.

'Wait,' he snapped. 'I've got this.'

He stood tall for a moment, and rubbed his palms together vigorously. He puffed, once, twice, and on the third outward exhalation bent forwards and seized hold of the iron bars. This time when he heaved, his forearms bulged, and a vein pulsed at his temple. Even by just the light of the torch beams, Ollie saw Flea's entire face turn red.

But it was working. There was a crunching sound, a patter as the crumbling concrete started to rain down into the hole, and then an almighty plume of dust as the grille finally came away. Flea staggered backwards, the mesh of iron in his hands, and it took Ollie, Song and Erik to hold him up.

Once Flea had regained his balance, Ollie and the others collapsed into a fit of coughing. Flea, meanwhile, roared his delight. 'Behold the mighty Flea!' he intoned, brandishing the metal grille above his head like a trophy. 'A boy with the strength of a thousand men!'

Still coughing, Erik looked at Ollie through the haze. 'He really does think he's one of the Avengers,' he spluttered.

Song was already moving back towards the hole. She flapped a hand in front of her to clear the air, and shone her torch into the cavity. 'You can see even less now than you could before.'

Ollie crouched down at her side. What she'd said was true. In the stillness of the crypt, the dust from the displaced concrete hung in the tunnel opening like a mist.

'Here,' he said, holding out his arms. 'Lower me down.'

Flea seemed about to protest, to insist that *he* go first, but when he leant over the hole and peered into the impenetrable gloom, he evidently thought better of it.

'You're the boss, PJ,' he said. He clamped hold of Ollie's right arm roughly, and Ollie offered his left to Song.

She shook her head. 'I'll go first,' she said. 'I'm lighter than you are, for one thing. Plus, no offence, Ollie, but I've spent a few more years in the dojo than you have. If it turns out the tunnel *is* being guarded, I'll have a better chance of defending myself than you will.'

Ollie frowned and looked at Flea, but there was no time to argue. Song was already moving into position.

It took all of Ollie's effort once she reached the edge just to hold her weight.

'Tell us . . . when your feet . . . touch the bottom,' Ollie grunted. His hands were latched around one of Song's wrists, as Flea stood beside him gripping the other.

Song dangled into the empty space, her legs already wrapped in darkness.

'Not yet . . . Still nothing . . .'

Ollie and Flea had lowered her as far as they could without toppling into the tunnel themselves. 'It's no use,' Ollie said. 'We'll have to pull you up, look for some other way to—'

'Wait,' said Song. 'I think I see something. Below my feet.'

'Are you sure?' Ollie said.

'Let me go,' Song instructed.

'Wait, Song,' answered Ollie. 'You don't know what's—'

But with a simple twist of her wrists – a trick to escape an arm grab that Song had shown Ollie in the dojo – Song made the decision for them. Ollie found himself clutching thin air as his friend dropped out of sight.

'Song!'

Ollie fell to his knees and peered into the hole. There was no sign of her. No sound either. For one awful moment, Ollie assumed she must still have been falling.

But then a torch beam shone weakly up at him through the haze.

'I'm down!' Song called. She'd obviously landed like a ballerina, light-footed from all those years studying karate. 'It's not that far, actually. Only a couple of metres. And it looks as if there used to be a set of steps. They've crumbled away, but if you're careful you could use what's left of them as rungs.'

Ollie held his own torch tight to the cavity wall and noticed the footholds Song was talking about. They began about a metre below the lip, but they would make the process of climbing down easier – not to mention climbing back up again.

Song led, followed by Flea, then Erik, and finally Ollie. There wasn't space at first for them to walk in anything other than single file.

Soon enough, however, the tunnel broadened, and instead of rubble beneath their feet, they found themselves stepping on a worn stone floor. At the crypt end, the tunnel had obviously collapsed in on itself, covering those steps Song had found and partly blocking the space. Now, it was more the underground passageway Ollie had first imagined. They were even able to reduce the brightness of their torch beams now that they were past the worst of the dust.

'So what's the plan when we get inside the grounds?' said Erik, who was clearly relieved to have put the crypt behind them. He was panting, and Ollie realised he was slightly out of breath as well. It wasn't immediately obvious, but the tunnel floor was on an incline, leading up as it burrowed beneath the hill.

'We find Errol,' Ollie answered. 'Somehow. And we bring him back to the Haven. Once Errol's safe, and he's told us everything he knows, we decide what to do about Forest Mount.' He wished their plan wasn't quite so vague, but the uncomfortable truth was, they still had no idea what they were really up against.

'We do have one thing on our side,' said Song. 'Once we get past those outer defences, we'll at least be able to blend in. The one place kids can generally walk about without being noticed is a school.'

'As long as we don't draw too much attention to ourselves,' said Ollie. 'Which reminds me: turn your jackets inside out.'

Without slowing their pace, they all did as Ollie had instructed. Their jackets were waterproof on the outside, but on the inside they'd been rigged back at the Haven to look like the blazers the pupils wore at Forest Mount. They each wore a plain white shirt as well, with black trousers to match the blazers, meaning their clothes would pass at first glance for the Forest Mount uniform. The only thing missing was the coat of arms that should have been on the Forest Mount blazer, which was a grander version of the one Ollie remembered from St Jerome's, his school before he'd joined the Haven. Both coats of arms were a long way from the much simpler logo that had become the Haven's symbol: an 'H' framed by a triangle.

'Um . . . Ollie?' said Song from up ahead. 'What now?'

Ollie squeezed past the others until he was alongside her. The passageway they'd been walking along continued straight ahead. But two new tunnels had appeared, forking both left and right.

Ollie looked at Song, who shrugged. 'The school is to the north, right?' she said. 'So let's go north.'

The problem was, the tunnel from the crypt hadn't exactly run in a straight line, meaning they could no longer be certain which way north was.

Ollie pulled out his phone and selected the compass app. The needle refused to settle, though. First it showed north as one way, then another. Ollie shook the phone and tried again, but the result was the same. His phone was as confused as he was.

Seeing Ollie struggling, the others tried their phones as well.

'That's odd,' said Ollie, when it became clear none of the others was having any more luck than he'd had. He looked at the tunnels. 'I guess we vote then. I say . . . right.'

'Left,' said Flea immediately, fixing Ollie with a defiant stare.

Rather than voting straight away, Song sniffed the air. 'Right smells fouler,' she judged. 'And there's something foul going on at Forest Mount, isn't there? So I'm with Ollie.'

They looked at Erik, who shook his head. 'I can't believe I'm about to say this,' he said, sniffing the tunnel and then wrinkling his nose in distaste. 'But foul makes sense. Kind of.'

'Right it is then,' Ollie said, and he moved into the lead.

They came to three more intersections, and each time elected to follow their noses. With their phones continuing to malfunction, it was their only option.

They rounded a corner, took another fork, and were about to take a further turning when all of a sudden Ollie felt Song's hand hauling him back.

'*The torches*,' she hissed. '*Turn them off!*'

'What is it?' Ollie said, crouching instinctively and flattening his torch beam against his chest.

'Up there.'

Ollie peered around the corner, tracking the path laid out by Song's finger.

It was a security camera, tucked against the ceiling of the passageway, and so well concealed, Ollie was amazed Song had spotted it.

'PJ . . .' urged Flea from across Ollie's shoulder.

'I'm on it,' Ollie muttered. He killed his torch, and tapped to open another of the apps on his phone. This one ran CCTV interference. Jack had developed it, and Ollie had seen it in operation before, so he knew it worked – but this time it was having no effect. It was like with the compass: something was causing the app to go haywire.

'It's not working,' Ollie muttered, as he tried desperately to find the right setting. He peered around the corner again. A little red light on the CCTV camera indicated it was still very much in operation.

'You're doing it wrong,' hissed Flea. 'Give it here.'

He snatched the phone from Ollie.

'Something's wrong,' Ollie said. 'I can feel it.' As he looked at the light on the security camera, it started to blink.

'Do you think they saw us?' Erik whispered.

'Not us, but maybe the torches,' answered Song.

'It's not working,' said Flea, who was fiddling with the app. He looked at Ollie. 'You broke it. You must have.'

'I didn't break it, Flea. I think maybe there's something down here interfering with the phones. Like a jammer or something. That's why the compasses didn't work either.'

'So what now?' said Song.

Ollie looked again at the winking camera. They couldn't go on, that much was certain. Not this way at least. But he didn't like the idea of going back, either. He thought about how upset Jack had been, how terrified for her little brother. There was no way Ollie was prepared to let her down.

'Maybe we could—' he started to say – but he got no further. A whirring noise interrupted him, and Ollie had time when he glanced up to see a small panel slide open on the ceiling above them. And then, as Ollie and the others watched on helplessly, the entire tunnel began filling with gas.

8 SNAKE PIT

'*Run!*'

At Ollie's command, they began to scramble through the passageway in the direction they'd come. Someone – Erik? – managed to switch on their torch, and Ollie saw the gas billowing in the tunnel right behind them.

'Tear gas,' choked Flea, and the burning in Ollie's eyes told him that Flea was right.

'Back to the crypt,' Ollie said. '*Quickly.*'

'Which way's the crypt?' gasped Erik, and Ollie realised he had no idea. He'd tried to keep track of the turnings they'd taken on their way out, but in their panic to run from the gas he'd already become completely disoriented.

'Straight on,' he coughed. 'I think.'

But even as he spoke there was another whirring sound, and then a hiss as more gas flooded into the tunnel right ahead of them.

'Left! Turn left!'

Ollie stopped and ushered the other three ahead of him, into a passageway that was mercifully clear. But the gas was being pumped out with such force in the tunnel behind them, they'd barely made the turning before this way began filling with noxious fumes, too. Ollie's eyes were already streaming. With the gas funnelling them one way and then the other, he felt like a rat running blindly through a maze.

'Faster!' he urged the others. Ollie was at the rear of the group. Flea had passed him first at the junction, meaning he was now the one leading. Ollie could only hope that Flea had a better idea of the way out than he did himself.

For a second or two it felt as though they were making headway. But then there came a hissing noise from up ahead. They'd each managed to power on their torches, and when Ollie swung his beam towards the ceiling he saw more gas being pumped into the tunnel just ahead of them. With the hissing noise all around them, it was as though they'd stumbled into a pit of sleeping snakes.

'What now?' yelled Song.

Ollie searched desperately with his torch beam, but there was no junction to save them this time. Between the gas filling the tunnel just behind, and the new plume polluting the air ahead, there was nowhere for them to go.

'PJ!' shouted Flea. 'Grab hold of Erik! And, Erik, catch hold of Song!' Squinting through the dimness, Ollie saw Flea in turn take Song's hand, so that together they formed a human chain. 'Hold your breath and shut your eyes!' Flea instructed. 'All of you! And whatever you do, *don't let go*.'

'Flea, wait!' Almost before Ollie had uttered the words, he found himself being dragged the way they'd been running, directly into the new cloud of tear gas. He clamped his mouth shut and tightened his eyes, silently praying that Flea knew what he was doing. Twice he clipped Erik's heels, almost sending them both sprawling, but somehow Erik managed to keep his feet.

They turned left, right, left again, blindly stumbling in the direction Flea was leading them.

When Ollie could hold his breath no longer, he let go of Erik and staggered to a standstill. The air in his lungs burst out of him, and he found himself gulping for oxygen. He expected to immediately start coughing, and braced himself to wretch against the fumes. But the air tasted almost normal, and when Ollie opened his eyes, he saw only a thin haze of gas in the space around them. The hissing had faded into the background.

Were they in the clear? Had Flea brought them through?

Still half blind, Ollie turned his attention to his friends. Erik was doubled over just ahead of him, spluttering and wiping his eyes. Song was a few paces on, holding herself up on the wall. And Flea . . . Where was Flea?

Ollie dialled his torch beam to full, wincing at the onslaught of light, and swept the tunnel up ahead. But Flea was nowhere to be seen.

'Flea!' he called again. 'Fl—'

And then he saw him. He was just ahead of Song, bent forwards on his hands and knees.

'*Flea!*'

At Ollie's cry of alarm, the others looked up. From the way their eyes were pinched tight – just like newborn kittens' – Ollie could tell they were having as much trouble seeing as he was.

He squeezed past Song and dropped to the ground beside Flea. His eyes, Ollie saw, were swollen completely shut. When Flea had instructed Ollie and the others to close their eyes and form a chain, he must have kept his own eyes open so he could guide them.

'Are we through?' Flea wheezed. 'The gas . . .'

From the fractured sound of Flea's voice, it was clear he'd inhaled plenty of the tear gas, too. And all to get them to safety.

'We're through,' Ollie said. 'I think.' He swept his torch beam across the ceiling. He couldn't be sure, but he thought if there had been another gas valve nearby, they would have triggered it by now. 'You did it, Flea. You saved us. But we can't stay here. There might be—'

'*Listen*,' said Erik.

Ollie and the others strained to hear. Voices filtered through the darkness.

'. . . that tear gas. They're probably lying in a heap just up ahead.'

‘That’s assuming they haven’t suffocated already. Did anyone recognise them? On the monitor it looked as if they were wearing uniform.’

‘Probably some dimwit year sevens. God knows how they stumbled into the tunnels.’

‘They were too big to be year sevens. And stop the chatter, you lot. Put on your gas masks, or in a minute you’ll all be crying like little babies.’

The voices went quiet, and Ollie shared a glance with Song and Erik. Without anyone needing to be told, they swiped their torch beams to low. Ollie helped Flea to his feet.

‘Put your hands on my shoulders,’ he whispered. ‘We need to move. *Now*.’

The gas was behind them, and the voices had come from somewhere up ahead, meaning they needed to find a junction, and quickly – before whoever was hunting them closed in.

They hurried on, moving as soundlessly as they could. Ollie was in the lead and guiding Flea, who was still blind from the tear gas. Ollie didn’t like the sound of his breathing, either. Flea’s mouth was only centimetres from Ollie’s ear, and every time he exhaled, Ollie heard a sound like broken bagpipes. It reminded him of the little girl back in the Haven, the one who’d been hospitalised with croup.

They reached a T-junction, and Ollie hesitated.

'Why have you stopped?' Flea croaked, and Ollie sensed Song and Erik shuffling uneasily further back.

'Just . . . give me a second.'

As well as listening for those voices, Ollie was trying desperately to recall the way back to the crypt. They'd turned right first, then right again, and after that two lefts. But when they'd fled the gas they'd also gone left. Hadn't they? Or maybe it was right, in which case—

It was no use. Ollie was hopelessly confused. And he knew it would be useless to evade the people hunting them if they couldn't also find their way back to the chapel. If they got lost down here, it would only be a matter of time until they were caught.

'This way,' he said, with far more decisiveness than he felt. He hoped the others wouldn't detect the uncertainty in his tone.

As they continued along the path Ollie had chosen, there was no sound of anyone coming after them. And the passage began to slope slightly downhill, giving Ollie a sense of hope. Soon enough they began to taste something else in the air – not the traces of the tear gas, but the earthiness of the dust they'd stirred up when they'd first broken into the tunnel.

'We're going the right way,' Ollie said, as much to himself as to the others. 'I know we are.'

But almost as he spoke, they reached a crossroads in the underground network that they hadn't come across before. The tunnels leading off it went in four different directions, but otherwise appeared identical. How was Ollie supposed to choose?

'Straight on,' he muttered. 'It has to be.'

With Flea wheezing at his back, he started moving again, crossing the intersection and continuing the way they'd been travelling. Right away he felt he'd made the right choice. That earthy smell got stronger, and the slope ahead appeared to descend more steeply.

He glanced across his shoulder to make sure Song and Erik were behind them. They were a few paces back, but had started to follow Ollie and Flea across the intersection.

And that's when it happened.

Without warning, the junction was flooded with light. Ollie and Flea had crossed into the shadows, but Song and Erik were only halfway across the gap. They froze like animals caught in headlights.

'There they are! Get them!'

It sounded as though their pursuers were right on top of them.

'Go,' croaked Flea. 'Just *go*!'

Ollie started to sprint. It wasn't easy with Flea clutching his shoulders. But it was flight or fight, and with Flea unable to see, and Ollie and the others half blind as well, there was no way they'd win if it came to conflict. Apart from anything, they had no idea how many people they were up against.

Ollie staggered, found his feet, continued running. His torch beam danced frantically in front of him, as Flea's breath whistled in his ear. Ollie had no time to check behind him. He just had to hope Erik and Song were keeping pace.

Another junction, and this time Ollie took them to the left. The tunnel was narrowing, the air thickening, but with dust, Ollie thought, not gas.

They were nearly there. *Surely.*

There was a shout behind him: a cry of alarm. It was Song's voice, and Ollie stopped running and swung his torch. He was just in time to see Song dispatch a boy who'd grabbed her with a back kick, her foot landing in her attacker's groin. The boy doubled over, and Song pushed him to the floor, directly into the path of another boy who was closing from behind. The second boy tripped, cursing as he fell, and for a moment the tunnel behind them was blocked and Ollie and the others were in the clear.

'Keep going!' yelled Song.

Ollie did as she'd instructed. He took them right, left, straight ahead, and then finally saw what they'd been searching for: those steps in the collapsed tunnel wall.

He took Flea's hand and guided it to the first of the rungs.

'Climb,' Ollie said. '*Quickly.*'

Flea moved with such assurance, it was hard to believe he couldn't see. In moments he was through the hole above their heads.

'You next,' said Ollie to Erik.

Just as Erik was about to start climbing, they heard footsteps pounding towards them along the tunnel.

'Get up into the crypt,' said Song. 'I'll deal with this.'

'But you can barely see!' Ollie protested.

'I can see enough,' Song answered, and with that she was off, back the way they'd come and towards whoever was closing in.

'Ollie!' Erik was halfway up the makeshift ladder. 'What are you waiting for?'

'But . . . Song,' Ollie responded, shining his light the way she'd run.

'Song will be fine. You've seen her in the dojo. Now *climb*.'

Reluctantly Ollie followed Erik up. But he lingered near the top of the steps, frantically shining his torch into the tunnel to try to see. He heard a holler, and Song's battle cry, and then what sounded like a third person joining the fight. There was an *oof*, and something heavy falling to the ground, and then an unmistakeable scream of pain.

'I'm going after her,' Ollie said. He started down, but when he felt with his foot for the rung below him, he found his sole being forced back up.

Song was standing right below him.

'I'm here, Ollie. But so are those Forest Mount kids. I dealt with two of them, but there's another four or five at least.'

'Grab a hold, Ollie!'

Erik was dangling his hand. Ollie seized hold of it, and with Erik's help, clambered on to the floor of the crypt. Then he spun to help Erik haul Song up, too.

'Where's the tomb?' said Flea, behind them. He was feeling about him blindly, searching for something in the room.

'The what?' said Ollie.

'The tomb! There was a tomb right beside the hole in the floor. Where is it?'

Ollie saw what Flea intended to do. He scrambled to his feet. 'Here,' he said, directing Flea towards the big stone tomb that dominated the room. 'But it's too heavy. There's no way you'll be able to—'

Flea wasn't listening. He'd positioned himself at one end of the tomb and was pushing with all his strength. But Ollie was right: it was too heavy. And the hole into the tunnels was filling with light, meaning Crowe's army had finally caught up.

'Song!' Ollie called. 'Erik!'

As one, the three of them moved to Flea's side. They started shoving with all their might. To Ollie it felt as though they were trying to move a solid wall.

And then it shifted. Just fractionally, but when they heaved again, the lid from the tomb started sliding, until all at once it was slipping forwards and they wouldn't have been able to stop it if they'd wanted to. It toppled with an almighty crash, filling the air with ancient dust, and blocking the entrance to the tunnel.

There were yells below them, shouts of frustration, until these too were completely shut off.

It was over. They were safe.

Ollie cast around at the others, daring to show his relief. But Song's face was a picture of horror, and when Ollie followed her gaze, he realised what she was staring at. Flea had fallen forwards, and he was lying lifeless on the floor.

9 CROWE'S NEST

Errol heard it all through the ventilation shaft. The desperate shouts, the scurrying feet, the distant crash, and then . . . silence.

For a short while he'd experienced a surge of hope. Someone was coming for him. Rufus, his stepdad? It seemed unlikely, as much as Errol would have loved to believe it. But maybe Jack, and her friends at the Haven . . .

Except after that final crash, Errol's hope had settled like falling dust. It was just him, all alone, in the dungeons below Forest Mount.

When Colton Crowe and the others had hauled him down from the boundary wall, they'd dragged him back through the undergrowth all the way up the hill to the main building. At the school Errol had been blindfolded, and led through passageway after passageway, down stairwell after stairwell, until finally he'd been tossed into his cell and the blindfold had been removed.

There were no windows in the cell, and just a single, solid-looking door. The handle had been removed on Errol's side, and when he'd tried kicking at the door he realised it was made of metal, and all he'd managed to do was hurt his foot.

His eyes kept returning to the vent on the wall. It was his one connection to the outside world. But in the wake of the commotion he'd heard, there was no further sound of any kind, no shift in the light when he peered through the mesh, just a slightly acrid stench in the air, like burnt bleach. It made his eyes water.

'Hello?' he called. '*Anyone?*'

He waited, ear pressed against the vent.

'Jack? Are you out there?'

'Who's Jack?'

Errol spun to the sound of the voice. The door into his cell had opened without him even hearing it, and there, at the threshold, stood Colton Crowe. His hair looked all the blacker in the dimly lit dungeon, and his smile glinted in the lamplight like jagged glass.

Errol pressed his back against the wall, and wiped his eyes to try to stop them streaming.

Crowe took a step into the room. 'I said, who's Jack? Answer me, or I'll give you something else to cry about.'

'I'm not crying,' protested Errol. 'And Jack's no one. Just . . . just my invisible friend.' Almost subconsciously, his hand went to his pocket. The photo of his sister was still in there. The prefects who'd led him to his cell had frisked him before they'd shut him inside, but they'd overlooked the thin slip of paper.

Crowe's smile broadened. He stopped halfway into Errol's cell, and cast his steely eyes around the grimy surroundings.

'Well, I could hardly blame you for inventing someone to talk to. These aren't the most salubrious of quarters, I will admit.'

Errol had no idea what 'salubrious' meant. It sounded like a prefect's word, and for some reason it made him furious.

'You can't keep me here,' he found himself saying. He'd edged slightly forwards from the wall. 'It's not . . . not *right*.'

'You're a fine one to talk about what's right,' said Crowe. 'Do you consider it *right*, for instance, when snivelling little year sevens go nosing about in other people's business? When they *spy* and *eavesdrop* and *interfere*?'

The smile had dropped from Crowe's face. In its place was something like a snarl. For half a moment, Errol could picture Crowe himself as the monster in the woods, like a werewolf or something, bounding about on all fours and howling at a blood-red moon.

'I wasn't spying,' Errol said, shrinking back. 'And anyway, I didn't see *anything*.'

It was a lie and both of them knew it.

'So why did you run?' said Crowe. 'If you saw nothing, what made you so desperate to get away?'

'I . . . I was homesick. That's all. I missed . . . my stepdad, and . . .'

'Ah, yes. Your stepfather. Rufus, isn't it? A very busy man, by all accounts. Too busy to look after his only child, from what I've gathered, or even to see him in the summer holidays.'

'He was away . . . on business. And— '

Crowe's smile spread slowly across his face.

'I'm afraid that isn't true, Errol. I looked into it, you see. It's easy enough to check on a person's travel history if you know where the information is kept. And the reality is, your stepfather hasn't left the country in months. He could have brought you home for the holidays, but he chose not to.'

Errol couldn't help but show his confusion.

'You thought he cared for you, didn't you?' said Crowe. 'I'm afraid the truth is your stepfather doesn't want you. He's *never* wanted you. Which makes you just the sort of person I've been looking for. You see, I have a task for you, Errol. A very *special* task.'

Errol shook his head. All he could think about was Rufus. What Crowe was saying couldn't be true. Could it?

'You don't know what you're talking about,' he said. 'You *can't* know.'

'Oh, but I do. When it comes to interfering little brats, I make it my business to know. When a student proves particularly meddlesome, they need to be dealt with, and in the most appropriate way. If their parents are going to ask questions, we need to come up with a story that will stop them looking too closely at the school. If, on the other hand, the parents are merely likely to shrug their shoulders . . . Well. Let's just say it makes my job a whole lot easier.'

Errol felt like pressing his palms against his ears. *It's not true*, he wanted to shout. *It's* not.

Instead, he dropped his eyes to the floor. Jack was right. All this time, Jack had been right. Rufus had never wanted *her*, just as he'd never really wanted *him*.

Errol had never felt like such an idiot.

'He isn't coming for you, Errol,' Crowe told him. 'Even if he knew you were down here in my little . . . nest, let's call it. I doubt he would come for you even then.'

'So why am I even still alive?' said Errol, bitterly. 'I don't know anything. There aren't any secrets I can give you to write down in that little black book of yours.'

Crowe, for a moment, looked impressed. 'My, my. You have been busy, haven't you? I bet you think you've got things all figured out.'

'I've figured out enough,' Errol said. 'I know you're using the kids here to spy on their parents so you can blackmail them. And I know you keep people who refuse to help you trapped down here, and torture them until they tell you what you want to know.'

'Torture?' said Crowe. 'Come now, Errol. This isn't the Middle Ages. I admit that sometimes we need to use a little . . . persuasion, but torture seems a rather dramatic way of putting things. Mostly we find people join our cause willingly. In the end.'

'Tell me what you did to George,' Errol demanded, suddenly livid – at Crowe, at Rufus, at *himself*. 'Tell me what you did to my friend. Have you got him locked up down here, too?'

Crowe feigned an expression of regret. 'There are one or two others in accommodation like yours, it's true. But George . . .' He shook his head sadly. 'George suffered an unfortunate accident. It seems he got a little . . . out of his depth,' he added, with a glimmer.

Errol couldn't mask his shock. 'You . . . you *killed* him? *Why?*'

'Don't you know? I thought you had this all figured out.'

'You want . . . money, obviously,' Errol answered, trying to sound more certain than he felt. 'Why else do people resort to blackmail?'

Crowe barked out a laugh. 'Money,' he scoffed. 'This isn't about *money*.'

Errol was trying to keep things straight in his mind, but all he could think about was George. *An unfortunate accident. Out of his depth . . .*

Errol shook his head to clear it. 'It doesn't matter what you're after. The only thing that matters is that you're not going to get it. People will find out. *Someone* will. And they'll stop you. *I* will!'

'You're right, of course,' said Crowe. 'Someone will find out. Eventually. But by then it will be too late. Because we *can't* be stopped, Errol. Everything's already in motion. What you've seen – what you *think* you've seen – is only the beginning.'

Errol couldn't stop himself asking the obvious question. 'The beginning of what?'

'The beginning of the end! By the time this is over, we'll be living in a country reborn. A *world* reborn, with a new power at its heart, and the right people in charge. Not the fools who run this country now.'

Crowe sneered at Errol's confusion.

'It will all become clear to you soon enough. The only thing you need to do is what I'm asking you to.'

'You mean . . . join you? Become *one* of you?'

'It's as I said to you, Errol,' said Crowe. 'We have a job for you. Something that would cement your place in history.'

Errol found himself shaking his head, slowly at first, but then with vigour. 'I'll never join you. Never!'

Crowe appeared unperturbed. 'So you say. And yet you don't even know what it is you're turning your back on.'

'It doesn't matter. I don't care. You're just bullies. That's all. Why would I ever want to join *you*?'

'Because you have no choice,' said Crowe. 'Not if you ever want to see daylight again.'

Errol swallowed. How long had he been locked up already? A day? A week? He had no way of telling. He knew he had to hold out, but faced with the sentence Crowe was threatening him with, he could already feel his resistance crumbling.

But then he thought of his sister, and it was as though he could hear her whispering, telling him exactly what *she* would do.

'I told you,' Errol said, his hand pressing against the photograph in his pocket. 'I said to you before. I'll never join you. You *are* bullies. You, and Strain, and . . . and whoever else you've got involved in your stupid *cause*.'

For a moment Crowe said nothing. Then his smile blackened. He hammered on the cell door with the back of his fist. 'In that case,' he said, stepping aside, 'I have no choice but to attempt more persuasive methods.'

Behind him, the door eased open. Slowly, gradually, so that Errol had time to realise what he was seeing.

And then he screamed.

10 BLAME GAME

Ollie sat alone on the empty platform, his feet dangling towards the tracks. The rails were mainly rust now, and the platform itself didn't lead anywhere – the entire tunnel was blocked off at either end. There were worrying cracks in the arched ceiling as well, meaning few people ever came down here.

Which today suited Ollie just fine.

He couldn't get what had happened to Flea out of his mind. It had been Ollie's plan. He'd led them down into the tunnels. In a way, he'd even been responsible for the tear gas. After what Errol had said in his emails, and what Flea had discovered on his reconnaissance mission, Ollie should have been prepared for *anything*.

So it was Ollie's fault, plain and simple. Flea had been right all along. Ollie should never have been elected the Haven's leader. More than that, he should have left after what had happened to Nancy, and after they'd dealt with Maddy Sikes. If he had, none of this would ever have happened.

'Ollie?'

At first Ollie didn't recognise the voice. There were lanterns strung along the walls of the abandoned platform, but they served as warning signs, mainly. They weren't bright enough to totally dispel the dark. And the person who'd called his name was approaching without a light of their own.

'Aunt Fay? Is that you?'

The Haven's founder was the one person within the community's walls who could navigate even the darkest tunnels without a torch to guide her. In fact she moved so sure-footedly, it was often easy to forget that she was blind.

'There you are,' said Aunt Fay, as she stepped into a puddle of light. She seemed to have pinpointed where Ollie was sitting from just the handful of words he had spoken. 'Do you mind if I join you?'

'I . . . No. Of course not.'

Ollie watched with concern as Aunt Fay moved towards the edge of the platform, readying himself to help her if she stumbled. He needn't have worried, though. She lowered herself gracefully to his side. Watching her move so easily, it was hard to believe she was approaching eighty years old.

'Is there any news?' Ollie asked, almost before she'd fully settled.

Aunt Fay showed Ollie her smile, which had the effect of lighting up even the darkest of rooms.

'There is *good* news,' she said. 'Galen says Flea will make a full recovery. He won't be running to catch a bus any time soon, and his sight will remain blurry for a while. But he is on the mend, and that is the main thing.'

Ollie dropped his head towards his lap, and sighed his intense relief. And then, abruptly, he sat up straighter.

'I should go and see him. I should . . . apologise, and . . .'

'Apologise?' echoed Aunt Fay.

'It was my fault,' Ollie explained. 'He got hurt because of me. *Twice* now.'

'The tear gas was your doing? You were the one to set the trap?'

'What? No. Of course not. But I led Flea in there. It was my idea to try the tunnel in the first place.'

'And you forced Flea to come with you. Is that what you mean?'

'Well . . . no. He wanted to come. But I should have . . .' Ollie shook his head, unable to finish the sentence.

'Should have . . . what?' asked Aunt Fay. 'Done nothing, perhaps? Because as I understand it, that was the only alternative. Yours was the only plan on the table.'

'That's what I mean, though! It was *my* plan. Which means it was all my fault.'

Aunt Fay laughed, not unkindly. 'You have a lot to learn, Ollie Turner. About many things. One of them being the limits of your responsibility. Dodge exhibited the same failing, if you recall. He believed it was beholden on him to solve *everything*.'

For a moment Ollie wasn't sure what to say. Whenever he thought about his former friend, he felt a perplexing mix of respect, gratitude, sadness and anger, which occasionally bubbled into outright fury. But the one thing he never considered Dodge was a *failure*.

'Dodge . . . made a mistake,' he said at last. 'That's all.'

Aunt Fay bobbed her head. 'That he did. A big one. One for which he paid very dearly. Fortunately, the cost of your mistake has turned out to be far lower.'

'So you admit it?' said Ollie. 'You agree I made a mistake?'

'I concede it looks that way now,' said Aunt Fay. 'But it is far easier to judge a decision when you already know the consequences. If you had asked me this time yesterday, before you went into that tunnel, my answer might well have been different.'

Aunt Fay was just trying to make him feel better, Ollie knew. He wouldn't let her change his mind.

'I'm stepping down,' he told her. 'As leader, I mean. And I think . . . I think it would be easier for everyone if I went away. Somewhere else.' Quite where, Ollie hadn't figured out yet. The truth was, even though he knew his leaving would be for the best, he couldn't quite bring himself to face up to the implications. *Leaving the Haven*. The only place in the world he'd ever truly loved. It would be unbearable – and yet easier, in many ways, than staying.

For a moment Aunt Fay said nothing. Then, 'It is your decision of course.'

Inside, Ollie wilted. He felt something between heartbreak and relief.

'But remember this, Ollie,' Aunt Fay went on. 'Failing is a part of living. It is only by failing that we learn.'

Ollie shook his head, determined not to be dissuaded.

'Flea should be leader. He should have been leader from the start.'

'And yet the children here voted for *you*, Ollie.'

'That's because they didn't know me properly. They thought I was something I'm not.'

'It sounds to me as though you might say the same thing about yourself,' said Aunt Fay.

Which Ollie didn't understand at all.

He shook his head again. 'Flea saved us. He got us out. And he sacrificed himself to do it. All I did was . . . was . . .'

'Try?' suggested Aunt Fay.

'Right,' Ollie answered, growing frustrated. 'I *tried*. And I *failed*. I've had more than two months of trying and so far I've managed to achieve nothing. We're still stuck down here in this stupid ghost station, people are still getting ill. Jack's brother is in trouble and there's nothing I can do to save him. And there are other kids at Forest Mount who are probably in as much danger as Errol is – not to mention whatever Colton Crowe and Professor Strain are up to! I just . . . I can't . . . I can't do it. I can't do what everyone wants me to. I don't know *how*.'

All at once, Ollie had never felt so exhausted. For weeks there'd been this weight pressing down on him, and he no longer had the strength to hold it up.

He missed Nancy. So, so much. He wished he could talk to her, just for a few minutes. He wished he could have cried and let her hold him, instead of having to pretend all the time that he was in control.

Now Aunt Fay was the one to sigh, and when she did so she finally looked her age. It was as though all the cares and worries she'd ever felt had simultaneously caught up with her.

'You poor children,' she said. 'You expect so much of yourselves. And all because of the burdens we adults place on your shoulders. The truth is, Ollie, *none* of you should be here. The Haven shouldn't even *exist*. That it does is a testament to a much greater failing: a collective one. One of society as a whole.'

For the first time since Ollie had known her, Aunt Fay sounded genuinely angry. Not with him, though. Rather, she sounded angry at the world.

'Will you accept one piece of advice, Ollie? And no matter what you choose to do, will you promise me one thing?'

Ollie didn't know what else he could do but nod. And then, when he remembered Aunt Fay couldn't see him, he said, 'I promise.'

Aunt Fay's hand worked its way around Ollie's. She squeezed so tightly it almost hurt.

'Keep faith in yourself,' she said. 'That's the best piece of advice I can offer you. I've found in this long life of mine that if you manage to do *that*, solutions often present themselves from the most unexpected of quarters.'

Keep faith in yourself, Ollie repeated in his mind. But what if others didn't feel the same way? What if you believed in yourself, but no one else did?

'As to the promise I'd ask you to make,' Aunt Fay went on, 'swear to me you won't ever walk away from something that isn't finished.'

Ollie was about to reply, when Aunt Fay raised a hand. 'I don't mean you shouldn't ever move on,' she said, seeming to anticipate what Ollie was about to say. 'Priorities change, times end, and . . . and people die.' At this she squeezed Ollie's hand again, no doubt aware that Ollie's thoughts had immediately turned to his lost loved ones. To Nancy. To his mum and dad.

'But there's a difference between walking away when you know it's time to, and giving up because something feels hard. Do you know, the only regrets I have in life are from the times I've turned my back on something when I've known, deep down, I was only doing so because it felt easier. Because keeping on was too difficult, even though I knew it would have been worth the effort in the end.'

It was an uncomfortable echo of what Nancy used to say, her lesson about never giving up. It had got Ollie through his karate grading, and plenty of other challenging times in his life. But this – leading the Haven – was the hardest thing he'd ever had to do.

And the most worthwhile, Ollie? The most important?

Ollie flinched at the voice in his head. It had sounded so much like Nancy speaking, she might have been standing at his shoulder.

'You want me to promise to stay at the Haven,' he said to Aunt Fay. 'That's what you're saying. You want me to promise to keep on being leader.'

To Ollie's surprise, Aunt Fay shook her head. 'No, Ollie. I want you to promise me that if you decide to leave, it's because you know it's the right time to do so in your heart. I want you to be certain that you are leaving for the right reasons, and won't look back on it one day as another mistake.'

Ollie fell silent. He stared, unseeing, at his lap.

Aunt Fay spoke gently at his side. 'It seems you have lots to think about, Ollie. But don't think too hard,' she added, her pale eyes twinkling in the lamplight. 'That's another regret I have, now I come to think about it. Sometimes – oftentimes – I've found thinking too much only makes things worse. It's often better just to trust your gut.'

She made a move to get to her feet. Seeing her struggle, Ollie rose to help her.

'Thank you, Ollie,' she said, once she was standing, and slightly breathless from the effort. 'Getting down is always easier than getting back up. Don't you find?' Her pale eyes sparkled again, and Ollie had the sense she was imparting another lesson.

She smiled then, and placed a hand on Ollie's cheek. He felt the warm smoothness of her palm and, for the briefest of instances, closed his eyes.

'I would stay and talk longer, Ollie,' said Aunt Fay. 'But it seems I'm not the only person who wanted the chance to speak with you.' She made the faintest of movements with her head, and Ollie looked across her shoulder.

Aunt Fay was right. Ollie hadn't heard anyone approach, but someone else was waiting in the shadows.

11 PLAN B

They walked slowly, side by side, back towards the heart of the Haven. Aunt Fay had already made herself scarce, vanishing into a nearby passageway as stealthily as Keya had appeared.

'No offence, Ollie,' Keya said, breaking the slightly awkward silence. She wrinkled her nose. 'But you kind of stink.'

Ollie sniffed his clothes, recoiling when he realised Keya was right. His hoodie reeked of the tear gas from the tunnels. It was the same smell they'd detected below the crypt – the foul stench Song had identified, and that had led them towards Forest Mount. Ollie reckoned his hoodie – his favourite – was beyond saving. He would have to raid the clothes store on his way to the shower block, and hope there was something in his size.

'Is that why you came to find me?' Ollie said. 'To tell me I smell?'

'Well, *someone* had to say it,' said Keya, returning his smile. 'And Aunt Fay is obviously too polite.' Her smile faltered. 'Also,' she went on, 'I wanted to apologise. For what happened in the canteen the other day. It wasn't Imani's fault. She only got involved to even up the sides. The fight itself – that's on me.'

'I reckon Flea's mates probably had something to do with it,' Ollie answered.

Keya's grateful expression told Ollie he was right. 'Even so,' she said. 'I let you down. And I came to tell you that I'm sorry.'

Ollie shook his head. 'You didn't let me down. If anything it's the other way around.'

Keya's eyebrows joined at the middle. 'What are you talking about?'

'I'm the one who should be apologising to you,' Ollie insisted. 'To everyone. The Haven is supposed to be a sanctuary. Right? A safe place. But all anyone's done since I took over is argue. And it's hardly surprising. Life down here in the ghost station . . . it kind of sucks.'

'It beats living on the streets,' Keya countered. 'It beats being part of some stupid *gang*.'

'Yeah, but—'

'No buts, Ollie.' She shook her head, exasperated. 'Honestly, for someone who's normally so smart, it's hard to believe you can also be such an idiot.'

'An idiot?' Ollie echoed.

'That's right,' said Keya, stubbornly. 'Aunt Fay thought so, too, I could tell, but she was too nice to say it. I told you, she's too polite.'

'You were listening? To what we were saying?'

Keya wriggled awkwardly. 'Not listening, exactly. I just heard, that's all.' She stopped walking, and Ollie was forced to face her. 'You can't leave, Ollie. You *mustn't.*'

'But—'

'I told you, no buts. The Haven is a better place because of you. End of story.'

Ollie frowned. Ever since he and Keya had escaped together from Maddy Sikes, she'd been one of his closest allies. More than that, she was one of his best friends. But there was no way anyone could realistically claim the Haven was a better place since Ollie took over as leader.

'You're doing it again,' said Keya.

'Doing what?' said Ollie, surprised.

'Acting like an idiot.'

'I didn't even say anything!'

'You didn't have to. Look, if you're not going to listen to anything I say, what's the point me even saying it?'

'But . . .' Ollie began, and Keya glared at him. 'I mean, I *am* listening. It's just, you're the only one who thinks that. Everyone else would agree with me.'

'Everyone? Like who?'

'Like . . . Flea. And all his supporters. And Aunt Fay, sort of. And . . . Lily.'

Keya stopped again, so abruptly that Ollie walked into her.

'Lily.'

Ollie had the feeling he'd said something he shouldn't have. 'Well . . . yeah. She can't even look at me, most of the time.'

Keya pressed her lips into a pout. 'Why do you care so much what Lily thinks?'

'I don't care. I mean, I do, but . . . Look, all I'm trying to say is, I don't see how me being leader helps. That's all. We've gone backwards since I took over. Maybe someone else would have a better idea about how to move things forwards.'

'Like *Lily*, for example?'

'Will you stop going on about Lily? I mean her brother, obviously. Flea.'

Once again Keya rolled her eyes. 'Flea. You think Flea would make the Haven a better place?' This time when Keya stopped walking, she stepped across Ollie's path. 'Listen to me, Ollie Turner. Are you listening to me?'

Ollie nodded, too taken aback to speak.

'That boy called us street rats. In the canteen. Do you remember?'

Once again Ollie bobbed his head.

'And what did you say? When you heard Flea's mate say that?'

'I said—'

'You said we were *all* street rats. Every one of us.'

'Yes, but I didn't mean—'

'And you were right,' Keya said. 'Do you see? You were *right*.'

'I was?'

Keya nodded. 'And *that's* why you need to stay on as leader. Some of Flea's supporters, they've been whispering about the former gang kids behind our backs, trying to make out they're better than us, that we don't really belong.'

'They have?' Ollie said, frowning now. Keya's expression, in response, seemed to soften.

'Don't you see, Ollie? Flea's Haven – it would be a place of *them* and *us*. A place where some people are more equal than others.'

'But Flea wouldn't want that to happen any more than I do,' Ollie protested. 'He cares about the Haven as much as anyone I know.'

'Maybe he does. But you didn't hear him sticking up for us the way you did, did you?'

'No, but . . . he probably didn't even notice. What that boy said – it probably didn't even register.'

'And that's exactly my point. *Flea didn't even notice*. He's too busy thinking about being in charge. About missions and adventures and . . . and collecting *scars*.' Keya had been waving her arms about as she spoke, but all of a sudden she dropped them to her sides. 'But you, Ollie: you care about the important stuff. About what the Haven stands for. *That's* why so many people voted for you. Not because of what happened with Maddy Sikes. They voted for you because they saw you for who you are. A *good* person. Who wants the best for *everyone* at the Haven, and for all the kids out there who need our help. Like Errol, for instance.'

Ollie opened his mouth to speak, but found himself at a loss for what to say.

'You're the only person who has a chance of keeping the Haven together, Ollie,' Keya pressed. 'Flea wouldn't. I don't mean he wouldn't want to,' she added, when she saw Ollie about to interrupt. 'What I mean is, he *couldn't*. He'd be like . . . like a president or a prime minister or whatever – someone who sounds good on TV, who promises to "Make Everything Great Again", but in the end only makes things fall apart. Not necessarily on purpose. Just because he turns people against each other. And when times are tough, like they are now, people need to stick together. Right? We're all on the same side, after all. We're all working towards the same goal. So *that's* how we move on. By joining hands, just like you and the others did down in that tunnel. That's how you get through the dark, Ollie Turner. Not by all pulling in different directions.'

When Keya had finished speaking, all Ollie could do was stare.

'What?' said Keya, defensively. 'What are you looking at?' She raised a hand to her face. 'Have I got a bogey or something?' She sniffed and brushed at her nose.

'No, I . . . It's not that. I'm just . . . impressed, that's all. Maybe *you* should be leader.' Ollie wasn't joking. He'd made the suggestion once before. But Keya dismissed the idea as rapidly as she had the last time.

'I'm too hot-headed,' she said. 'Just in case you hadn't noticed. And besides, there's only one person who deserves to be leader. And that's why I don't want to hear any more talk about you leaving. Understood?'

Ollie hesitated before answering.

'I said, *understood*?' Keya demanded, prodding his chest with a finger.

'OK, OK,' Ollie said. He held up his hands in mock surrender. 'Understood.'

Keya allowed her finger to fall away. 'Well . . . good. That's settled then.' Her eyes narrowed. 'Right?'

'Right,' Ollie agreed, smiling at his friend's relentlessness.

Keya seemed to relax slightly. 'We're all in this together, Ollie. Every one of us. Rescuing Errol, finding somewhere else to move the Haven – it's not all on you, you know. It's not your responsibility to solve everything.'

Ollie recalled how Aunt Fay had said exactly the same thing. But he was also thinking about something else – about something Keya had just said. *We're all in this together . . .*

'Ollie?' said Keya. 'What is it? You've got a weird look in your eye. You'd better not be having second thoughts, because I swear if you make me tell you how great you are again, I might start campaigning for Flea after all.'

'No, I . . .' Ollie grabbed hold of Keya's hand. 'Come on,' he said. 'We need to find the others.'

'What? Why?'

'Because you've given me an idea.'

'So what do you think?'

They were back in the infirmary, gathered around Flea's bed. Galen was lingering just out of earshot, keeping a watchful eye on her patient, and making sure Ollie and the others did nothing to hinder Flea's recovery. *No over-stimulation*, she'd warned them. *No exertion, do you hear?*

Even so, Ollie had struggled to keep the excitement from his voice as he'd outlined the idea he'd come up with. He watched in anticipation as the others exchanged anxious glances.

Erik was the first to speak. 'Personally I think you should hop into bed next to Flea,' he said. 'Clearly that gas had more effect on you than we thought. It's messed with your brain or something.'

Sol was the only one to chuckle. The rest of them – Lily, Jack, Song and Flea – appeared deep in thought. Keya and Imani, who weren't on the investigations team itself, but who Ollie had wanted present when he briefed the others, shifted uneasily at Ollie's shoulder.

'I think . . .' Lily began, not quite meeting Ollie's eye. 'I think it *could* work. If Jack can find a way to get the paper trail in order.'

'The paper trail would be the least of our problems,' said Jack, who looked more concerned than any of them. 'You know the stakes, Ollie. You know what happened to Errol. Are you sure you want to do this?'

'But that's just the point,' Ollie countered. 'We *don't* know what's happened to Errol. We think he's being held at Forest Mount somewhere, but we don't know where or why. This would give us our chance to find out.'

'You said . . . the same thing . . . about your last plan,' wheezed Flea. He was lying on his back beneath the bed covers, doing his best to wriggle on to his elbows. Slightly incongruously, he was wearing a pair of sunglasses, which Galen said would help to protect his eyes while they recovered.

Galen herself twitched nervously when she noticed Flea attempting to sit up.

'I did,' agreed Ollie, holding off Galen with a palm. 'And I was wrong, I admit it. I underestimated how far Strain and Crowe would go to keep whatever they're up to hidden, but that just goes to show how important it is we find out what's really going on. And just because we got knocked back, doesn't mean we shouldn't try again. Right?'

Flea gave up attempting to sit, and lay back down again with a huff.

'And look at it this way, Flea,' Ollie went on. 'If I fail, chances are you'll be leader before the week's out. And if I succeed . . .' Ollie glanced at Keya. 'If I succeed, we'll have that leadership election anyway. I promise. I reckon you've earned it.'

He offered Flea his hand, and waited – until Flea raised his own hand and pumped Ollie's once.

'It's your . . . funeral . . . PJ,' he grunted, and then folded his arms across his chest.

'I'm coming with you, Ollie,' said Sol, stepping forwards. 'You're not leaving me on the sidelines this time.'

'Me, too,' said Lily, this time looking Ollie straight in the eye. 'You're going to need help, and given that Song and Erik got spotted in the tunnel, you've got no choice but to let us come along.'

'But . . .' Ollie began. He'd intended to go it alone – the last thing he wanted was anyone else getting hurt – but then he remembered what Keya had said. *We're all in this together*. It was what had given him the idea in the first place.

'I'm coming, too,' said Jack. Then, when she saw Ollie about to protest, 'Just try and stop me.'

Ollie looked at Jack, Sol and Lily in turn. 'Fine,' he relented. 'If you're sure you can get us all in, Jack?'

Jack gave an easy shrug, attempting to hide her delight. 'If I can get one of us in, I can get four of us in.'

Which made sense, Ollie figured. Kind of. And secretly he was glad he wouldn't have to face things all alone. With four of them gone, however, and Flea out of action, Erik and Song would need help running things at the Haven.

'Keya?' he said. 'Imani? Can I trust you to help keep the peace while we're gone?'

Keya and Imani exchanged sheepish grins. 'I reckon so,' said Imani. 'Just don't get too comfortable in your posh new surroundings. Any of you. You're street rats, remember?'

Ollie couldn't help but grin. 'We were,' he said. 'But you know what they say: if you can't beat them . . . join them.'

[illegible] Odd figure! [illegible]

was glad he wouldn't [illegible] alone. [illegible]

[illegible]

would [illegible] the streets.

[illegible] keep the

[illegible]

[illegible]

[illegible] remember?

[illegible] 'We were,' he said. 'But you

know [illegible]'

12 NEW RECRUITS

It was like stepping into a different world.

Having lived for most of his life on the edge of a notorious north London estate, and studying at a regular state-run school, Ollie had never experienced anything like it. It was like walking into a palace or something. Or on to a set of one of those boring period dramas Nancy had always insisted on watching on Sunday nights.

Even in comparison to the old Haven, Forest Mount was lavish beyond anything Ollie could have expected. He recalled how astonished he'd been when he'd first seen the former Haven's entrance hall, with its enormous oak staircase and triple-height ceiling. But whereas the Haven had been light and full of quirky character, Forest Mount was what he imagined an old gentlemen's club might have looked like. It was all dark wood and parquet floors and oil paintings, any one of which, Ollie would have guessed, was worth more than his and Nancy's old flat. It wasn't welcoming, the way the rundown library had immediately felt to Ollie. Rather, it was more like a stuffy old museum, the kind of place you just knew you were forbidden from touching anything, or talking in anything more than a whisper.

Above all, it was creepy, just as Errol had said it was. The eyes on those paintings – of grim old men in robes, every one of them – seemed to follow you, tracking you with their disapproving glares. The heavy lead on the windows looked like prison bars, and the woods outside loomed darkly, as though it were only the glass on the windows themselves that was preventing the trees from reaching in with their spindly branches. To think, Ollie and the others had judged Forest Mount scary on the *outside*. Inside, he'd decided, it was even worse, and so far they'd got barely any further on their 'welcome' tour than the assembly hall.

'The main auditorium is where students gather for instruction every morning,' their guide was saying. He was a boy of about fifteen, who walked with his nose half pointing towards the ceiling and his over-stuffed belly leading the way. 'Professor Strain commences his daily address at a quarter to seven on the dot.'

Ollie heard a splutter at his shoulder.

'A quarter to seven?' said Sol, an appalled expression on his face. 'As in, *A.M.*? What about breakfast?'

Ollie jabbed him with his elbow, careful not to let anyone else see. They were in the middle of a group of about a dozen boys, and he and Sol were side by side. The girls had been taken on their own tour. Although lessons at Forest Mount were mixed, the dorms and certain other facilities were not. As far as anyone knew, Ollie, Sol, Lily and Jack were simply a few of the new intake, their arrival at the school perfectly timed for the start of the academic year. As part of their cover, they weren't supposed to know one another. More importantly, Ollie had made it clear they were to avoid doing anything that might attract unwanted attention.

'Who said that?'

The guide turned abruptly, causing the entire group to come to a stop.

'Um . . . I did,' admitted Sol.

Unfortunately for him, he stood taller than most of those around him by half a head. Jack had seen to it that Sol and the rest of the Haven kids were being admitted into year ten. The majority of the new arrivals were year sevens, meaning the prefect pinpointed Sol easily.

'*Breakfast*,' he explained, scornfully, 'is served between six and six-thirty. Not a minute earlier, not a minute later. And I suggest you get in the habit of eating quickly. Professor Strain does not take kindly to tardiness.'

'Right,' said Sol, with a nod that was almost a bow. 'Um . . . sir,' he added.

The prefect narrowed his eyes, as though wondering whether Sol was mocking him. He swung his gaze around the rest of the group, alert for any sign of disrespect.

Ollie hunched lower. He was younger than Sol by almost a year, so he was shorter anyway. Technically, he should have been entering year nine, with only Sol, Jack and Lily going into the year above. But when Jack had forged their applications online, she'd also tweaked Ollie's birth date to ensure they would all be taking lessons together. Ollie was thankful he wouldn't be on his own, but feeling the withering glare of the prefect, he almost wished he could have passed for a year seven.

After studying Ollie for an uncomfortable few seconds, the prefect finally turned away, intent on resuming the tour.

'Forest Mount is a renowned institution,' the prefect intoned as he resumed walking. 'If you have been accepted as a student here, that means you will be expected to behave at all times in a manner that befits the school's illustrious reputation.' He glanced at Sol across his shoulder, who twitched a smile and gave something between a thumbs up and a salute.

Ollie, watching, could only wince. It wasn't Sol's fault, but the truth was, for all the talk of avoiding attracting attention, all four of them stood out as plainly to his eyes as one of the Forest Mount prefects would have at the Haven. Even dressed in official Forest Mount uniforms this time – which, incidentally, had cost the same as it would have to feed a dozen Haven kids for over a month – they didn't fit in. They were street rats, after all. They weren't posh enough, rich enough, brash enough, meaning it was inevitable they'd be found out eventually. It was just a question of whether they would be able to rescue Errol, and uncover what was really going on here, before anyone unmasked *them*.

'The classrooms are all located on the ground and first floors,' the prefect was saying, loosely waving a hand towards a passageway that led off to their right. 'The dorms are on levels two and three. You have all been issued with maps in your orientation packs, so I suggest you study them, and memorise the quickest routes between lessons. Note that in Forest Mount you walk on the *right*-hand side of the corridors, but the *left*-hand side of the stairwells. During extensive trialling, this has been found to be the most efficient way to disperse traffic and ease congestion.'

Sol had been drifting towards the left-hand wall of the corridor. Surreptitiously, Ollie tugged him back towards the right. One of the year sevens noticed and glanced at the two of them contemptuously. Already the boy was walking the way the prefect was, nose high and shoulders back, as though he was doing his best to try to fit in.

All of a sudden the prefect spun and raised a finger, startling Ollie to a standstill.

'Don't dawdle, don't loiter, don't shout, don't chew, don't laugh, don't eat outside the refectory, don't drink anything other than water and *don't* remove your blazers unless given explicit permission by your teacher,' he recited. 'To forestall any needless questions, this will *only* happen when the temperature in the main courtyard exceeds twenty-nine point six degrees Celsius. And be warned,' the boy added, a weird expression appearing on his face, which Ollie belatedly realised was intended to be a smile, 'in my time at Forest Mount, this has happened only *twice*, and on both occasions we elected to keep our blazers *on*.'

This seemed to be a joke, because one or two members of the party – those most eager to create a good impression – chuckled appreciatively. Ollie and Sol exchanged baffled looks, and Ollie noticed others in the group doing the same. Clearly some of the other kids were as unprepared for Forest Mount as he and Sol were.

The tour continued, and by the end of it Ollie was horribly disorientated. The school had a central courtyard, which should have made the layout easy to navigate. But none of the corridors were straight, and the majority of the stairwells ran in spirals. Ollie hadn't tried it on his own yet, but already he had the impression that trying to get from one end of the school to the other would be like playing a game of blind man's buff. You'd get to keep your eyes open, but he reckoned he would do just as well wearing a blindfold.

For all its bewildering rules and disorienting layout, however, Forest Mount was astonishingly well equipped. In contrast to the situation at the Haven – even before the fire had claimed so many of their resources – the classrooms were all kitted out with personalised workstations. There were too many computers for Ollie to count, and tablets on virtually every desk. Jack, he knew, was probably going into meltdown. There were plenty of ramps to help her get around, as well – something the ghost station sorely lacked.

They'd passed the gymnasium, too, which was as fancy and well appointed as a professional sports hall. There were basketball hoops (with *nets*, something Ollie hadn't witnessed in all his years of schooling), hockey goals and an indoor cricket pitch, as well as mounds of footballs and rugby balls for use on the 4G pitches to the rear of the main building outside. To top it all, not one of the balls Ollie saw showed the slightest sign of having a puncture. At St Jerome's, you'd have been lucky to find a tennis ball to kick around at lunchtime. A full-size, fully inflated leather football, which wasn't coming apart at the seams, was as rare a thing in Ollie's experience as a physics lesson that didn't send half the kids in the class to sleep.

Needless to say, there wasn't a trace of graffiti anywhere; no broken windows or mouldy sills. The bathrooms were gleaming, the refectory pristine. And the food Ollie saw being prepared for that evening's meal actually looked *edible*. There was fish, and pasta, and fresh fruit and vegetables, and even steak. 'Things are looking up,' Sol had whispered to Ollie when they'd seen what was on that night's menu. Watching as one of the cooks brought a tray of steaming bread rolls out of an oven, Ollie had been too busy salivating to disagree.

When he and Sol finally reunited with Jack and Lily in the year-ten common room, Ollie found himself in a mild state of shock.

'How can a place like this even exist?' he said. 'Who *pays* for it all?'

They were gathered around the open fire, another extravagance given that it was September, and it wasn't *that* cold outside. The common room was abuzz with excited chatter among pupils returning from the holidays and isolated pockets of new arrivals, meaning the Haven crew wouldn't have appeared out of place. So long as they kept their voices down, Ollie figured, they'd give the appearance of being four new students simply trying to make friends.

'You do,' Jack said, in answer to his question. 'Or at least, Forest Mount *thinks* you're paying for it. As it was, the money we had left over from Maddy Sikes's watch was barely enough to buy these uniforms for us all. The fees themselves were *way* out of budget.'

As well as being the Haven's technical whizz, Jack was also in charge of the purse strings: a job, these days, that basically involved watching their savings get smaller and smaller.

'I set up dummy payments instead,' Jack went on, 'but it won't be long before whoever runs this place realises the money isn't really in their account. They'll trace the bogus payments back to us, and when that happens—'

'We'll be back to eating beans on toast for every meal, and trying to pretend the drinking water down in the ghost station doesn't taste of mildew,' finished Sol, obviously mulling his forthcoming steak.

'Is that all you think about?' snapped Lily. 'Your stomach? You're as bad as Flea.'

Sol appeared taken aback. 'What's bugging you?'

Lily glared for a moment, then crossed her arms. 'Sorry,' she muttered. 'It's not your fault.'

'Lily took exception to some of the things our tour guide was saying,' explained Jack. 'She was talking about how amazing the facilities are at Forest Mount, then said something about it being nothing less than the children here deserved.'

'It was more than that,' put in Lily. 'She was basically saying that Forest Mount kids were better than the rest of us. That it was right they were eating steak for dinner every night, while kids just a few streets away might be lucky to get a meal at all. That snotty, pompous, overfed . . .' Lily was trying so hard to find the appropriate word to finish her sentence, she gave the impression of being about to burst.

'Windbag?' suggested Sol.

'*Windbag*. Thank you.'

Sol nodded, pleased to be back in Lily's good books.

Ollie found himself wondering, from Lily's description, whether she hadn't somehow confused their guide with his and Sol's. She clearly hadn't: one of the guides had been a boy, the other a girl. But they obviously shared the same snobbish attitude.

'And it's all nonsense anyway,' Lily was saying. 'That girl talked about *class* and *breeding*, but really it's all about *money*. That Jack got *us* in here proves it. If you can afford to join the club, you're welcome. If you're poor, you're written off as undeserving riff-raff.' She was pacing in tight circles in front of the fire, and stopped when she realised her friends were staring at her. 'Sorry, I . . . It's just so different from what I'm used to, that's all. From how things are at home.'

Ollie nodded sympathetically. He'd only been here a day, and already he found himself missing the Haven, too. Not the draughty, smelly ghost station. It was as Aunt Fay had told him after the old library had burnt down. The Haven wasn't a building, it was an *idea*. And that was what Ollie missed: the feeling that, no matter who you were, you belonged.

'Talking of money,' said Sol, 'you do realise we're going to get found out long before they start questioning those dummy payments, right? I mean, we've got Ancient Greek tomorrow morning. The only thing I know about ancient Greece is what I read in *Percy Jackson*.' He was looking down at a photocopy of their timetable, and Ollie peered over his shoulder.

'And "discourse and deliberation",' he read aloud. 'What's that when it's at home?'

'It means arguing,' said Jack. 'I reckon we should be OK at that. Maybe Lily could step in if it looks as if one of us is struggling.'

Lily was still visibly fuming, her arms latched tightly across her chest, but she couldn't help smiling through her fury.

Ollie, though, remained worried. Maybe they could bluff their way through a few lessons if they had to, but at some point their luck was bound to run out.

As if in response to Ollie's darkening mood, a shadow fell on their group. When Ollie raised his head, he saw three older boys standing in front of them. They were prefects, and as well as their solid-black uniforms, all three of them wore a scowl. The boy in the middle was the tallest, and from his dark hair and steel-grey eyes, Ollie guessed immediately who he was.

'You four,' said Colton Crowe. 'Come with us. There's somebody who'd like to have a word with you.'

13 IMPOSTORS UNMASKED

Crowe led them from the common room. The other two prefects hung back, then followed behind, and Ollie had the distinct impression they were there to ensure the Haven kids didn't try to make a run for it. Was it really that obvious they didn't belong here? If their cover had been blown already, on the very day of their arrival, they must have stood out even more than Ollie had realised.

He exchanged anxious looks with Jack and Sol. Lily, meanwhile, had pulled slightly ahead of the rest of them. She was keeping pace with Crowe's purposeful strides by scurrying along at his shoulder.

'Are you Colton Crowe? *The* Colton Crowe?'

Crowe turned, irritated, but when he saw Lily's face, his expression softened into something like a smirk. 'At your service,' he responded, dipping his head.

Lily giggled, and fluttered her pale brown eyes. Ollie found his own gaze tightening.

'I'm Lily,' she said. 'I only arrived today, but already I've heard *so* much about you.'

Crowe's smirk crept wider. 'And what exactly have you heard about me, Lily?'

Lily shrugged, swinging her shoulders slightly from side to side. Ollie bit down, hard.

'Just that you basically run this place,' Lily simpered. 'And some of the other girls said . . .' She giggled again, and blushed.

'What did the other girls say?'

'Just . . . that you were handsome. That's all. *And* that you didn't have a girlfriend.'

Ollie could hardly believe what he was hearing. What was Lily playing at? If she was faking – merely pretending to flatter Crowe to try to get in his good books – she was doing an uncomfortably good job of it. And why bother trying to impress Crowe in the first place?

'I don't know about the handsome part,' Crowe replied, his modesty as transparent as a sheet of glass. 'But it's true that particular position is currently vacant. Why? Do you know anyone who might be interested in applying?'

Jack, next to Ollie, made a gagging sound. Fortunately, neither Crowe nor his cronies appeared to notice. If Lily had heard, she did nothing to acknowledge it either.

'Maybe,' she tittered. 'We'll have to see. I suppose it depends on what perks come with the job.'

Crowe smiled appreciatively.

'Is it true, by the way,' said Lily, 'that your father is like, a *knight* or something? He must be really important.'

If she was trying to flatter Crowe further, this time her words fell flat. Crowe's smile flipped into a scowl.

'Who told you about my father?'

'What? I mean . . . I can't remember. I just heard, that's all.'

'Well, *un*hear it,' snapped Crowe. 'And get back in line with the others. There's no talking in the East Wing.'

Recoiling, Lily dropped her pace, until she was trudging along beside the rest of them. She met Ollie's eyes briefly, and then focused her confusion on the floor.

Still trying to work out what had just happened himself, Ollie tried to concentrate on what Crowe had said. *The East Wing*. Errol had mentioned the East Wing in his emails. And if Ollie remembered correctly, somewhere on this side of the building was—

'Professor Strain's office,' said Crowe.

He stopped abruptly beside a set of double doors and, before Ollie or any of his friends could react, rapped twice to announce their presence.

'*Enter*,' boomed a voice.

Crowe, on hearing it, recovered his smile. To Ollie's eye he looked exactly like Sol had back in the refectory, when he'd been contemplating his evening meal.

Ollie and the others had no choice but to file inside.

*

Beyond the set of double doors was a room as opulent as the ghost station was decrepit. One wall was bricked floor to ceiling with books, all in red leather covers. Opposite was an enormous fireplace, with a gilded mirror above it and two imposing reading chairs beneath, each of which could have passed as a small sofa. The fire was raging, and the room was stiflingly warm. Immediately Ollie felt an uncomfortable prickle around his shirt collar. His blazer seemed to be tightening around him. It felt like a straitjacket made of wool.

Directly in front of the doors through which they'd entered was a vast bay window, overlooking Forest Mount's impressive central courtyard. Ollie could see the gargoyles on the ramparts outside, all leering in his direction. Just as Crowe had in the corridor outside, they looked hungry – but excited too, as though they could tell they were just about to feast.

A single figure stood in front of the glass. He was looking out, his hands linked behind him. When he turned, Ollie had to fight the urge to step back. Instead he forced himself to meet Professor Strain's coal-black eyes, which peered out from beneath eyebrows that were as thin and colourless as his narrow lips.

'It seems we have some impostors in our midst,' said Strain, the sonorous voice they'd heard through the door reduced to something like a hiss. But for the slight shadows on his gaunt cheeks, his skin was the colour of skulls.

Strain stepped slowly from behind the desk, and Ollie realised for the first time how tall he was. And he didn't hunch, like most tall people Ollie knew. His headmaster's robe hung pristinely from his wide shoulders, and for a moment Ollie had the impression that, were Strain to spread his arms, the material that enveloped him would form into thick, black wings.

'Well? What have you got to say for yourselves?'

Up until this point, Ollie had been clinging to the possibility that he'd misinterpreted what Crowe coming for the four of them might have meant. But there was no scope for uncertainty any more.

He sensed movement at his back, and turned to see Crowe closing the double doors behind them, his two goons stationing themselves sentry-like outside. Then Crowe took up position himself, blocking the exit from the inside and folding his arms across his chest.

'I-impostors?' Ollie stammered. 'What do you mean?'

Strain linked his bony hands in front of him, his long fingers as pale as the rest of him. 'What I *mean*, young man,' he said, with a treacherous smile, 'is that it already seems obvious that the four of you are *not* Forest Mount pupils.'

'But . . . we are,' said Jack. 'We have . . . acceptance letters, and—'

'Acceptance letters?' interrupted Strain, the mockery evident in his tone. 'Oh, well then. If you have *acceptance letters*, then clearly I am mistaken. Never mind that all four of you were the *only* new arrivals who failed to present themselves at the *mandatory* induction assembly. And never mind that you have chosen to present yourselves to me in a state of undress.' Like a snake striking, Strain whipped out a hand, flicking a yellow fingernail against Sol's tie knot. 'If you have *acceptance letters*, then of *course* you must be Forest Mount pupils. How *foolish* of me to believe it was your *comportment* that determined your status.'

His sarcasm was so thick, it positively dripped from his words as he uttered them. Even so, Ollie felt a flicker of hope. Why would Strain be concerned about Sol's tie if he knew the four of them had faked their way into Forest Mount in the first place? And why was he going on about some assembly they'd apparently missed?

'Ties are to be fastened in a *Windsor* knot,' Strain continued, fixing his narrowed eyes on Sol. 'Did you not read the rules and regulations in your handbook, young man?'

'I . . .' Sol's hand found his tie knot, which looked OK to Ollie. And he would have bet Sol had no better idea what a Windsor knot was than Ollie did.

'It's my fault,' Ollie said. 'I . . . borrowed his copy. Of the handbook, I mean. He didn't know about the . . . knot thing.'

Strain's attentions snapped to Ollie. 'And yet your tie is incorrectly fastened as well. Pray, what is *your* excuse? It seems you have had access to two copies of the handbook: the one you borrowed, and the one you presumably lost. Tell me . . .' Strain turned to read a note on his desk. 'Tell me, Ollie Chambers, is this the standard of behaviour we are to expect of you? I count *three* misdemeanours already, on your very first day of attendance.'

Ollie was right. Strain *didn't* know who they were. If he did he wouldn't have used the fake surname Jack had allocated to Ollie on his application for Forest Mount. But it would hardly matter if they escaped being uncovered as spies if instead they were expelled for breaking school rules. Either way their mission would end in failure.

'N-no, sir,' Ollie said. 'I'm sorry. We all are. About the assembly, I mean. We didn't know about it. And we'll read the regulations, I promise.'

'You will indeed,' Strain agreed. 'In fact you will copy them out. All thirty-seven pages. I will see four handwritten copies on my secretary's desk by this hour tomorrow, or your time at Forest Mount will be over before it has even begun.' He looked at Jack, and added, '*Acceptance letters* or not.'

Ollie groaned inwardly. *Thirty-seven pages?* It would take them all night.

'This is a very important term for Forest Mount,' Strain was saying, delivering the words as though he were addressing an audience much larger than the five children who were with him in the room. 'We are on the cusp of achieving something great, and I will not – I repeat, *not* – permit the behaviour of four unruly upstarts to distract me from my plans. Have I made myself perfectly clear?'

Instinctively Ollie and the others bobbed their heads. 'Yes, sir,' they responded in unison. Ollie hadn't noticed until then, but during their audience with Strain they'd shuffled closer together, so that they were gathered almost elbow to elbow.

'I have my eye on you, young man,' Strain said to Ollie, having seemingly marked him out as the group's leader. 'I have my eye on *all* of you. And believe me, there is *nothing* in this institution that escapes my notice. Now get out of my sight.'

14 NIGHT PATROL

They'd drawn straws.

Two of them were to stay behind, and work through the night to try to finish the task Strain had set them. The other two would steal downstairs and investigate the corridor along from Strain's office, to see if they could locate the secret door Errol had mentioned in his emails. They still had no idea what was really going on at Forest Mount, but their immediate priority was Jack's brother, and if it was true the door led to the dungeons, it was also their most likely route to finding him.

Neither assignment was particularly appealing, but in the end only Jack appeared disappointed with her lot. She and Sol had each drawn the short straws, meaning they were to stay behind and copy out the regulations chapter of the school handbook. It would be mind-numbing work, and Jack did nothing to hide her frustration. She was dying to do something practical to help her brother, whatever the risk.

Sol, on the other hand, couldn't disguise his relief. Following Jack's lead, he'd tried to act disappointed that he'd miss out on the 'excitement', but Ollie could tell he'd been dreading the prospect of sneaking around Forest Mount in the middle of the night.

And Ollie didn't blame him. It wasn't just the building itself that was so menacing. It was everything about the place: the fear inspired by Professor Strain, which seemed to have contaminated the entire school. It was exactly as Errol had described. Some of the kids – the prefects and the Colton Crowe wannabes – appeared to revel in it, taking delight in the oppressive atmosphere, like alien beings who breathe best in a cloud of noxious gas. But there were others, too, who clearly found the environment as poisonous as Ollie did. They were the kids you didn't really notice at first, because they were so determined to keep their heads down. But when Ollie and the others had returned to the common room after their encounter with Strain, for example he'd spotted them clustered in corners, trying to gauge what had happened to Ollie and his friends with knowing, terrified eyes.

There was something awful going on here, Ollie could feel it. Errol and the others had been silenced for a reason. And it was down to Ollie and Lily to try to find out why.

They'd arranged to meet at the bottom of the main staircase in the entrance hall, but to get there Ollie had to slip out of his dorm and then work his way downstairs without being seen.

As he slid from his bunk, he noticed Sol beneath the covers in the bed across from his, already hard at work copying out the handbook by the light from his phone. With his eyes on the warm orange glow, Ollie couldn't help but feel a pang of envy. The night air in the draughty old school was sharp and unwelcoming, the stone floor beneath his feet like a slab of ice. It was a relief to slip his toes into his school shoes, hard and uncomfortable as they were.

He tiptoed from his bunk to the threshold of the room, but as he made to step into the corridor outside he almost ran headlong into a pair of prefects. He had another close shave on the staircase, but soon enough he reached the main entrance hall, and his rendezvous point with Lily. The only problem was, Lily was nowhere to be seen.

'Lily?' Ollie hissed. 'Where are you?'

There was no answer. Ollie was alone.

He cursed inwardly. After her performance with Crowe, Lily had given the impression of being back to her usual self. In truth, though, Lily hadn't seemed herself to Ollie for weeks, not since he'd taken over as the Haven's leader. If he was honest, that was another reason he'd been so reluctant to leave his bed: he was more than a fraction uneasy at the thought of being alone with Lily. Did Lily feel the same way, he wondered? Was that why she hadn't shown up?

All of a sudden, a voice whispered out in the darkness.

'Ollie? Is that you?'

It was coming from the recess behind the main stairwell.

'Lily?'

Lily poked her head out of the shadows, into a moonbeam filtering weakly through an overhead window. 'Thank god. I thought you were a prefect. I've almost been spotted once already.'

She emerged fully. Like Ollie she was dressed all in black. Partly to provide camouflage. Partly so that if they were seen, the other prefects might assume they were prefects, too.

'Come on,' Ollie said. 'Let's get a move on.'

It came out more abruptly than he'd intended. He noticed Lily recoil slightly, but he didn't know what to say to put things right. He turned away, and when he heard Lily fall in behind him, he tried to focus on the task that lay ahead.

On his way down from the dorm, Ollie had got a sense of the prefects' routines. They patrolled in a loop, with a four or five minute gap between pairs, meaning it was easy enough for him and Lily to avoid being seen. Finding their way proved the trickier part. Ollie had drawn a map on the underside of his arm, but it was hard to decipher in the dark, and already the felt-tip lines were beginning to blur as a result of his nervous sweat.

Eventually they found the corridor they were looking for, and the wood panelling that Errol had claimed masked the secret door. But the panelling stretched twenty metres at least, and neither Ollie nor Lily had any idea where to begin looking.

'You start here,' suggested Lily. 'I'll work towards you from the opposite end. If neither of us finds it, I guess we'll meet in the middle.'

'Right,' agreed Ollie. He was a little disconcerted by how rapidly Lily turned away from him, but it was also something of a relief when the space opened up between them.

For a short time, Ollie was able to put Lily from his mind. The wood panelling was incredibly ornate, and any one of a thousand tiny protrusions might have concealed a switch that would trigger the secret door. Ollie ran his finger everywhere he could, pressing and prodding as he worked, but he had no luck. Steadily he and Lily drew closer together, until once again they were side by side.

'Nothing?' Ollie said, knowing already what Lily's answer would be.

'Nothing,' replied Lily, exasperated. She stepped back, and surveyed the wood panelling with a frown. 'Are you sure we're in the right corridor? I must have pressed *everywhere*.'

'You read Errol's emails,' Ollie answered, his frustration carrying in his tone. 'If you didn't think we were in the right place, you should have said.'

Now Lily turned her frown on him. 'I was only asking. There's no need to snap.'

'I wasn't snapping,' Ollie snapped. 'And keep your voice down, will you?' he added, lowering his own. 'Someone could hear.'

Lily folded her arms and turned her head, huffing angrily into the silence.

'Look,' said Ollie, 'let's just . . . check again. OK?' He returned his attentions to the wooden panels.

'What are you doing?' said Lily, from across his shoulder. 'I've already checked there. Or don't you trust me to have done the job properly?'

Ollie had been working left to right. Without thinking how it would look to Lily, he'd continued the way he'd been moving, and was now searching the panels Lily had already inspected.

Rather than stopping, though, Ollie carried on working. 'It's not that,' he replied. 'I'm just being thorough, that's all.'

'Meaning I wasn't?' Lily answered. 'Why don't you check your own panels if you're so keen on being *thorough*.'

This time Ollie turned. 'Why don't *you*?' he retorted. 'It would be more useful than standing there having a go at me.'

'*I'm* having a go at *you*?' said Lily, her hands finding her hips. 'You're the one who—'

They heard the prefects at exactly the same time: hissed, urgent voices carried on a beat of approaching footsteps. There were torch beams bobbing towards them from around the corner.

'Quick,' said Ollie, 'this way!' He tried to pull Lily with him.

'No, wait,' said Lily, resisting. '*This* way.' She was tugging

Ollie in the opposite direction, *towards* the approaching prefects.

'But—'

'Look, just stop *arguing*, would you?' Lily said, cutting off Ollie's objection. 'Trust me for once!'

Before he could protest further, Lily was off and away. She stopped halfway to the corner. When Ollie caught up with her, she was pulling something from her pocket.

Unable to keep the horror from his expression, Ollie realised what she was doing. 'This is the door to Professor Strain's office,' he said. He looked down at what Lily was holding. 'And that's—'

'My brother's lock-picking set,' finished Lily. 'He gave it to me before we left the Haven. He figured it might come in useful.'

'But if the prefects catch us in Strain's office, we'll get kicked out of Forest Mount for sure!'

'We'll get kicked out if they catch us full stop,' countered Lily, as she started to fiddle with the lock. 'You heard Crowe: we've already had our last warning. And maybe Strain's office is the one place those prefects wouldn't *dare* look.'

Ollie checked the corridor. Those lights were getting closer, the voices louder.

'You probably imagined it,' someone was hissing.

'I didn't, I swear. It sounded like . . . like *arguing*. And it came from somewhere down here.'

As soon as the prefects reached the corner, Ollie and Lily would be in plain sight. The only reason they hadn't been spotted already was that the prefects seemed to be searching the rooms they passed along the way.

'Hurry, Lily. They're coming.'

Ollie could only watch as Lily fumbled to decipher the lock. 'Flea always makes it look so easy,' she was muttering. 'Wait, I think I've . . . *No*. Damn it!'

Ollie checked the lights. From the look of it, the prefects were already on the final classroom before they reached the corner. And it was too late for Ollie and Lily to run. They'd never make it around the far corner in time.

'Lily . . .' Ollie urged.

'Maybe I'm using the wrong pick.' Lily was waggling the tool in the lock furiously. Ollie had never picked a lock himself, but he was fairly sure that wasn't the technique Lily's brother used. When Ollie had watched Flea break through the lock in the crypt, for example, he'd worked slowly, delicately, as though he were trying to crack a safe. In her desperation, Lily was resorting to brute force.

Ollie checked the lights again. They had seconds left at best. 'It's no use, Lily. We have to go. *Now*.'

But Lily wouldn't be moved. 'Flea said every lock was different,' she was mumbling, 'and that sometimes you just have to . . .'

There was a click.

'. . . give it some welly,' said Lily, grinning.

The torch beams reached the corner. Ollie saw the shadow of the leading prefect emerge not ten metres from where they were standing.

There was no time to think.

As Lily turned the handle to the door, Ollie grabbed her arm and dragged her across the threshold, into the gloom of Strain's office. Quickly, silently, Ollie shut them inside, and then collapsed with his back against the door.

He closed his eyes and let out a breath. They were safe, for the time being at least.

But when he opened his eyes, Lily's face was a picture of horror.

Ollie looked up, and saw a robed figure standing over them.

15 TOP SECRET

Ollie wrapped a hand around Lily's mouth. He was sure his friend was about to scream. Not surprisingly – Ollie had almost cried out himself.

But the figure they'd mistaken for Professor Strain was just the outline of his headmaster's robes, which were draped pristinely around a hanger inside the door.

Ollie saw Lily register their mistake, and he allowed his hand to fall away.

Lily clutched her heart, silently gasping her relief. Ollie's own chest felt as though it was about to burst.

He raised his finger to his lips and pressed his ear against the door.

'You were right,' he whispered. 'They've gone straight past. We'll give it another thirty seconds, then head the way they came. So much for finding that secret door,' he added bitterly. He hated the idea of going back to the others empty-handed, but he knew they had no choice. It would be suicide to push their luck any further.

He got to his feet and gripped the handle of the door, ready to sneak back outside.

'Ready?' he said to Lily.

'Wait.'

Lily was drifting further into Strain's office. The room was dark, and the curtains were drawn, so they couldn't have been spotted from the courtyard. Even so, Ollie was aware those prefects might return at any minute.

'Lily,' he hissed. 'What are you doing?'

'Looking,' she answered, stating the obvious. She switched on the torch beam of her phone. Even set to minimum, it was disconcertingly bright.

'Looking for what?'

'Anything,' Lily hissed back. 'If we can't find that secret door, we might as well try to accomplish *something* useful. And when are we going to get another chance to search Strain's office?'

Ollie was about to protest, to insist they had to get out of there *now*. But Lily had a point: they wouldn't get an opportunity like this one again. He pressed his ear to the door once more, listening out for any indication those prefects were on their way back.

He got out his own phone.

'Two minutes,' he conceded. '*Maximum*. And then we're out of here. Agreed?'

There was a flash of the old Lily in her smile. 'Agreed.'

Ollie started at the nearest corner, making his way past the bookshelves. Lily headed straight for Strain's enormous desk.

‘These books are all written in gibberish,’ said Ollie, his torch beam sweeping the wall of red-leather spines.

Lily swung the light from her own torch across the room. Even with the second beam illuminating the titles of the books, Ollie couldn’t decipher the writing. He flicked between screens on his phone, and opened one of the apps Jack had been working on recently. Since the fire, they didn’t have the resources at the Haven for Jack to do much more than keep on top of basic operations, but she’d managed to hone a few of the toys she’d already had in development. This app was one of them. When you pointed the camera at something written in a foreign language, the app cross-referenced the text with Google Translate, and the image on screen adjusted to display the writing in English.

‘It’s Russian,’ Ollie declared, looking at the screen. ‘The letters are all Cyrillic.’ He opened one of the volumes and flicked the pages, using Jack’s app to decipher the text’s meaning, then ran the camera across the spines on the shelf. ‘They’re history books, mainly, from the look of them. Politics, too.’

‘Maybe Russia is his speciality,’ suggested Lily. ‘He has to be a professor of something, I suppose.’

‘Lily. Look at this.’ Ollie had moved on to a photograph that had been framed and pinned to the wall. He hadn’t noticed it the last time he’d been in Strain’s office. He’d barely been able to divert his eyes from Strain’s hypnotic gaze.

'Isn't that—?'

'The Russian president. Shaking hands with Strain.'

Ollie peered closer. The face of the president of Russia was unmistakeable. Ollie had seen his image a thousand times on television. In the picture he and Strain were clasping hands, and Strain was almost smiling. The image was slightly washed out, as though it had been bleached by the sunlight, making Strain resemble a grinning skull.

'Over here, Ollie.'

Ollie was about to join Lily at Strain's desk, when a noise drew his attention towards the door.

'Two minutes, Lily. That's what we said. We should go.'

Lily was flipping pages on Strain's desk. 'I know, but seriously: you need to look at this.'

Ollie moved reluctantly to her side, his eyes half on the door. But when he saw what Lily was looking at, he forgot about the prefects entirely.

On the surface of Strain's desk was a manila folder. Lily had been flicking through the contents, but when Ollie moved to peer across her shoulder, she closed it so that Ollie could see the front.

'Top Secret', read the stamp on the cover. And when Lily showed Ollie the pages inside, he immediately understood why.

'This can't be right,' he muttered. 'Can it?'

'It's there in black and white,' Lily replied. 'And it *looks* real.'

‘The prime minister,’ Ollie said, ‘coming *here* to announce the start of her re-election campaign.’ He turned back to the opening page, then forwards to the document’s conclusion. ‘But what’s Strain doing with the security details of the PM’s visit? Shouldn’t this be classified?’

‘According to the cover, it is,’ said Lily, pointing at the big red stamp emblazoned on the document’s front page. ‘But maybe Strain has to be in the loop. Probably he’s partly responsible for the PM’s safety when she gets here.’

‘I guess,’ Ollie muttered. He was using his phone to spotlight the pages, and he swiped the screen to open the camera.

‘Wait, Ollie – should you be doing that? If you get caught with top secret government documents on your phone, you could—’

Before Lily could finish her sentence, Ollie dragged her to the floor. He covered her phone with his hand, and pressed his own against his chest. Just in time – the door into Strain’s office had cracked open. Those prefects who’d been hunting them were right outside.

‘Um . . . Professor Strain?’ came a nervous voice.

Ollie peered out from beneath the footwell of Strain’s desk and saw one of the prefects poke his head through the doorway.

‘He’s not in there, you idiot,’ came a second voice, a girl’s this time. ‘Professor Strain would have used a *key*.’

Ollie could tell from Lily's expression that she'd realised the same thing he had. The lock pick. It was still in the keyhole on the corridor side of the door. That was what had given them away.

The door opened fully, and the gloom of the office was pierced by two torch beams. The prefects were silhouettes in the doorway.

'Who's in here?' said the girl. 'Show yourselves.'

Lily stared at Ollie helplessly, her wide eyes showing white in the shadows. They were hidden behind the desk for the time being, but there was nowhere for them to go without breaking cover.

'I said, *show yourselves*,' the girl repeated.

Ollie's eyes swept the space around them. They were beside the windows. Could they climb outside and escape across the courtyard? But the sashes were likely to be locked, and even if they did manage to get a window open, they would almost certainly be caught before they could climb through. At the very least they would be *seen*, and then the game would be up anyway.

'Harry,' said the girl, who seemed to be in charge. 'Stand here and guard the door. And find the light switch, will you?'

The girl continued into the room, sweeping her torch beam as she went. Her focus seemed to be on the two large chairs beside the fireplace. But it hardly mattered that she was looking in the wrong direction. As soon as the other prefect turned on the overhead light, Ollie and Lily would be—

The light.

Ollie had an idea.

He signalled to Lily, tapping a fingertip against his phone. Then he pushed the air with a palm, desperately trying to convey his message. Lily frowned, mystified – until her eyes broadened, and she nodded to show she understood.

Ollie knew they had to get the timing just right. He counted down with his fingers. One, two . . .

Three.

As one, Ollie and Lily stood up, raising their phones in front of them and dialling the modified torch beams to maximum. At the same time they hit the strobe function Jack had installed – another recent modification. They rushed forwards, taking advantage of the dazzling light to hurtle into the two prefects. Lily went left, towards the fireplace. Ollie ran straight for the prefect beside the door, driving his shoulder into the boy's midriff before he could have realised what was happening.

Ollie heard Lily's prefect call out, and there was a crash as she toppled into the companion set beside the fire. Ollie knocked the other prefect straight into the coat stand, which tipped like a falling tree. The boy became entangled with Strain's robes, trapping himself beneath them as he tumbled.

Ollie spun, ready to help Lily if she needed it, but his friend was already at his side. This time she was the one to haul Ollie across the threshold, dragging him into the corridor outside. Ollie's instinct was to keep running, but Lily turned on her heels. She grabbed the door and slammed it shut. Flea's lock pick was still in the keyhole, and Lily made to twist it in the lock. Ollie was about to tell her to leave it, to pull her away as he should have done before, but this time the latch clicked immediately.

The door was sealed, trapping the prefects inside.

16 MYSTERY GUEST

Ollie didn't sleep a wink all night.

When he'd finally made it back to his dorm, after parting with Lily in the entrance hall, it was all he could do to lie restless on his bunk, listening for the sound of footsteps marching his way. When none had come, he'd crept over to Sol, only to find his friend asleep with his torch on beneath the covers. Ollie didn't have the heart to wake him, as much as he wanted to tell Sol about everything that had happened. Instead, sleepless with nervous energy, Ollie had taken the handbook back to his own bed, and continued copying it out where Sol had left off.

By dawn, exhaustion was catching up with him, but when the morning bell rang to raise the Forest Mount pupils from their beds, the adrenalin kicked in once again, and Ollie was the first in the dorm to find his feet.

On the way downstairs to the refectory, and as he filled Sol in on the events of the night before, he expected to feel a hand fall on his shoulder. He would turn and see Colton Crowe, or even Professor Strain himself, with the two prefects from the previous night in the background, pointing accusing fingers in Ollie's direction.

But now, having made it through breakfast (Ollie and Lily hadn't eaten a thing, though Sol had been only too pleased to help them out) and then their first lesson at Forest Mount, Ollie was beginning to accept that maybe Strain *didn't* know Ollie and Lily were responsible. He was fairly certain those prefects hadn't seen their faces, so maybe they'd got away with it after all. On the other hand, they would know that *someone* had been sneaking around last night, meaning it was more important than ever that Ollie and the others did nothing to attract attention.

Fortunately, in terms of the lesson they'd just attended, they needn't have worried about showing themselves up. If any one of them had been called on in class, their lack of knowledge of Ancient Greek would have been immediately obvious. Instead, like all the other pupils in the class, all they'd had to do was sit there and copy down what the teacher was writing on the board. It was nothing like lessons at the Haven, where all the kids worked together to find the solutions to the tasks they set themselves. Here, there was no interaction, no questions and answers. Ollie had never been so glad to be forced to endure a lesson that was quite so boring.

'Do you reckon all the lessons are like that?' said Sol, as he and Ollie waited outside the classroom for Jack and Lily to catch up. 'I wonder if they ever get around to teaching anything that's actually useful.'

'Why would you care about learning anything *useful*?' sniffed a prefect who was walking by. 'It's passing the exam that counts. And it's Ancient Greek. Nobody speaks it any more *anyway*.'

She flounced off, clutching her books to her chest.

'That was kind of my point,' muttered Sol, as he watched her go.

Another group of students buzzed past them. These kids were younger, and in their evident excitement they seemed to have forgotten the restrained demeanour that was expected of them.

'Did you hear the news?' one of the girls was saying. 'I hope I get to meet her!'

'You won't get to meet her,' said the only boy in the group. 'It'll just be the prefects, I expect. It's *always* just the prefects.'

As the group babbled off along the corridor, Jack and Lily appeared from out of the classroom. Lily looked as exhausted as Ollie felt.

'What was all that about?' said Jack, her eyes on the group of younger kids.

'It sounds to me as if the news is out,' said Sol. 'Come on, let's see where everyone's going.'

A flow of students had begun to channel purposefully along the corridor. Ollie and the others fell in step, and when they reached the entrance hall they found a crowd gathered around the noticeboard. They had to shove their way through the press of people to be able to read what was posted there.

'The news is out all right,' said Sol. In front of them was a notice of a special assembly to take place that lunchtime in the main auditorium, at which the details of a 'very special visit' by the prime minister of Great Britain to Forest Mount would be announced.

'Maybe we'll find out when it's actually happening,' said Lily. 'There were no details in that document we saw. None that I spotted anyway. Ollie tried to photograph the pages, but the prefects walked in on us before he could.'

Ollie glanced across at her. Was there a note of accusation in her tone, or was he imagining things now? Despite their shared adventure last night, they'd barely said a word to each other all morning. Neither one of them had confessed to the others about the argument they'd had.

'It's probably a good job they did,' said Jack. Then, noticing Ollie's confusion, she added, 'Didn't you read the rules and regulations while you were copying them out, Ollie? It says the authorities here at Forest Mount have the right to access a pupil's mobile phone at any time. Meaning they could confiscate it right now if they chose to, and if they found pictures of a document that was locked in Strain's office . . .'

'They'd know it was you who'd broken in,' finished Sol.

Even so, Ollie wished he'd managed to get a copy of those pages. The prime minister coming to Forest Mount *had* to be linked to what was going on here. Maybe whatever was in that document would have helped them work out how.

And there was something else that was niggling at him. Something obvious he felt he was missing.

The problem was, he was too exhausted to think straight. On top of everything else that was going on, he kept worrying about what was happening back at the Haven. Was everyone safe? And Flea – what was he up to? He'd probably already started campaigning ahead of the election Ollie had promised him. Ollie couldn't help but wonder how many people would be on his side by the time he got back, regardless of whether they managed to complete their mission successfully. And if he lost the vote, Ollie had decided, he would *have* to leave the Haven. He would be too ashamed to stay.

'It says the assembly is at one,' said Jack, checking her watch and interrupting Ollie's thoughts. The rest of the pupils around them were already drifting off to their next lessons. 'That's three hours from now.'

Sol looked at his own watch. 'And I reckon we should try to make this one. Don't you?'

Three interminable lessons later, and having given in their handwritten copies of the rules and regulations, Ollie and the others filed into the main auditorium with the rest of the school. They sat in the third row: close enough that they would be able to see everything that was going on, but far enough from the stage that their faces would blend into the crowd. Or so they hoped.

The audience was chattering excitedly, but at a signal from somewhere, the noise dwindled, until the auditorium was filled with an expectant hush. Suddenly, through the doors at either end of the hallway, two lines of black-shirted prefects marched in. They were led by Colton Crowe, who stationed himself at the corner of the stage. The rest of the prefects took up position along the rear and sides of the room, standing to attention like beefeaters at the Tower of London.

Because of her wheelchair, Jack was at the very end of the row, with Ollie just beside her, then Sol, then Lily – meaning two of the prefects ended up standing disconcertingly close. One was a girl, the other a boy, and Ollie was convinced just from the look of them that they were the very prefects who'd walked in on him and Lily in Professor Strain's office. He began to wonder whether the prime minister's visit was the *only* reason for the special assembly. Or whether he and the others were about to be publicly unmasked.

When the doors at the front of the hall swung open once again, Professor Strain swooped into the room, his robes billowing behind him. The students in the auditorium burst into applause. There was no whooping or hollering – Ollie had a feeling such behaviour would have been deemed beneath Forest Mount pupils – but even so, the outburst of approval was the last thing Ollie had been expecting.

He felt a nudge in his ribs, and he turned to see Jack clapping, too. She moved her eyes meaningfully towards the prefects standing beside her, and Ollie took the hint to join in the applause.

As Strain took up his position behind the lectern on stage, he raised a hand for silence. The clapping stopped immediately.

For the first time Ollie noticed that another man had accompanied Strain on to the platform. Ollie didn't think he was one of the teachers. There were photographs of each of the members of staff in the handbook, and that was a section Ollie *had* studied closely. Rather, the stranger was a thin, oily-looking man, with black, greasy hair. He'd sat down on a solitary chair to one side of the stage, but even seated, Ollie could tell he was a good head shorter than Strain. The man's eyes, though, seemed just as sharp as the headmaster's, and they roamed the area in front of him as though he was hunting for something. Or some*one*.

'As you will no doubt be aware by now,' intoned Strain, 'I have a very special announcement to make.' He gripped the lectern with both of his hands as he spoke, and trained his nose on the children in front of him like a gun sight. 'In three days' time, the prime minister herself will be coming *here*, to Forest Mount, to announce the start of her general election campaign. She will give an address in this very hall, at 6.15 p.m., which will be televised live to the nation, and every Forest Mount pupil will be present. Which *means*,' he went on, cutting off the murmur of excitement that filled the hall before it could develop into anything more substantial, 'that we have three days to prepare for her arrival. *Three* days to ensure we are ready to demonstrate to our honoured guest exactly how a community *should* be run: with order and discipline and control.'

He allowed a pause.

'I can promise you all,' the headmaster continued, 'the prime minister's visit will be an event to remember – a day in your lives you will never forget.'

Ollie looked over at Colton Crowe, who lowered his eyes slightly. But there was no mistaking his expression before he did. He was smiling slightly – sneering in fact, as though he had gleaned a meaning in the headmaster's words that Ollie, for one, had not.

The headmaster continued his address, but after turning his attentions from Crowe, Ollie found himself concentrating on the mystery guest. The man's eyes didn't rest. He seemed to be scouring every inch of the room, and every face within it.

And then his eyes fell on Ollie, and rather than moving on this time, they tightened in what Ollie took to be recognition.

But that was impossible – wasn't it? Ollie was sure he didn't know the man. So how was it possible that the stranger would know him?

Ollie looked down, then up again, hoping he was simply mistaken. Yet when he raised his eyes towards the stage once more, the man was still staring at him.

'Mr Ross here . . .' Strain said, and the man on stage had no choice but to release Ollie from his gaze, '. . . will be on hand over the next three days to ensure everything goes according to plan. Mr Ross is the prime minister's personal assistant, meaning you are to afford him the respect you would offer the prime minister herself.'

Ross tipped his head in acknowledgement, his sly eyes narrowing further. Ollie shifted in his seat slightly, so that Ross's view of him would be blocked by a taller boy in the second row.

Sol glanced at Ollie quizzically, and Ollie realised he was almost certainly being paranoid. He was just on edge, that was all – because of Lily, because of the Haven, and because of everything that was going on at Forest Mount. Surely if anybody *did* know who Ollie was, and what he and his friends had been up to, there was no way they would have been allowed to just sit there.

As if to prove the point, Strain brought the assembly to an end without any mention of the break-in to his office. Once the headmaster and his guest had left the stage, the prefects began to file out, followed by the other students, leaving Ollie and the others sighing in relief.

Except as Ross had left the room, he'd definitely glanced once again in Ollie's direction. And Ollie realised what it was that had been bothering him before. They'd broken into Strain's office and found the dossier about the prime minister's visit, but Strain had made his announcement this morning without any hint that anything untoward had happened last night. There'd been no lecture, no witch hunt, no confiscated phones. None of the things Ollie would have expected to happen.

All of which led him to the only conclusion that made sense: Strain was trying to cover it up. They would be searching for those responsible, but secretly, because Strain didn't want anything to stop the prime minister from coming to Forest Mount. If he admitted someone had broken into his office and found the security plans for her visit, he would have *had* to call it off. But for whatever reason, Strain couldn't allow that to happen. He wanted the PM's visit to go ahead. He *needed* it to.

And for the first time, Ollie thought he might have understood why.

17 AFTER DARK

For the next two days, Ollie and his friends had no choice but to try to keep their heads down. There may not have been an obvious witch hunt, but there was no question the prefects were being unusually watchful. When Jack and Sol had taken their turn to try to find the secret door the night after Ollie's and Lily's failed attempt, they'd barely made it as far as the East Wing before they'd been forced to retreat back to their dorms. The night patrols seemed to have been doubled, and a permanent guard had been set along from Strain's office.

On the third night, they thought about trying again, but Jack convinced them they would all be better off getting some sleep, and attempting to work out some other way of breaking into the dungeons. The problem was, none of them could.

Even sleep proved hard to come by. Ollie was exhausted, but he kept thinking about the PM's visit, about the theory he'd come up with during Strain's assembly. On the one hand, he struggled to believe it himself, and he was reluctant to confide in his friends until he was certain. But he also recalled everything Jack had told them about Strain's history, and how Errol had overheard Crowe talking about a 'revolution'. And Strain himself, bragging to the audience in his assembly. *An event to remember*, he'd said. *A day in your lives you will never forget . . .*

On the evening of their fourth day at Forest Mount, the night before the prime minister's visit, Ollie called a meeting with the others in the common room. A group of prefects had colonised the space by the open fire, so Ollie, Jack and Sol dragged some chairs together in a corner by one of the windows, as far from prying eyes and pricked up ears as they could get.

'Where's Lily?' Ollie asked.

'Last time I saw her she was talking to Crowe,' said Sol. 'She said she'd join us later. If she could.'

Ollie found himself frowning. Not only had he witnessed Lily flirting with Crowe on their very first morning at Forest Mount, more than once over the past two days he'd seen her hanging around in Crowe's vicinity, clearly trying to get him to notice her. Whether she was faking her interest in Crowe or not, the one thing they could be certain of was that Crowe was the enemy. Whatever was going on at Forest Mount, there was no question Crowe was at the heart of it, doing Professor Strain's bidding. And Ollie had made it clear they needed to keep a low profile, particularly after what had happened in Strain's office. Lily, though, seemed determined to do just the opposite.

'So what was it you wanted to talk to us about?' said Sol, getting down to business. 'It sounded as though it was important.'

Ollie hesitated. He'd made up his mind to share what he was thinking with his friends, to explain to them his theory about why George had been murdered, why Errol and the others had been silenced, and how it all tied in with the prime minister's visit. But sitting there with an empty seat across from him, Ollie felt the confidence drain out of him.

'I just . . . I think we need to try the secret door again,' he said. 'Tonight.'

Sol and Jack shared a look.

'But I thought we'd decided?' said Jack. 'There's no way we can get close, not now the door is under guard. And even if we could, you and Lily have already tried to find the switch.'

Sol nodded grimly. 'I hate to say it, mate, but when it comes to that secret door, I think we've blown our only chance.'

Ollie heard the prefects laughing together by the fire. He glanced again at Lily's empty chair, and felt frustration welling up within him. 'Look, you two can do whatever you want,' he said. 'Go hang out with Colton Crowe, for all I care. But I'm going down there again. As for the guards, I'll . . . I'll distract them. Somehow. It would be easier with a bit of help, that's all.'

Immediately Ollie felt ashamed for having lost his temper.

‘We didn’t say we wouldn’t help, Ollie,’ said Jack. ‘There’s no one who wants to solve this thing as much as I do, I promise you.’

‘Right,’ agreed Sol. ‘Me, too. I mean, it’s Jack’s brother who’s gone missing, but that’s not to say I’m any less determined to find him. We’re with you, mate, honestly. The same goes for Lily.’

‘So what’s she doing spending her free time hanging around with Colton Crowe?’ Ollie said, his hackles rising again in spite of himself. ‘She should be here, with us. The PM’s visit is *tomorrow*. And when she gets here, when she steps up on that stage to deliver her address . . .’

Ollie swallowed what he’d been about to say.

‘Ollie?’ said Jack. ‘What is it? It sounds as if you think you know what’s going to happen.’

Ollie shook his head. ‘I don’t, though. That’s the point. All I know for certain is that the clock is ticking. For Errol, for all of us.’

At the mention of her brother’s name, a tear formed in Jack’s eye. She turned her face to the corner. She didn’t want anyone else in the common room to see her crying, clearly. But Ollie had a sense she didn’t want him or Sol looking at her either.

‘Look, Jack, I’m sorry,’ said Ollie. ‘I didn’t mean to snap. I know this is harder on you than it is on anyone. But we’ll find your brother, I promise we will.’

'That's right,' said Sol, squeezing Jack's shoulder. 'Let's just give Lily some time. OK? She'll be here, I know she will.'

They waited for over an hour. Eventually the common room began to empty out, as the rest of the students drifted off to bed. Ollie was so worn out his eyes were burning, and not just from the heat of the fire. He'd been nodding off in his armchair as they waited for Lily, but every time he closed his eyes, his semi-conscious mind assailed him with weird, mashed-together images: of Professor Strain sprouting wings and taking flight, soaring high above Forest Mount; of Flea's body lying in an open coffin, the room around it swirling with smoke; of Colton Crowe chasing him with gnashing teeth, and Lily laughing in the background.

'It's curfew time, newbies,' said a prefect who was standing beside the door. Ollie and the others were the last ones in the room.

'Nighty night,' said the prefect, 'don't let the vampires bite.' And without warning he switched off the overhead light, leaving Ollie and his friends smothered in darkness. The prefect cackled off along the corridor, and the door swung shut behind him.

'Not much of a turn-down service here, is there?' said Sol through the gloom. 'I suppose it's too much to hope for chocolates on our pillows.'

'Come on,' said Ollie, getting up. 'We should grab a couple of hours sleep if we can before we try to find that secret door.'

'What about Lily?' said Jack.

It was the very question that had been playing on Ollie's mind. 'I guess she had better things to do,' he said.

Already the ground floor was deserted, and with only the emergency lights aglow in the corridors, it was barely any lighter in the passageway than it had been inside the common room. To Ollie's mind, Forest Mount had never felt creepier. There was no moon visible through the leaded windows, just a barely penetrable blackness. Other than the silhouettes of the nearby trees, the only thing Ollie could see when he tried to look outside was his own ghostly reflection looking back at him.

'We'll walk you to the girls' dorm before we split up,' said Ollie to Jack. 'And not because you're a girl, before you say anything. And not because we don't think you can't handle yourself. I'm just not sure it's a good idea for any of us to be wandering around after dark on our own. Not if we can help it.'

There came a scraping sound at one of the windows they were passing, as if something outside was clawing to get in. All three of them whipped their heads towards the glass.

But it was just a tree branch stirring in the wind.

'Er . . . OK,' said Jack, her eyes wide. 'You know, if it will make you feel better.'

They continued along the corridor, more warily than they had before. Ollie's gaze kept being drawn towards the windows.

He found himself recalling Flea's warning, about the thing he'd heard growling in the woods. An animal of some kind? A *monster*? Or just a figment of Flea's imagination?

'Are you sure this is the right way?' said Sol.

Ollie surveyed the corridor. The passageway that led from the common room towards the girls' dorm was lined with portraits of Forest Mount's former headmasters. This corridor had the same stone walls, the same blood-red carpet – black in the midnight glow – but the walls were bare.

'We must have taken a wrong turning,' said Ollie. 'I was just following you.'

'Me? Why on earth would you follow me?' replied Sol. 'I assumed Jack knew the way.'

'I was following Ollie!' said Jack. 'I figured he knew a shortcut or something.'

The wind outside was picking up. Another tree tried to scratch an opening in the glass, and the sound was like nails being dragged down a blackboard.

'*Ollie, look*,' hissed Jack, and she pointed towards the window.

'What is it?' said Ollie, his heart thumping at the thought of what Jack might have spotted.

'Not that way,' Jack said. 'Over *there*. And get down, both of you. He'll see us.' Jack grabbed Ollie and Sol by their arms, her urgent fingers pinching Ollie's skin as she tugged him down to her level.

'Is that . . .' Sol said.

'Colton Crowe,' Ollie finished. 'What's he doing outside at this time of night?'

Crowe was illuminated by a pool of light spilling from an upstairs window. His black hair flashed momentarily silver, before he stepped once again into darkness.

'Is Lily with him?' said Jack. 'I can't see her.'

'I don't think so,' said Sol. 'No, he's definitely alone. But where's he going? He hasn't even got a torch with him.'

'Because he doesn't want to be spotted,' Ollie said, and even as he spoke, Crowe turned to check in their direction.

'*Down*,' urged Ollie, and he and the others ducked lower.

Ollie counted to three before daring to peek again. This time when he looked, Crowe was concentrating on the path in front of him, which was leading him away from the main building.

'I'm going to follow him,' Ollie said. He scanned the corridor and spotted an exit sign glowing faintly up ahead.

'Wait,' said Jack. 'What happens if he sees you?'

'I'll make sure he doesn't,' Ollie answered.

'I'll come with you,' said Sol. 'We'll all come.'

'No, you two stay here. There's less chance he'll notice if it's just me.'

'But what about what you said earlier?' said Jack. 'About not wandering around at night-time on our own?'

Ollie checked again through the window. Crowe was veering from the path and cutting across a patch of grass, heading directly into the forest.

'You two go on ahead,' Ollie said, deliberately failing to answer Jack's question. 'Try to find that secret door without me. Or *something* that will lead us to Errol.' He made to move off, then turned back. 'You were right what you said before, Jack. I do have an idea what's going on. George's "accident", Errol and the others going missing – that's just a sideshow. It's the prime minister who Strain is after. I think . . . I think he plans to kill her. Here, at Forest Mount. And *that's* only the beginning.'

18 MIDNIGHT MEETING

By the time Ollie got outside, Crowe was nowhere to be seen. Even the light in that upstairs window had been extinguished, leaving the grounds on the forest side of the school in darkness. Above him, not a single star penetrated the inky blackness. The only lights Ollie could see were at the base of the hill, in the sprawl of the city itself. London was all around him, he knew, but from where he was standing, it was as if he were looking down at life on another planet.

For a brief, disconcerting moment, Ollie felt such a longing to be back at the Haven, safe beneath the ground at the city's heart, it was all he could do to stop himself sprinting for the gates.

Instead he stood quite still, waiting for his eyes to adjust. He turned his gaze towards the tree line, in the direction he'd last seen Crowe. He let his vision go slack, alert for some sign of movement. And then he saw it: a shadowy figure weaving between the trees.

Ollie was off.

He ducked his head and cut straight across the grass, and was soon amid the trees himself. From what Ollie could make out, Crowe was heading right into the centre of the forest.

Why? What was he doing? Was there something hidden among the trees that nobody else knew about?

Ollie didn't think so. Jack and the rest of the investigations team had scoured the school's grounds on Google Earth before embarking on their mission, and although it had been hard to see past the tops of the trees, they'd spotted nothing that appeared out of place. Certainly there'd been no space in the forest for buildings of any kind, not even a woodshed or a hut. In fact there was only one clearing in the whole of the wooded area, and that was taken up by the lake – the place George's body had been discovered.

An owl hooted overhead, and Ollie gave a start. He'd slowed his pace since entering the forest. Partly because he had no choice: tree roots crossed the ground like trip wires, and the undergrowth was so thick in places, it was like trying to wade through a crowd of grabbing arms. Also, though, the determination he'd felt when he'd been with Jack and Sol was in danger of deserting him. Out here, in the forest, there was nothing but shifting shadows all around. The air was cold like a grave, and the autumn wind cut mercilessly through the branches of the groaning trees. Plus, of course, there was the wildlife. Ollie couldn't see any of it, but he could hear plenty. From the howls in the canopy above his head to the rustles in the decaying leaves at his feet, the forest was alive with unseen movement.

Ollie heard Flea's voice once again in his head. *There was something out there. Something big . . .*

Crowe had a fifty-metre head start, but he didn't seem to be in any particular hurry, meaning Ollie was able to narrow the gap between them. He didn't want to get *too* close, though. Part of the reason Crowe was moving so slowly was that he was pausing every few steps to make sure he wasn't being followed.

Ollie couldn't help but wonder again what he was up to. Was it possible he would lead Ollie directly to Errol? Perhaps this was where they would find another route into the dungeons.

Ollie crept as near to Crowe as he dared, closing the gap to less than ten metres. The last thing he wanted was for Crowe to disappear into a hidden entranceway, leaving Ollie stumbling blindly in the dark.

Instead, Crowe appeared to be slowing. They'd almost reached the lake. A thin, sharp moon had appeared through a gap in the clouds, casting a silver light on the depthless water. When they reached the bank, Ollie couldn't help but shiver. He was thinking about George, picturing his body trapped beneath the reeds . . .

Suddenly a light flicked on up ahead, flashing three times and then vanishing. For a moment Ollie thought he'd been spotted, and that the light was being directed at *him*. But it was coming from the far side of the lake, a good twenty metres away. The pattern repeated, and Crowe spotted it himself. It wasn't a searchlight, Ollie realised. It was a *signal*.

So that was why Crowe was out here. He was meeting someone. Someone he didn't want anyone else at the school to know was there.

Crowe signalled back with his own torch, then he and whoever he was meeting kept their torches on as they made their way towards one another. This deep into the woods, they were obviously satisfied that no one back at the school would be able to see them.

Ollie waited until the two lights drew closer together before daring to creep any nearer. He kept as tight to the lake as he could without breaking cover, using the softness of the bank to stifle his footsteps. He crouched beside a patch of reeds, and peered out at the midnight meeting.

The stranger was about Crowe's height, and no broader, but from his slouched shoulders and heavy footsteps, Ollie could tell immediately that he was a grown-up.

For some reason, Ollie's first thought was that Crowe was meeting Mr Ross, the man Strain had introduced as the prime minister's personal assistant. Ollie couldn't help remembering the way Ross had been looking at him during Strain's assembly. There was a slyness to the man that Ollie didn't trust.

But when the stranger walked into the glow from Crowe's torch, Ollie realised it was a man he had never seen before. He had dark stubble and hooded eyes, and wore a heavy black overcoat that didn't quite disguise his bulging belly. Ross, in contrast, had been thin and wiry, with slicked back hair and the same skeletal appearance as Professor Strain.

'You are late,' the stranger said. He had an accent Ollie couldn't immediately place. There were kids from all corners of the world at the Haven, many of whom had fled their homelands to avoid famine or war or persecution – and sometimes all three – so Ollie had grown accustomed to telling their accents apart.

'It is not polite to keep guests waiting,' the man went on. 'Particularly when they come bearing gifts.'

This time there was a smirk in his words. His accent wasn't Scandinavian, like Erik's, Ollie decided. Was it Eastern European? All of a sudden Ollie thought of those books in Strain's office, the photo he and Lily had spotted on the wall. Russian. That was it: the stranger's accent was Russian.

'You have it?' said Crowe. He sounded nervous, Ollie thought. And for some reason, he seemed to be keeping his distance. The Russian had stepped clear of the trees, on to the bank of the lake, but Crowe hung back at the forest's edge.

The Russian raised an arm, and Ollie saw he was holding a briefcase. But it was bulkier than the sort of case you saw business people carrying, and it seemed to be made of metal.

Crowe took half a step backwards.

'Is that it? Is it . . . is it safe?'

The man let out a throaty cackle. 'If it is not, my friend, then you and I are both already dead.'

He swung the case, and it arced in the air towards Crowe. Crowe dived to catch it, ending up on all fours in the slime of the river bank, the briefcase clutched like a baby in his arms.

'Are you crazy?' Crowe spluttered, his eyes wide in obvious fear.

The Russian laughed his rusty laugh. He was clearly taking pleasure in Crowe's discomfort. What was Crowe so afraid of, Ollie wondered? What was in that case?

'Of course I am crazy!' the Russian said. 'Do you think I would be carrying around such – how do you say? *Knick-knacks?* – if I were not? Relax, my friend,' he added, chuckling. 'It is safely protected in the case, but *deadly* the moment it is released. You will find it does exactly what you need it to.'

Crowe was struggling to rise. He had both arms wrapped around the case, and his feet kept slipping from under him as he tried to stand. The Russian laughed again and offered out his hand. Crowe ignored it, and finally staggered to his feet. He backed towards the trees. One side of his school uniform was completely covered in mud.

'You are not leaving so soon I hope,' said the Russian. 'You have something for me also, yes?' He was still smiling, but there was an unmistakeable warning in his tone.

Crowe seemed to sense it, too. Wrapping one arm more tightly around the metal briefcase, he fumbled with his free hand to pull something from his pocket. It was an envelope, stuffed so full it was as thick as a dictionary. Crowe tossed it and the Russian caught it one-handed. He tested its weight in his palm, then looked at Crowe with narrowed eyes. There was no trace any more of his smile.

'What is this?' he said, his accent thickening in his anger.

The man tore an edge of the envelope and peered inside, then ripped it open fully and emptied its contents over the forest floor. Ollie watched as pieces of newspaper the size of fifty pound notes fluttered confetti-like to the ground.

The man took a furious step towards Crowe. The envelope was behind him, discarded on the floor, and instead his hand was reaching for something concealed inside his overcoat. Rather than cowering away this time, Crowe straightened his shoulders. 'Personally,' he told the Russian, 'I would be heading in the other direction right about now. And rather quickly.'

There came a growl.

Halfway towards Crowe, the man came abruptly to a stop. His head whipped towards the trees.

His own terror budding in his stomach, Ollie followed his gaze.

And then he saw it.

It emerged with red eyes blazing. Its skin was raw, its nose scabbed and bleeding. It looked like something newly born, similar to a rat maybe, except it was the size of a lion or a tiger. And it had teeth: vicious, nicotine-coloured needles, each the length of Ollie's middle finger. They were bared as the beast padded into the glade, one clawed foot at a time.

Flea's monster, Ollie realised: it was *real*.

The Russian appeared frozen in fear. From his coat he'd retrieved a revolver, but in his terror he appeared to have forgotten all about it.

The beast took another step, and Ollie could see its hindquarters. They were pink and raw like the rest of its body, but here and there on its mottled skin were patches of soot-coloured fur. Only its hind legs were fully coated, but here, instead of black, the beast's fur was thunderstorm grey.

The Russian took a stumbling step backwards, raising his weapon to fire.

But he was too late.

The beast launched itself into the air. There was a hollow crack, like a branch breaking, as the man's weapon went off, but the shot went wild, and even before the beast landed on him, the Russian was falling on to his back.

There was a scream, high pitched and shrill, cut off an instant later by the sound of something tearing.

Ollie had no choice but to look away. He crouched lower, and focused on controlling his panicked breathing. What *was* that thing? And why didn't Crowe appear afraid of it?

Ollie moved to peer once again through the reeds. He had to focus. He had to find out what was in that briefcase.

But he barely got a chance to steal another look. His gaze caught on the stranger's body, and the beast standing salivating over it – its blood-red eyes now fixed directly on Ollie.

19 BLOOD HUNT

Ollie didn't hesitate. He'd seen what the monster had done to the Russian, and he'd been a fully grown man, with a gun in his hand ready to fire. Ollie himself wouldn't have stood a chance. And so he took the only option open to him.

He *ran*.

He had no idea whether Crowe had seen his face. It seemed unlikely – impossible, even, given that Crowe's torch was pointing in the opposite direction – but at that moment Ollie didn't much care.

As soon as he found his feet, he sprinted for the tree line. With every step he expected to be caught. He was braced for a searing pain down his back, or an explosion of agony in his trailing foot.

Yet he made it to the first trees unscathed, and as he crashed his way through the branches he found himself praying he'd been mistaken. Maybe the beast *hadn't* spotted him. There was no sound of anything pursuing him: none of the snarls and snuffled growls he'd heard before.

But soon enough he realised why.

'Go!' yelled Crowe. 'Get him! *Kill* him!'

The beast was merely waiting for a command.

There was a howl, like a wolf baying at the moon. The sound was so chilling, Ollie almost froze in his tracks. But immediately afterwards there was another crash, as the beast broke through the first row of trees.

It was coming for him.

The faster Ollie tried to run, the more the branches seemed to want to hold him back. They snatched at him, snagging his clothes and tugging his hair. It was almost as though the forest itself was on Crowe's side, as ready to obey him as the monster was.

As if to prove it, a tree root hooked around Ollie's toes, and would have felled him had he not caught himself against the trunk of a nearby tree. For three or four paces, he was half sprinting, half falling, until he recovered himself and stumbled on.

He ducked and dipped as he ran. He knew he should be heading uphill, but when he tried to do so it felt too slow, like trying to run through water. In the end he simply aimed himself at whichever slight pathway was open to him.

And then he tripped.

His foot had snagged again and this time there was no saving himself. He tipped forwards, rolling in a tangle as he landed, and then slamming kidneys first into a tree.

For a second, two, he couldn't breathe. The wind had been knocked out of him, all of his remaining energy, too. It was only instinct that pulled him on to his hands and knees, the knowledge that if he were to lie there, the beast would be upon him in a matter of seconds. And then . . . then . . . Ollie thought about that tearing sound he'd heard, the way it had ripped through the Russian's blood-curdling scream.

He tried to force himself standing, ignoring the clamour in his lungs and the slimy feel of the leaf mulch below his palms. But his hand slipped, costing him time he didn't have . . . and when he finally regained his feet he was already too late.

The beast was here, now, its red eyes glowing in the darkness from no more than pouncing distance away.

It snarled, and crept from its hunting place amid the shadows.

Cornered, Ollie backed against the tree. The beast continued towards him, clawing its way across the leaf-strewn floor. Its upper lip was curled backwards to reveal its teeth, and in the moonlight its gums appeared the same colour as its skin. The redness showed up as shades of black, and there was something even darker sticking wetly to the beast's whiskers.

'Where are you?' came a voice. Crowe's, from some distance away. 'You won't get away, you know, whoever you are. If I don't find you, then *it* will. Assuming it hasn't already.'

Crowe's cackle carried through the trees. From the sound of it he *hadn't* seen Ollie's face at the lakeside – although to Ollie, in his current predicament, it was scant consolation.

With his hands gripping the tree trunk behind him, he scoured desperately for an escape route. The beast was coming at him head on, but when Ollie tried to slide around the tree, it altered its path, cutting off any chance Ollie might have had of getting away. It was bearing down on him slowly, steadily, as though savouring the thought of its upcoming kill.

Except . . . just as Ollie was sure the beast was about to pounce, it instead started pacing from side to side, as though suddenly uncertain. It kept its raging eyes on Ollie, cannily blocking his escape route, but for some reason it was holding off on its final attack.

What was it waiting for? Another command? But Crowe had already given it an order to kill.

Making the most of his momentary reprieve, Ollie scanned the ground around him, searching for something that might help him. A stick, a stone, *anything*.

But then the beast started forwards once more, its snarl deepening, and its teeth coming slightly apart. It coiled its legs, readying to pounce, and it was all Ollie could do to raise his hands. It was instinct more than anything, a futile gesture of self-defence – and yet in response the beast wheeled away, whimpering slightly, and gazing back at Ollie with its bloodshot eyes.

And this time Ollie wasn't mistaken: there was *fear* in those eyes, he was sure of it. But why would the beast be afraid of *Ollie*?

He didn't stop to consider. He'd spotted a branch at his feet. It had been just out of reach before, but now he dived for it. The beast was facing him again, crouching, and caught in some kind of confusion Ollie didn't understand. But when it saw Ollie make a move, its killer instincts kicked in and it leapt, its claws outstretched and its muzzle aiming for Ollie's throat.

Ollie tightened his grip on the branch, and swung.

The branch was heavier than he'd been expecting, one end clumsy with leaves. It arced agonisingly slowly through the air, as though it were tethered with elastic.

It hit the beast on the side of its head. The wood reverberated in Ollie's hands, and the beast fell as Ollie did, collapsing in a heap on the mulchy floor.

The beast was so close to Ollie that he could smell it. It stank of blood and gone-off meat – and something else. Something smoky and bitter and pungent, the way the old library had smelt after the fire.

At first Ollie thought the beast might be dead. It lay utterly motionless, not even a breath rippling its hairless body. But then its left eye popped open.

In a heartbeat Ollie was up and running again, onwards through the trees, and not caring that he'd lost all sense of direction. The only thing he was concerned with was putting as much distance as possible between him and that *thing* before it got back on its feet.

And there was Crowe, of course. He was out there somewhere, too.

Breathless and sweating in the cold night air, Ollie stumbled on. The school. He had to get to the school. There were dangers within Forest Mount as well, but right now its walls were his only chance of safety.

He veered uphill, pumping his legs to try to keep from slowing down.

And then he heard it again: the sound of something in pursuit. The beast? Or Crowe?

The sound was coming from his right, so once again Ollie changed direction. In the back of his mind he heard a warning, a nagging voice from somewhere in his subconscious. It was trying to remind him of something – something it was important he remembered, even in the midst of his flight.

But the noise behind him was getting louder, meaning his pursuer was closing in, and for the time being the voice was lost in a clamour of competing fears. It was the beast Ollie was most afraid of: the monster with the blood-red eyes.

And it was gaining.

Ollie was so tired he could barely lift his feet. He tripped, staggered on. He raised his head, then ducked manically to avoid a low-hanging branch. *The school. I have to get to the school.* But the building was nowhere in sight, and Ollie could hear panting right behind him. *Not the beast then. Crowe.*

Ollie tried to increase his pace, but his energy was spent. And something was holding him back. Not the undergrowth this time, but that voice again. *The grounds*, it was saying. *Remember about the grounds . . .*

But Ollie *couldn't* remember, and by the time it came to him it was already too late.

The cliff.

He only saw it when he broke through the tree line. And even then it took a second for his brain to catch up with his eyes, and a second after that for the message to be relayed to his feet.

As the trees finally receded, the ground opened greyly in front of him. Beyond that was a sudden blackness, and before Ollie could register what was happening, the world disappeared from under him. He had a sensation of falling, of feeling nothing, and then there was an explosion in his head, and Ollie was aware of nothing more.

20 HUMAN SACRIFICE

Colton Crowe knew the boy would be dead by now, but the knowledge did nothing to diminish his irritation. As he marched from the forest towards the school, the metal briefcase he'd collected from the Russian in his grip, he simmered with barely contained fury.

That was the third time outsiders had attempted to interfere. Not just outsiders: *children*. It had been kids they'd chased from the tunnels, until the roof had come crashing in. It had been children, too, who'd broken into Professor Strain's office, which also meant they'd somehow infiltrated the school. They must have done, for the boy – whoever he'd been – to have followed him to his rendezvous at the lake.

And security was Crowe's responsibility. That had been made perfectly clear to him. And failure, he knew, would not be tolerated.

Inside the building now, Crowe headed directly to the East Wing. Despite the hour, he wasn't challenged on the way, which only angered him further. But then he remembered that the prefects had their own task to accomplish tonight, a special job for Professor Strain, meaning the patrols Crowe had set up were temporarily suspended.

It couldn't be helped, he supposed. Strain's wishes had to be obeyed. And actually, given what Crowe was carrying, it was probably a good job he was able to pass through the school without being seen. Most of the prefects knew better than to ask questions, but there were one or two who hadn't quite learned their place yet, and Crowe didn't have time to remind them.

He reached the corridor with the wood panelling and triggered the secret door. It opened noiselessly, and Crowe slipped quickly across the threshold. On his way through he banged the case carelessly against the door frame, and for an instant his anger gave way to terror.

You and I are both already dead . . .

The Russian's words came back to him. Was it really possible that something so small could kill so stealthily? Without being seen, heard or smelt?

Sweating now, in a way that had nothing to do with the temperature, Crowe carried the case more carefully down the steps into the dungeon. He passed through the corridor where the 'runaways' were being kept prisoner. Behind the final door in the row was the cell in which their most recent guest was being held.

Errol.

At the thought of him, Crowe's anger resurfaced. Errol was central to the plan, but so far he was proving infuriatingly stubborn. Crowe had been so sure he could be broken, but the boy was braver than Crowe had realised. Even when he'd let the beast into Errol's cell, the boy hadn't given in. He'd screamed, yes, and cowered in terror, but still he'd refused to do what Crowe had demanded.

Crowe had half a mind to open the cell door right now, to have another go at breaking him, but he knew he had to be cleverer than that. There had to be *something* he could use. Something dear to the boy, which Crowe could hold over him, and blackmail him into doing Crowe's bidding.

Crowe reached the wall at the end of the dank passageway. Here he paused, and glanced briefly over his shoulder. He knew there was nobody watching him, but even so he needed to make sure. Most of the prefects knew about the secret door up in the corridor, but none were aware there was a *second* secret entranceway down in the dungeon itself.

Crowe located the catch that would release the secret door. A crack appeared in the damp stone wall, and he slipped stealthily through the gap.

'Do you have it?'

The passageway beyond the door was in shadows, and the voice carried through the darkness.

Crowe froze in his tracks, the sweat on his brow all of a sudden feeling like ice.

'I . . . I thought you'd be upstairs,' he said.

'*Do you have it?*'

'Yes, I . . . I have it here.' Crowe held up the case and took a step forwards.

'Stay back, you idiot. Keep it away from me.'

'Of course,' Crowe said. 'Sorry, I . . .'

'And don't grovel. Haven't I taught you better than that?'

Crowe's instinct was to apologise again, but instead he forced himself to stand a fraction straighter.

He caught a glimpse of a smile then, like a knife waiting in the dark.

'What of the boy? Has he been . . . persuaded?'

'He'll do as he's instructed,' Crowe answered, hoping he sounded more confident than he felt. 'There won't be any further problems.'

'Problems like the brats who've been sniffing around my school, you mean.'

'They've . . . they've been dealt with,' Crowe said. 'One of them has, anyway. As for the others, by the time they figure out what's really going on, it will be too late.'

The shadow in the dark loomed nearer. 'Assuming you can convince the boy to deliver our package, of course.'

Crowe swallowed. 'He will. Count on it.'

'He better. Because if he refuses, that particular honour will fall to *you*, Colton. I suggest you think about what that would mean.'

A hand fell on his shoulder, the fingers thin and pale, and it was all Crowe could do not to flinch.

And then it withdrew. There was a swish, a retreating shadow, and Crowe was left standing in the darkened passageway all alone.

He felt the hatred rise up in him. He would show them. Every one of them. Professor Strain, who thought Forest Mount was *his*, and Crowe just another minion at his command. The other prefects, too, who thought they were special, that *they* would be permitted to share the spoils when this was over. The over-privileged, self-righteous fools. They were just like their parents, every one of them. Crowe couldn't wait to see the expressions on their faces when they realised how comprehensively they'd been duped.

And then there was his father, of course. *Sir* Sebastian Crowe. So respected among his peers. A close supporter of the prime minister, with a seat on her front bench. But in reality nothing more than a bully. What would his friends, his allies, say if they knew how the esteemed Sir Crowe treated his only son? How he hit him, humiliated him, *hated* him. As far as his father was concerned, nothing Colton did was ever good enough. All he cared about was his precious career.

Well, if everything went according to plan, his career might very well end up being the death of him. At the very least, Crowe would be able to watch as it was transformed to dust and ash.

But it all depended on Errol.

It was less than twenty-four hours until the prime minister's visit, and if Crowe failed to break Errol in time, the final task in the plan would fall to him. And as much as he believed in what he was doing, he wasn't willing to offer himself as sacrifice. He wanted to be there to see their objective achieved, to witness the expression on his father's face when he realised what his son had set in motion . . .

And Errol was threatening to ruin everything.

In a flash of irritation, Crowe lashed out in the darkness, slamming a fist against the wall.

There must be *something* the boy cared about. Some*one*, even. But his real parents were dead, and now that George had been dealt with, by all accounts Errol had no real friends. It was hardly surprising he'd invented an invisible companion. What had he called him?

Jack. That was it.

Cursing under his breath, and flexing his now-bleeding knuckles, Crowe closed his eyes and tried to focus. To *think*. But his anger clouded his thoughts. It hadn't escaped his notice that all the trouble, all the interference from those pesky kids, whoever they were, had only begun after Errol had been taken captive. It was almost as though the two events were connected, that Errol being locked in his cell and those kids trying to break in through the tunnels had—

All of a sudden Errol's words came back to him. *Jack*, he'd said. *Are you out there?*

Not, 'are you there?' Rather, 'are you *out* there?' And he'd been pressed against the wall. Beside the air vent, his eyes watering. *I'm not crying*, Errol had insisted, and he hadn't been, not in the way Crowe had assumed.

For the first time since his meeting beside the lake, a smile crept across Crowe's face.

When he returned to the passageway outside and opened the door into Errol's cell, the boy was already on his feet. And right away, Crowe could tell this wasn't going to take long.

Ignoring Errol's terrified expression, Crowe strode across the cell, straight to the vent high on the wall. He raised his nose, sniffing the air. The scent was faint now, but unmistakeable.

'That's tear gas you can smell, in case you were wondering,' he said. 'The vent must be connected to the tunnels.' He faced Errol. 'What did you hear, I wonder? How much did you allow yourself to hope?'

The boy's skin was marked and grimy, his eyes puffed from tears. But he did his best to appear defiant. Crowe could almost admire it.

'I'm not saying anything else to you,' Errol said. 'I've decided. You can do what you want to me. Feed me to that . . . that *thing* if you want. I don't even care any more.'

'But you care about Jack, don't you, Errol?' Crowe responded, and the flicker of alarm that showed on the boy's face dispelled the last of Crowe's remaining doubts.

'Who's Jack?' Errol tried to bluff. 'I don't know a Jack.'

His eyes twitched tellingly, and his hand drifted to his pocket.

'Come now,' Crowe said, as he closed the gap between them. 'Your invisible friend. Remember?'

'Oh,' said Errol. 'Right. Yes. Her. I thought you meant . . . that you were talking about . . .'

Errol's words tailed off as Crowe backed him against the wall. *Her*, Crowe was thinking. That was interesting. He'd been assuming Jack was a boy.

'What's in your pocket, Errol? You were touching it before, I remember. The last time we spoke.'

'My pocket? Nothing. I . . .' Errol snatched his hand to his chest, allowing Crowe to seize hold of it effortlessly.

Errol tried to break free, but Crowe was much too strong for him. Crowe used his bodyweight to drive Errol against the wall. Hard, so that the breath – and the fight – went out of him.

With his free hand, Crowe retrieved what turned out to be a slip of paper. No, a *photograph*, he realised when he flipped it over.

'That's not mine,' Errol gasped. 'I just . . . I found it. On the floor. I assumed it was—'

This time Crowe cut off Errol's words by driving his fist into the boy's solar plexus.

As Errol slumped breathless to the floor, Crowe studied his prize.

And it was a prize indeed. What was that expression? Two birds with one stone. Two problems solved for the price of one. The boy must have had the photograph with him all along. Those idiot prefects who'd dragged him from the forest must have missed it when they'd frisked him.

Honestly, thought Crowe, smiling. *Must I do everything myself?* Although as it had turned out, the task that lay ahead of him now was one he reckoned he was going to enjoy.

21 DARKEST SECRETS

Ollie woke to see the monster staring down at him.

He panicked, tried to wriggle himself backwards, but a hammering in his head stopped him moving. He screwed his eyes tight, until gradually the pain at his temples began to ease.

'Easy, Ollie. Take it easy.'

When Ollie looked, he saw those eyes again.

'Ollie? It's me. Are you OK? Don't try to sit. Not yet.'

'Sol?' Ollie said, realising who it was gazing down at him. 'Where . . . where are we? Why does my head—'

An explosion of pain interrupted him. He reached and located a bump the size of an apple beneath the hair on his crown.

And then it came back to him. The woods, the Russian, the *beast* . . .

The cliff.

'I fell,' he said. 'Someone . . . someone was chasing me.' Gradually Ollie took in his surroundings. He was in his bunk, in the dorm at Forest Mount.

'Um, about that . . .' said Sol. 'Don't get mad or anything. But . . . that was sort of me.'

'You?' Ollie tried to sit again. The pain came abruptly, like an axe splitting his skull, but this time he forced himself through it. He shuffled until he was upright against his pillows. 'I thought it was Crowe,' he said, wincing. 'And . . . the monster. The beast . . .'

'What beast?' said Sol, frowning. He leant closer. 'Better keep your voice down, Ollie. Most of the others have gone down to breakfast, but we're not alone.'

He gestured with his eyes, and Ollie saw two Forest Mount pupils in the far corner of the dorm. The dawn light was barely breaking through the windows, but already the pupils were up and dressed, and they were looking over every so often at Ollie and Sol, no doubt wondering what Ollie was doing still in bed.

'The beast,' Ollie repeated, lowering his voice. 'You didn't see it?'

Slowly, Sol shook his head, his worried eyes never leaving Ollie. 'I saw Crowe, that's all. He was heading back to the school. He was carrying something, like a briefcase. I waited to see if you were following him, but when there was no sign of you I went looking in the woods.'

'I thought . . .' Ollie winced again. Even though he was whispering, his voice was like thunder in his head. 'I thought you'd gone with Jack. To find . . . to find the secret door.'

'I did. At first. But when we got there, Jack said she'd handle it on her own. She was worried about you heading off after Crowe. We both were. So I came back.'

'What about Lily?'

Sol shrugged, almost apologetically. 'I didn't see her all night. I'm sure she's fine, though. She's probably been, like . . .'

But it was clear from the way Sol floundered to finish his sentence that he had no idea what Lily had been up to.

'Anyway,' Sol said instead, 'when I spotted you in the woods, you ran straight past me. You were motoring, mate, I can tell you. I didn't dare call out, in case Crowe heard. So I . . . I ran after you. I wasn't *chasing* you. I was just trying to catch up.' He frowned again. 'What did you see out there? Why were you running so fast?'

It came back to Ollie then: the panicked sensation as he'd fled through the woods. At the time it had felt as if he was running through treacle, but he must have been moving faster than he'd realised.

'I . . . it doesn't matter what I saw. Not right now. But we need to find the others.'

'They'll be waiting for us downstairs,' said Sol. 'That's why I woke you. I figured sleep was more important than breakfast – for you, anyway,' he added, rubbing his growling stomach. 'But we need to be there for morning assembly. Strain will have kittens if we don't show our faces. Do you think you're up to it?'

'I'll manage,' said Ollie, moving to get out of bed. When he pulled back the covers, he saw he was in the clothes he'd been wearing last night. Sol had removed Ollie's blazer, but even the shirt he'd had on beneath it was marked and muddied, and his trousers were shredded. He whipped the covers back across him before the other pupils in the dorm could see.

'Don't worry. I pinched you some spares,' Sol said, indicating a pile of clothes on the chair at Ollie's bedside.

Doing his best to ignore the pounding in his head, Ollie started to change into the clean uniform underneath his duvet.

'What happened, Sol?' he said, as he wriggled. 'I remember falling. And I definitely must have hit my head.' He patted his pocket. 'Damn. And I lost my phone.'

'You fell all right,' said Sol. 'A good ten metres. But you picked the right section of the cliff to aim for. It was more of a steep slope, really. Another step or two to the left, though, and you'd have been a goner. A bit like your phone, I'm guessing. As it was, you landed in a gorse bush. Which reminds me, we'll have to think of a way to explain the scratches on your face.'

Ollie's hand drifted to his cheek. He felt a coarse line of blood beneath his fingertips. 'You pulled me up?' he said. 'How did you get me back to the school?'

'You don't remember?'

Ollie started shaking his head, then stopped abruptly when his brain rebounded against his skull.

'You walked for most of it,' Sol told him. 'If you can call it walking. You were slumped against me, your arm around my shoulders. And you kept mumbling something about a dog.'

'A dog?' Ollie tried to recollect. He must have been talking about the beast. Or maybe Sol had simply misheard.

'You were pretty out of it,' Sol said, testing a smile. 'To be honest I didn't fancy our chances of making it past the prefect patrols inside the school. But the thing was, there weren't any.'

Ollie paused in his movements. 'What? Why not?'

Sol twitched a shoulder. 'Search me. But I wasn't about to complain. If there had been, we'd probably have been forced to spend the night in a cleaner's cupboard.'

Ollie finished getting dressed. No patrols? It didn't make sense. Then again, there was very little about what was going on at Forest Mount that did. Until last night, Ollie had been beginning to think he'd got everything figured out. But it was clear to him in the cold light of morning there was a whole lot he still didn't understand.

Once Ollie was presentable, and stable enough on his feet to walk unaided, they made their way from the dorm to the entrance hall. It was here that Sol had arranged for them to meet the others. Assuming Lily decided to turn up this time, Ollie was thinking, although he kept the thought to himself.

They noticed the transformation immediately. The main wooden staircase had been buffed and polished, and the entrance hall was festooned with a giant banner, welcoming the prime minister to the school. The windows were gleaming, and the dark wood floor was so shiny, Ollie could almost make out the scratches on his face in his reflection.

'So that's what the prefects were doing all night,' said Sol. 'Strain had them scrubbing and scouring.' He smiled. 'It's a shame we came in the back way. I would have liked to have seen that. It's probably the first time they've had to clean up after themselves in their lives.'

Ollie wished he could have shared Sol's glee. The sight of the school transformed only served to remind him how little time they had left until the prime minister's visit. Her address was due to commence at just after 6 p.m., which was in less than twelve hours' time.

'Sol, Ollie. Over here.'

Jack was waiting for them at the bottom of the staircase. Ollie looked, but there was no sign of Lily.

'You should see the assembly hall,' Jack said, as Ollie and Sol drew near. 'There's another banner, Union Jacks all around and TV cameras being set up *everywhere*. Plus all the security, of course.'

She jabbed a thumb over her shoulder, indicating the top portion of the drive that was visible through the glass entrance doors behind her. There were police vans, dog units, armed officers, even a helicopter chopping at the air somewhere overhead.

'Whoa,' said Sol. 'It's as though they're expecting trouble.'

Ollie shook his head. 'That's just it,' he said. 'I don't think they are. Not the kind they *should* be looking out for anyway.'

He turned to the others.

'We need to talk,' he said, urgently. 'All of us. Although I guess if Lily is too busy, then it will have to be just us three.'

'I'm right here, Ollie.'

When Ollie looked around, Lily was standing at his shoulder. He hadn't noticed her approach.

'We've got things to tell you as well, Ollie,' Jack started saying. 'Last night, after you disappeared into the woods—'

But Ollie wasn't listening. The noise of the other pupils was only intensifying the pounding in his head. And Lily was standing there as though she'd been there all along – as though it was entirely reasonable of her to have abandoned her friends the previous evening, without a word of explanation about what she'd been up to.

'Your face, Ollie. Those scratches . . .' said Lily, concernedly. 'Are you OK?'

'Sure,' he answered. 'No thanks to you.'

Lily's features scrunched in confusion. 'What's that supposed to mean?'

'It means, it's nice of you to join us. Where the hell were you last night? You were supposed to meet us in the common room.'

'I know, but—'

'But you forgot?' Ollie suggested. 'You had better things to do? Like hanging out with Colton Crowe, for example?'

'Ollie . . .' Jack warned.

'No, it's fine,' Ollie said, holding her off. 'Lily's made it perfectly clear she doesn't think I'm cut out to be leader. So if she wants to do things her own way, that's up to her. It would have been nice of her to let the rest of us know, that's all.'

Lily turned an alarming shade of crimson. Her hands knotted at her side.

She was just about to speak, when Ollie noticed who was approaching from across her shoulder.

He turned abruptly, pulling Lily with him.

'Start walking,' he instructed.

Lily was too surprised to protest. Sharing a mystified glance, Sol and Jack fell in beside them.

'Stop,' came a voice. 'You four!'

'Ollie?' whispered Sol, facing forwards. 'What's going on?'

Ollie had hold of Lily's sleeve as he dragged her from the lobby and along the corridor. She wrenched it angrily from his grip, but thankfully kept pace at his side.

'I said, stop!' the voice repeated. But it was a thin, weaselly tone, easily lost among the clamour of eggs-and-bacon-fuelled pupils.

'It's Mr Ross,' Ollie hissed, resisting the temptation to look around. 'The PM's assistant. The man who was on stage with Professor Strain.'

'So?' Lily said, sharply.

'*So*, I think he knows who we are,' Ollie said. 'Who *I* am, anyway.'

'But how?' said Jack.

'I don't know. It's just a feeling. But there was something about the way he was looking at me the other day . . .'

'Ollie *Chambers*!' the voice called. It was tinged with both frustration and irritation. And there was something about the way he'd said Ollie's surname that made Ollie feel certain that Ross knew it was fake.

Ollie urged the others to move faster. He didn't dare glance behind him, but it sounded as though they'd opened up a slight gap. They reached a junction, and Ollie ushered the others around the corner, using the flow of pupils around them as cover.

'Quick, in here.'

The four of them hurried into an empty classroom. Ollie kept the door slightly ajar, and peered out into the corridor. Several moments later there was still no sign of Ross. With any luck, he'd assumed Ollie and the others had filed with the rest of the pupils into the assembly hall, and was busy hunting for them in there.

'We don't have much time,' Ollie said. They had the classroom to themselves, but he kept his voice low. Lily crossed her arms, and was glaring at Ollie with the same red-faced fury she'd shown in the entrance hall.

'Last night,' Ollie said, 'in the woods, I saw Crowe take delivery of something. Something *dangerous*. It was that case you saw him carrying, Sol.' Ollie went on to explain about Crowe's meeting by the lake, about the mystery Russian, and about how he'd met his end. He left out the gory parts, including the description of the beast, which Ollie had trouble believing really existed now himself.

'The point is,' he said, 'I think whatever Crowe was collecting is key to how they plan to do it.'

'Wait,' said Lily, 'what are you talking about?'

'If you'd been there last night you would have heard,' Ollie snapped. 'I think Strain's planning on assassinating the prime minister. *Today*. And after that, I think he's planning on taking over.'

'Taking over what?' said Sol.

'The *country*,' Ollie answered.

There was a moment of stunned silence.

'I don't know how exactly,' Ollie went on. 'I think . . . I think it's something to do with the secrets Crowe's been gathering. You remember what Errol said in his emails? That Strain was building an army of spies, gathering intel on some of the most important people in the country. Errol thought Strain was after money, but I think it's more than that. I think it's their *support* Strain is after. With the PM dead, the government will need to elect a new leader, and what I think is, Strain is planning on blackmailing them to elect *him*.'

Jack started shaking her head.

'But that's not possible,' she said. 'The ruling party can't just pick somebody at random to be prime minister, even if Strain *is* blackmailing them.'

'It's not random, though,' said Ollie. 'You've seen Strain's history. He used to be a politician himself. He wanted to get rid of democracy. Remember? And this is the way he's going to do it. Crowe said it himself. Errol overheard him. He talked about starting a "revolution". And maybe that's what Crowe and Strain have been promising the prefects. A place in the new regime, a position of power like the one they have here. Maybe *that's* how he's getting them to betray their parents. Maybe the prefects even think they're doing their parents a favour, guaranteeing them a place in Strain's government as well.'

'Strain wants to make the country like Forest Mount,' said Sol. 'A dictatorship, with secret police and everything, just like his prefects. He wants to be like . . . like what's his name. That Russian bloke. The one who murdered all those people.'

'Joseph Stalin,' Jack provided, thoughtfully. But Ollie could tell she wasn't quite buying it.

'Look, I don't know all the details,' Ollie admitted. 'And I can't *prove* anything. That's why I've been waiting to tell you. But it all makes sense, particularly after what I saw last night. It explains everything: Strain's history, Errol going missing, George and the other kids too, plus what Errol said in his emails. And I *saw* the Russian get murdered, meaning it's beyond doubt now that Strain is willing to *kill* to achieve his goal. You see that,' he said to Jack, 'don't you?'

'I agree it *looks* that way. That Strain is up to *something*.'

'But?' Ollie prompted.

'But he'd be blamed,' said Jack. 'Wouldn't he? If the prime minister is murdered here, at Strain's school, there'll be a massive investigation. Only one British prime minister has ever been assassinated, and that was more than two hundred years ago. There have been attempts since then, sure, but if Strain is actually successful, the authorities will tear the school apart. I just don't see how they wouldn't find out that he was responsible. And after that, there's no way he'd be taking over anything, other than a very small cell in a high-security prison.'

'Maybe he's planning on covering up his involvement,' suggested Sol. 'If he's blackmailing the police, for example. Judges. People like that. Maybe *that's* how he plans to get away with it.'

Jack tipped her head side to side uncertainly. 'I suppose it's possible.'

Ollie spun away, moving to check the gap beside the door. 'If only we knew what secrets Strain has been collecting,' he said, with one eye monitoring the empty corridor. 'And about who. Like, which people *exactly* he plans to blackmail.' Ollie thought for a moment, his eyes dropping towards the floor. 'Didn't Errol say something about Crowe writing it all down? Like, in a notebook or something, one he—'

There was a sharp slap behind him, like a palm smacking skin. Ollie whipped around, fully expecting to see one of his friends clutching their cheek.

Lily had taken a step forwards. In front of her, lying on one of the desks, was a thick, black notebook.

'You wanted to know what I've been up to, Ollie. Well, now you do. I only didn't tell you before because it's obvious you don't trust me.' Lily folded her arms, as Ollie moved to pick up the notebook. 'The entries are in code,' she went on, her voice clipped. 'But the names aren't. The police commissioner is in there, and certain judges just like Sol said. Even the home secretary is listed: Sir Sebastian Crowe. Colton Crowe's father.'

‘Crowe’s *father*?’ repeated Sol.

‘He’s one of the PM’s closest allies. And Crowe *hates* him. You saw how he reacted when I mentioned him that time on the way to Strain’s office.’

Ollie flicked through the pages of the notebook. Sol read across his shoulder. Just as Lily had said, the main text seemed to be in code, meaning they couldn’t tell what secrets Strain had collected. But it didn’t matter. The names were enough. The notebook proved that Strain was blackmailing some of the most powerful people in the country.

Ollie looked at Lily. So *that* was what she’d been doing flirting with Crowe, hanging around with him while Ollie and the others had been in the common room. She’d been getting close to him – close enough that she’d been able to steal his notebook.

Ollie opened his mouth, wanting to apologise, but unable to find words that would be enough.

‘So this is it,’ said Sol, who’d taken the notebook from Ollie’s hands. ‘This is the proof. All we have to do is take this to the police. Right? Or to Mr Ross, the prime minister’s assistant. And then it’s over, before it’s even begun.’

‘Not Ross,’ Ollie said, finally finding his voice. ‘For all we know he’s in on this, too. Maybe he’s Strain’s inside man.’

‘And we can’t take it to the police,’ said Jack. ‘Whatever code Crowe used, I haven’t been able to crack it in the time since Lily showed me the notebook last night. Maybe the police will have better luck – or maybe they'll decide it's just a bunch of gobbledygook, and we're making the whole thing up.'

'You knew about this?' Ollie said to her. 'You knew Lily had the notebook?'

'Only since about three a.m. this morning,' Jack replied. 'I tried to tell you in the lobby, but you . . . Well.'

Ollie hadn't been listening. He'd been too busy having a go at Lily.

He felt himself flush with shame.

'There's something else we were going to tell you, Ollie,' Jack said. 'While Lily was searching Crowe's room, and you and Sol were in the woods, I went looking for that secret door. There were no guards, and I found the hidden switch.'

'You did?' said Ollie. 'How?'

'I used this.' From her pocket Jack produced what looked like a circuit board, wrapped together with an antenna and a nine-volt battery. 'It's a homemade metal detector. The insides of a portable radio, basically. What you do is, you turn the frequency on the radio to the highest band on the AM setting, and then . . .' She seemed to realise Ollie was already lost. 'Never mind,' she went on. 'The point is, the catch on the secret door was always going to be made of metal, right? So I used this to locate where it was.'

'So you opened the door? You went into the dungeon?'

Jack shook her head. 'The button I found didn't work. But then I saw Crowe. He was carrying that case you mentioned, so I guess it was about the same time Sol was chasing you over the cliff.'

'Hey!' said Sol, looking hurt.

Jack ignored him. 'When I heard Crowe coming, I hid, and I saw how *he* got inside. There were *two* switches. Crowe pressed them simultaneously. That's why the switch I found didn't work on its own. There was another one higher up that I missed.'

'So we go back again,' said Sol, sounding excited. 'We need evidence, right? And if it's anywhere, it will be down in those dungeons. As will Errol,' he added, looking at Jack. 'I'm sure of it.'

'When, though?' Jack said. 'If what Ollie says is right, we can't wait until tonight.'

'We go *now*,' said Ollie. 'We don't have any choice. At least with everyone else in the assembly hall we'll have the corridor to ourselves. And hopefully the dungeons, too. For a while, anyway.'

'What if Strain notices we're missing?' said Sol.

'Even if he does, he couldn't do anything,' Ollie answered, 'not while he's up on stage. And later, if he wants to expel us, let him. It will all be over by this evening anyway.'

'One way or another,' Jack added, grimly.

‘So what are we waiting for?’ said Sol. ‘Let’s get moving.’ He led the others towards the door. Jack followed. Lily made to go after them, but Ollie took hold of her arm.

‘Lily, I . . . About what I said to you . . .’

But as she had the last time, Lily shrugged him off. ‘Save it, Ollie. We’ve got a job to do. Remember?’

And she marched away before Ollie could say anything more.

22 DEATHTRAP DUNGEON

Once they reached the corridor along from Strain's office, Jack led them to the spot on the wall where she'd witnessed Crowe opening the secret door. It was almost exactly halfway along, the point Lily and Ollie had converged the night they'd had their first argument.

Jack was facing the wall, running the antenna of her makeshift metal detector over the elaborate wooden panels. 'It was just . . . here,' she announced, as the drone being emitted from the radio circuit board changed to a higher pitched beep. 'You can actually see it if you look closely enough. This little circle is slightly lighter than the wood around it. And there's another one up there.'

Seated in her wheelchair, Jack couldn't quite reach where she was pointing, but Ollie followed her gaze. Now that he knew what he was looking for, he could hardly believe he'd missed it last time. Then again, when he and Lily had been searching it had been by torchlight. Now, the sun was creeping above the canopy of the forest, and it was filling the corridor with a watery, rose-coloured light. It seemed ironic given their situation, but for the first time in weeks, it promised to be a beautiful day.

'If you press one of the switches on their own, nothing happens,' Jack said, demonstrating. 'But if you and I press together, Ollie. One, two . . . *three*.'

Ollie and Jack pressed the two buttons in unison, and without any fanfare, or indeed any noise at all, a door revealed itself in the wooden panel in front of them. The door's edges had been completely camouflaged by the details of the engravings. Ollie was reminded of the entrance into the Haven down in the sewer tunnel, which was equally undetectable to the eye.

'Huh,' said Sol, giving the open door a gentle push. 'That was a bit less dramatic than I was expecting.'

'Drama is overrated, in my opinion,' said Jack, moving past him. She was grinning, no doubt in eager anticipation of finding her brother. 'I'm all for a nice, simple . . . Oh.'

Almost immediately on the other side of the secret door there was a steep stone staircase leading down. And unlike around the rest of the school, nobody had thought to install an access ramp.

'To be honest it's no less than I was expecting,' said Jack. 'Whoever built this place back in the Middle Ages probably didn't have fourteen-year-old girls in wheelchairs uppermost in mind.'

Ollie peered down. The steps disappeared into the darkness, so far below him that he couldn't see where they ended.

'It's fine,' said Jack, clearly struggling to contain her disappointment. 'You three go. Find Errol. *Please*. I'll stay here and keep a look out. I'll call if I hear someone coming, to give you a chance to hide.'

Ollie looked again at the staircase, then at Jack's chair. 'If someone comes, we'll be trapped down there, even if we do find a place to hide,' he said. 'Our only chance is to get in and out before the prefects return from assembly.' He bent down and took hold of Jack's chair. 'Sol, Lily, give me a hand. We're doing this together.'

Even with the three of them helping, it was a struggle to reach the bottom, mainly due to the steepness of the staircase. And the lower down they got, the darker it became. Soon Ollie could no longer see the steps themselves, and had to feel his way with his feet.

When they finally reached the bottom, Ollie was puffing heavily.

'That's one time . . . I would have been glad . . . to have Flea around,' Sol panted.

Doing his best to control his own breathing, Ollie held his finger to his lips. The corridor they found themselves in seemed deserted, but there was no way they could be certain.

They crept forwards, scanning the space around them. The passageway stank of damp, like mouldy laundry, and the only light was coming from a series of low-wattage lamps that had been placed every ten metres or so along the wall. The ceiling was low enough that Ollie could have touched it, and the floor below their feet was made of ancient, ill-fitting cobblestones, a bit like the floor in some of the tunnels they'd accessed when they'd first tried to break into the school.

'Wow,' said Lily, speaking for the first time since she'd stormed out of the classroom. 'It's like being in the London Dungeons or something.'

'Except this place isn't exactly set up for visitors,' said Sol. 'They could do with a snack bar or something. Maybe a gift shop? Something a bit more welcoming anyway than dripping walls and a stink like a pair of Ollie's socks.'

When Ollie turned, he saw Sol smiling. Lily might have smiled too, ordinarily, but it seemed even the mention of Ollie's name was enough to set her scowling.

'Seriously, you guys,' Ollie said, 'keep it down. We can't be sure there's nobody else around.'

He led the way along the passage, although in truth it was Jack who was forcing the pace. Now that they'd finally broken into the dungeon, she was clearly desperate to try to find her brother.

The passageway broadened, but the stench and the gloom only intensified. To Ollie, it felt as if they'd discovered Forest

Mount's dark underbelly. More than that, it was as though they'd unearthed the very heart of the place, the way the entire building would have looked had its true nature been allowed to seep through. Upstairs it was masked by the modern amenities: the lights, the heating, the paint and the pictures on the walls. Down here there was none of that, just a natural, inherent foulness. It was the perfect birthplace, it struck Ollie, for a twisted and evil regime.

'Look,' Jack said, pointing. Up ahead, the passageway kinked to the right. Just before the bend there was a door.

'Jack, wait,' Ollie hissed, but Jack was already propelling herself forwards, driving her chair across the ruts in the floor. Cursing, Ollie hurried to catch up with her.

Jack paused outside the half-open door. Ollie joined her in peering through. They looked at each other, then made their way cautiously inside.

'It's a control room,' Jack said. 'Just like ours back at the Haven. The old Haven, I mean.'

Unlike the corridor outside, this room had been plastered and painted, and within it there was computer equipment and a series of control panels. There were monitors displaying CCTV images, some showing the tunnels they'd accessed from the crypt. It was from here they'd been spotted on their approach, Ollie guessed, and that tear gas had been released to drive them out.

Jack was wheeling her way among the desks. 'This is high-end stuff,' she said. 'Strain's well financed, clearly.'

'Probably siphoning off half of those school fees,' Sol sniffed, his hand reaching to fiddle with the equipment.

'I wouldn't touch that if I were you,' said Jack, as Sol's fingertips came within centimetres of a big, red button. 'I wouldn't touch *anything*. Who knows what kind of security measures they've got in place here? If you try to operate something without first providing the right access code, you could trigger an alarm – or something worse.'

Ollie was shaking his head. 'I don't like this,' he said. 'The open door, the abandoned room. Surely someone should be monitoring this place, morning assembly or not.'

'Maybe it's automated,' said Jack. 'It looks sophisticated enough.' Ollie could sense Jack was itching to reach out just as Sol had. For her, the urge to play with the equipment here must have been as tempting as a pick-and-mix counter to a five year old.

'Guys,' came Lily's voice, and Ollie turned. He hadn't noticed that she'd failed to follow them into the room. 'Out here. Look.' She moved from the doorway back into the passage, and the others followed where she led.

Around the bend, there were more doors. Some were clearly the same age as the passageway itself, and looked flimsier than pieces of old driftwood. But the ones further on appeared to be made out of steel.

Sol squinted into the darkness. 'Do you think those could be—'

'*Cells*,' Jack finished, and once again she was moving before Ollie or either of the others could hold her back.

'Errol!' she called – softly, but loud enough that anyone close by would have heard. '*Errol!*'

After first checking back along the passageway to make sure no prefects had appeared, Ollie saw no choice but to follow Jack's lead. If anyone *was* listening out for them, they would already have given themselves away. And they didn't have time any more for subtleties.

Jack was beside the first of the metal doors, pumping the handle fruitlessly and then scouring the surface for any way of seeing through to the other side. Ollie went straight to the second door, as Sol and Lily began working their way along the opposite wall.

'Errol,' Ollie hissed, 'are you in there?'

As Jack's had been, Ollie's door was locked, and he ran his fingers around its edges searching for the slightest gap. But there was no way of prising the door open, and no response from within.

'*Quiet*,' said Jack, abruptly, and she held up a hand.

Ollie froze, sure that Jack had heard someone approaching. The prefects returning from assembly, or even Colton Crowe himself.

But then Ollie heard it, too.

'Jack?'

It was a boy's voice, weak and distant. Ollie looked at Jack, and saw her face suddenly light up.

'*Errol*,' she said. 'It's him!'

'It's coming from down there.' Lily was furthest along the corridor, and she hurried towards the next corner. Jack was right on her heels.

When Ollie and Sol caught up, the girls had paused just around the bend. This corridor was a continuation of the previous one, with more steel doors on either side.

'*Listen*,' Jack whispered, holding up her hand again.

'I'm here, Jack,' came the voice. 'Down here!'

'There.' Sol pointed to a door at the far end of the passageway. And like the door into the control room, this one was slightly ajar.

Which was the first indication to Ollie that something was wrong.

'No, don't . . .' he said, but the others were already speeding off.

Ollie had no choice but to run after them, hoping he could catch them before they reached that final door. If Errol was in there, and he'd heard them coming, why hadn't he come out into the passageway? And why was the door open in the first place?

'Jack, Sol, Lily . . .'

His friends had already reached the threshold. Before Ollie could stop them, they stepped into the room.

The *empty* room, Ollie saw when he caught up.

'Jack! In here!'

Errol's voice seemed to be coming through the walls.

Ollie exchanged a mystified glance with Jack. Warily, the four of them edged further into the room. It was an empty cube, bare but for a single bunk. There was a stained pillow on the bed, and a thin, fraying blanket.

'Up there,' said Jack, pointing. Just above Sol's head, on the wall furthest from the door, there was a small, rectangular air vent.

'*Errol?*' Sol hissed, raising himself on to his toes beneath the vent.

'I'm sorry, Jack. I'm *so* sorry.'

As one the Haven kids spun. Rather than from the vent, Errol's voice had come from right behind them. And when they turned, Ollie saw a boy of about eleven standing in the passageway outside the door.

'*Errol,*' said Jack.

But before Errol could speak again, he was gone, tugged roughly to one side by an unseen hand.

And then there was a growl, and Ollie knew what was coming. He could smell it just as surely as he could hear it.

'Is that . . .?' said Sol, as a bared set of teeth emerged from around the door frame.

'Uh huh,' agreed Ollie, swallowing.

The beast padded into the room, a bead of saliva dripping from its jaws. In the wavering light of the prison cell, its pale skin seemed to ripple, like melted wax that hadn't fully set. Its teeth glinted, and there was fire in those blood-red eyes.

But Ollie's attention quickly switched to what came after.

The beast was on a chain, a sequence of shiny, platinum-coloured links. And holding it was the beast's master. Not Crowe, as Ollie had first imagined. Not even Professor Strain. Rather, a figure as hideously deformed as the beast itself, with skin just as papery and raw. It was burnt skin, Ollie realised, scarred by flames, just as the hair had been singed from the figure's head. But the voice, when Ollie heard it, was exactly as he remembered it. It was a voice that haunted him in his dreams.

'Well, well,' said Maddy Sikes. 'If it isn't Ollie Turner. I was so hoping we'd get to meet again.'

23 OLD FLAME

'*You?* But you're . . .'

'Dead?' Maddy Sikes offered, and Ollie winced at her leer. Just like the beast's, Sikes's skin had a wax-like sheen, and her features were warped and twisted. From once being so coldly beautiful, she was now like a Madame Tussauds model of herself that had been left too close to an open fire.

And perhaps that wasn't so far from the truth.

'You escaped the burning plane?' Ollie said. '*How?*' He recalled the intensity of the heat soon after he'd leapt from Sikes's private jet, and the fireball that had erupted after the plane had collided with the fuel tanker.

'Your friend helped me,' said Sikes, as she took a step into the cell. The beast came with her, as behind her Colton Crowe appeared, holding Errol in an armlock.

'Dodge,' Sikes went on, speaking over the beast's low growls. 'That was his name, wasn't it?' At this, she focused on Lily. 'Oh, he's dead, my dear. In case you were getting your hopes up. But when he collapsed on top of me, he shielded me from the worst of the flames. And it wasn't long afterwards that I was rescued.'

Sikes brought the beast to heel, and she reached down and tickled its red-raw neck. Ollie caught a glimpse of Sikes's wrist. It was as flame-damaged as the rest of her visible skin, but it was also pitted with what looked like teeth marks.

Sikes caught Ollie looking. She bent forwards, so that she was talking into one of the beast's bat-like ears.

'They don't recognise you, Bullseye. They don't know how brave you were to save me, to drag me from the flames the way you did.' She stood straighter, studying her wrist and then smiling at Ollie. 'The pain of reconstructing the tendons was a small price to pay,' she said. 'Wouldn't you agree?'

Ollie stared at the beast, seeing it as though for the first time. That . . . *thing* was Sikes's *dog*? The *warg*. The hell hound which had once also sunk its fangs into Ollie's ankle. The last time Ollie had seen it, it had been covered in thick, white fur. That was gone, the only remnants patches of blackened hair on the beast's haunches. In that respect it was very much like Sikes herself. She'd had white hair before as well, but like her pet, Sikes was now almost completely bald.

And Ollie had known before. Hadn't he? His subconscious mind had already made the connection. According to Sol, he'd been muttering about a *dog* when Sol had hauled him from the cliff. Ollie must have realised why the beast had been afraid of him, just as it occurred to him now. The last time Ollie and Bullseye had come face to face, Ollie had given Sikes's pet an electric shock. Bullseye had been hesitant of attacking him in the forest because his animal instinct was to expect the same treatment.

But he was clearly over that now.

As Ollie stared at it, Sikes's pet growled and lunged towards him. Sikes allowed just enough slack in Bullseye's lead for the beast to snap its jaws within centimetres of Ollie's nose.

'Isn't life full of wonderful surprises?' Sikes said, with another smile. She was like the Joker in those old Batman movies, Ollie thought. Or, one of those Picasso portraits Nancy had taken him to see once in the Tate Modern, where the subject's features are all misshapen and misaligned.

And yet, somehow, Sikes's new appearance suited her. It was like with the dungeons: the way they represented the true nature of the school. Sikes had never deserved her beauty. Now, the way she looked was a genuine reflection of her soul.

Noticing Ollie staring, Sikes grinned wider and leant towards him. 'Do you like what you see, Ollie Turner? I hope so, given that you're responsible.'

Revolted, Ollie turned away.

'Which I suppose makes us even,' Sikes said, clearly revelling in Ollie's reaction. 'You created *me*, just as I created *you*.'

Ollie turned back then. He looked Sikes squarely in the eyes. She'd said something similar to him once before, he remembered. The first time they'd come face to face, in fact.

Sikes had gloated to Ollie that he was who he was because of her. She'd killed his parents, just as she'd killed Nancy. And Ollie hated her for it. Even when he'd thought Sikes had been dead, his loathing for her had not diminished.

It swelled within him as he stood before her now.

'It was you all along,' Ollie said, struggling to contain his fury. '*You're* the one who's behind what's been happening. You and Crowe and . . .' He paused. Professor Strain, he'd been about to add. But something about that didn't fit. 'Mad' Maddy Sikes didn't share power with *anyone*.

'Strain has nothing to do with this,' Ollie said. 'Does he? We just *assumed* he was behind it all, because he's in charge of the school.'

What was it Strain had said that time he'd hauled Ollie and the others into his office? *There is nothing in this institution that escapes my notice*. And Ollie had believed it, as wholeheartedly as Strain himself.

'*You're* the one who plans to take over,' Ollie said. 'You kill the prime minister, then use the secrets you've gathered to take control of the government *yourself*. That's how you plan to get away with it: by blaming Strain. He's your fall guy. Your decoy.'

Sikes clapped her hands together in evident delight. 'You see!' she said to Crowe. 'I told you he was bright. Brighter than those prefect buffoons up in the assembly hall, anyway. More money than sense, the lot of them,' she added, with a conspiratorial wink towards Ollie.

Crowe just scowled. 'This is the kid who stopped you last time? He doesn't seem so clever to me. He walked into my trap, didn't he?'

As though attempting to inflict pain on Ollie himself, Crowe gave a yank on Errol's arm. Jack's brother cried out.

'Leave him alone!' Jack yelled, but there was nothing she or any of the others could do. Bullseye was like a barrier of teeth and claws.

'Ignore Colton's rudeness,' said Sikes. 'He's just angry at you for all the problems you've caused. It was only belatedly we realised that it was you Haven brats who'd been snooping around, you see. Young Errol pointed us in the right direction, in the end.' She tilted her head towards Jack. 'You don't look a bit like you do in your photograph, you know. In real life, you're *far* more attractive. Although it *is* a pity about the wheelchair.'

Ollie saw Jack's fingers turn white around the push rims on her chair. Barrier of teeth and claws or not, he sensed his friend was ready to take her chances, and drive herself right into Maddy Sikes's shins.

'You're right, of course, Ollie Turner,' Sikes said, turning her attention back to Ollie. 'Strain is as clueless as everyone else as to what is about to happen. He thinks he's finally about to receive the public acknowledgement he feels he's always deserved. You know about his history, I take it? His past political ambitions? Well, over the years he's had to modify his expectations, although I suspect he's never quite accepted that a lonely, north London private school is about the only regime he'll ever get to manage.' Sikes shook her head. 'It's rather sad, really.'

She smiled.

'But now Strain will get his moment in the limelight. His political career remains in ruins, but he will finally be seen on a national stage standing *right beside* the prime minister. And he has no idea what . . . *secrets* I had to leverage to buy him the honour. He truly believes the prime minister is here to pay tribute to the system of leadership he's established in this nasty, fourth-rate institution.'

'Fourth rate?' Ollie said. 'I would have thought you would have approved of this place.' He looked around at the dank dungeon walls. 'If you ask me, you fit right in.'

'Oh, I approve of the system of leadership, certainly,' said Sikes, refusing to be bated. 'That's one thing Professor Strain and I do indeed see eye to eye on. I don't believe in *democracy* any more than he does. But Forest Mount itself . . .' Sikes shuddered theatrically. 'I used to be a student here, you know. My parents sent me here when I was Errol's age, and left me to rot. And I hated *every miserable moment*,' she added, with sudden venom. 'The bullying, the backbiting, the *loneliness* . . .'

Her bloodshot eyes seemed to glaze slightly, as her gaze turned momentarily inwards.

And then Sikes blinked.

'But I got my revenge. On my parents,' she said, her eyes glinting. 'And on this whole stinking place. I *bought* it. I fired every teacher who'd ever been cruel to me, and I trebled the fees. With all the children who were vicious to me already . . . dealt with, let's say, it seemed the best way to punish their pompous, over-privileged families. But do you know what, Ollie Turner?'

Sikes appeared suddenly pleased with herself, her expression like a cat's as it licks its paws beside an empty bowl of cream.

'The *fools* carried on paying! Not only that, they thought that because the school was the most expensive, it had to follow that it was also the *best.* And so children from the country's elites came flooding in, which is what gave me the idea to make use of them. You see, I've been planning this whole endeavour for quite some time now. I've had to accelerate the timing somewhat, thanks to your intervention last time. But as it happens, everything has worked out rather nicely. Wouldn't you say?'

Ollie could only glare, too disgusted to respond.

Sol spoke up beside him. 'So you appointed Strain?' he said to Sikes. 'You made him the headmaster here?'

'After his failure as a politician, the poor man was a laughing stock,' said Sikes, once again affecting sympathy. 'It seemed the *least* I could do. Plus, of course, his political past made him the perfect candidate. The perfect . . . what was it you called him, Ollie Turner? A *decoy*. A failed, fringe politician. An extremist, in fact, with noted links to Russia, and a public record of praising nasty dictators. Who *won't* believe he's responsible for the assassination of the prime minister? Particularly if he's not around to defend himself afterwards . . .'

'You mean to murder him, too?' said Ollie.

'Oh, many people will die, I'm afraid,' Sikes responded. 'It's regrettable, but unavoidable, given the way we intend to handle things. You'll find it's not easy to arrange the murder of a British prime minister. Many have tried over the years. Almost all have failed. The trick, as I say, is in the method.'

'The briefcase,' said Ollie, looking at Crowe. 'You mean to kill the prime minister with whatever was in that metal briefcase.'

Crowe smiled coldly.

'A Russian nerve agent,' said Sikes. 'A Soviet nerve agent, to be more accurate, left over from the Cold War. And as it happens, the preferred weapon for political assassinations of the current Russian administration.'

'Meaning Strain is implicated even further,' said Ollie, remembering the Russian literature in Strain's office, as well as the photo of him shaking hands with the Russian president.

Sikes tipped her head in acknowledgement.

'A nerve agent?' said Sol, as much to Jack as to Sikes. 'Is that like a poison?'

'Worse,' said Jack, who was glowering furiously. 'It's a lethal chemical. If you swallow it, or touch it, death is almost immediate, not to mention incredibly painful.'

'Unless you have the antidote,' said Sikes, with a glance at Errol, 'which our belated Russian friend was also good enough to supply.' She turned to Jack. 'One thing you neglected to mention is that nerve agents are also *undetectable*. They're colourless, odourless, tasteless. The prime minister won't even know what's happening to her. Not until it's already too late.'

'But it won't just be her, will it?' said Jack. 'It will be Strain and whoever else is with her on stage. Whoever else is in the *room*.'

Ollie looked at her quizzically.

'Nerve agents aren't like bullets,' Jack explained. 'They're more like . . . explosions. Think of the fumes spreading the way a blast would. You wouldn't be able to *see* them, but they also affect whoever is nearby. Maybe they wouldn't kill you right away, but you'd still succumb eventually.'

'So the other kids,' said Ollie, 'the prefects even – they'd all die, too?'

'It depends how close they're standing,' said Jack. 'But at the very least they'll get very, very sick.'

'Brains *and* beauty,' said Sikes, who was gazing at Jack admiringly. 'Aren't we blessed?'

'But those prefects were working for *you*,' Ollie said, looking at Sikes and Crowe in turn. 'You'd really just let them *die*?'

'Those idiots were working for *Strain*,' said Crowe. 'They thought they were anyway. That's what I told them: that Strain was the one who meant to take over. And they were under instructions to report only to me. Professor Strain needed to be *protected*, I said, which meant no orders would come from him directly.' He laughed cruelly. 'They have no idea what's really going on. The blackmail, the kids down here, sure – but not the nerve agent, the assassination . . . As far as they know, it's *Strain* who's planning a revolution.'

'Which is exactly what they'll tell the authorities,' put in Sikes. 'Those who survive, at least. And Professor Strain will go down in history after all. Just not in the way he's always imagined. Instead he'll be remembered as a political crackpot who managed to kill himself at the same time as assassinating the prime minister.'

'And then what?' said Ollie. '*You* take over? "Maddy Sikes, Prime Minister." It's not going to happen, Sikes. No matter how many people you blackmail.'

'Oh, I completely agree,' said Sikes. 'Appearances are so very important these days, and it hasn't escaped my notice that I no longer have a face for television.' She leered again, horribly. 'But power comes in many forms, Ollie Turner. With the secrets I've gathered, I'll be able to control the person who *does* replace the prime minister, just like a puppet on a string.'

'Sebastian Crowe,' said Lily. 'Your father,' she added, talking to Crowe. 'That's who Sikes is going to install as her puppet. And you mean to help Sikes control him, to tell him what to do. As . . . what? Some kind of *revenge*? Do you really hate him that much?'

'He hated me first!' Crowe spat. 'He's *always* hated me. That's why he sent me here: to get *rid* of me. But I know everything about him, all his dirty little secrets. For once in his life he'll do as *I* say!'

Sikes was smiling appreciatively. 'He will indeed, until such time as I am ready to get rid of him. Because eventually, Ollie Turner, I *will* take over. And not as prime minister, but as a *new* type of leader.'

'A dictator, you mean,' Ollie retorted.

'If you mean someone who has absolute power, then, yes. A dictator. Power isn't something that can be *divided*,' Sikes said. 'Just as money isn't something to be *wasted*. When I am in charge, there will be no more *charity* in this country, no more places like your precious Haven. We will not squander resources on those who are too weak to help themselves.'

'Instead you'll siphon off those resources for yourself,' said Jack. 'For your loyal supporters, too,' she added, turning her disdain towards Crowe.

Sikes inclined her head. 'There have to be *some* perks of leadership, my dear.'

'She'll betray you, Crowe,' said Ollie. 'We've seen it before. She murdered our friend, and probably the last person she called her assistant, too. What was his name, Sikes? Grimwig, wasn't it?'

'May he rest in peace,' Sikes responded, mockingly.

'She'll use you and then she'll get rid of you,' Ollie pressed, focusing on Crowe again. 'Think about . . . your other family. Your mother for example. What about *her*?'

Crowe and Sikes shared a look, and that was when Ollie saw it. The resemblance. It was well hidden. Even if Sikes hadn't been so hideously disfigured, she and Crowe would at first glance have looked nothing like each other. She was thin and fair, whereas Crowe was broad and dark. But there were pieces of them that matched: the sharp nose, the sly eyes, the set of their teeth when they smiled.

Sikes saw Ollie looking and her smile broadened. 'I would never betray Colton,' she simpered. 'Who else would I anoint as my heir?'

'Your heir?' Lily repeated. 'You mean . . .'

'I mean Colton is my son.'

Ollie and his friends were temporarily speechless.

'But you *hate* kids,' Sol finally blurted. 'How can you possibly have a *son*?'

'Perhaps you could ask one of your friends to explain the birds and bees to you later,' Sikes replied. 'And while it's true I have an aversion to your breed in general, Colton, you will have noticed, is almost a man. And as it turns out, he is very much a chip off the old block.'

Ollie was shaking his head. He looked from Crowe to Sikes, to the beast that was threatening to snap its flimsy-looking chain.

'Now,' said Sikes. 'As much as I've enjoyed our little reunion, it's time to get down to business. The notebook. The one you stole from Colton. You will return it to its rightful owner.'

She looked at Lily, and held out a blister-scarred hand.

Ollie caught sight of Lily swallowing. But she stared back at Sikes defiantly. 'I don't know what you're talking about.'

Sikes's hand struck Lily's face before Ollie knew what was happening. Lily cried out, and Ollie and the others lurched forwards to defend her.

'Stay where you are!' Crowe shouted. He slipped a forearm around Errol's throat. 'I can break his neck just as easily as I can break his arm.'

'Here,' said Sol. 'Take it.' He reached into his pocket and pulled out the notebook. He'd been carrying it since he'd taken it from Ollie back in the classroom.

Sikes flicked briefly through the pages. Her lips curled at one corner. 'Colton, the prime minister will be arriving in just a few hours. I suggest you take Errol and make the necessary preparations.'

Crowe only edged further into the cell, driving Errol in front of him. 'Let me kill them first, Mother. What's the point in dragging things out?'

'Colton, Colton,' said Sikes, soothingly. 'You're forgetting our promise to young Errol here. Didn't we assure him we would let his sister and her friends go if he did as he was asked?'

'That's right,' whimpered Errol. 'You said. You *swore*.'

'Don't do it, Errol! Whatever she's said, whatever she's promised you, don't believe a word she—'

This time Jack was the one to feel the back of Sikes's hand. Ollie winced at the sound the blow made, but Jack made no noise in response. She fumed with silent tears as Crowe tugged Errol from the room.

'I'm sorry, Jack,' Errol was saying. 'I'm so sorry!' The words faded as he was dragged away along the corridor.

Ollie and the others were left facing Sikes and her rabid-looking pet.

'What do you want with my brother?' said Jack. 'What is it you're making him do?'

'My dear,' said Sikes, '*someone* has to deliver our little gift. When the prime minister is up on stage, a Forest Mount pupil will be charged with filling her glass of water, and the nerve agent will be administered into that. As you said so eloquently earlier, even the fumes should be enough, but once the prime minister *ingests* the toxin, the effects will be so much more . . . spectacular.'

'But why do you need *Errol*? You said you had an antidote. So why can't Crowe do it? He's head pupil, so surely he's going to be up on stage, too?'

Sikes didn't respond – and her silence, for Ollie, was answer enough.

'There is no antidote,' Ollie said. 'Is there, Sikes?'

Sikes stared back at him, whether pleased with herself or with Ollie for working it out, Ollie couldn't tell.

'There is not,' Sikes affirmed. 'But your little brother is so pathetically *trusting*.' She tittered in Jack's direction. 'An *antidote*? For something as powerful as this particular nerve agent? It would be like trying to use mouthwash to cure cancer.' She sniggered again. 'No, when Errol opens that vial, he'll assume he's protected, when really he'll be as exposed as the prime minister herself. As everyone else who's up there on stage.'

'You'd really sacrifice so many innocent people?' said Lily. 'And Jack's brother . . . What did Errol ever do to you?'

Slowly Sikes wound Bullseye's leash around her wrist. 'I will sacrifice whoever I need to,' she said, leaning close. 'My own son, if I had to. The naive brother of a know-it-all cripple girl. And as for the four of you . . .' A bead of saliva ran from Sikes's twisted mouth, making her resemble her drooling pet. Until

Crowe had left the room, she'd acted as though she was in total control of her emotions, but Ollie could finally see the intensity of her anger. 'You will die a slow, agonising death,' she told them, 'right here in this cell. After the nerve agent is released, the school will be evacuated and locked down. It will be *weeks* before anyone is able to return, and far longer before these dungeons are discovered. Assuming they are ever found at all.'

Sikes drew back, wiping her chin with the back of her hand. Her eyes blazed: with fury for what Ollie had done to her, but with triumph, too. After Dodge, after the fire at the Haven, after everything Ollie and his friends had achieved, Sikes had won in the end.

She dragged her pet to the threshold of the cell. 'Goodbye, Ollie Turner,' she said. 'This time, I assure you, we will not be meeting again.'

And with that she swung the steel door shut, sealing Ollie and his friends in their tomb.

24 NO ESCAPE

The metallic clang reverberated around the cell.

Sol and Lily hurried towards the door, checking for some way to open it. But Ollie knew it would be hopeless. They'd seen how impenetrable the cell doors were from the outside. Inside there wasn't even a handle, just a solid, seamless piece of steel.

Ollie stood quite still, but inside he was a churning cauldron of emotions. *Sikes*. Maddy Sikes was behind this. She was *alive*, while Nancy and Ollie's parents were gone for ever. It wasn't fair. It wasn't *right*.

Sol and Lily turned from the door, defeated.

'Well,' said Lily. 'What now?'

Sol was checking his pockets. 'I've got my phone,' he said. 'There's no signal, but maybe . . . I don't know. Could you work your magic, Jack? Get our messaging app working at least, so we can get in touch with someone at the Haven?'

Jack didn't seem to hear. She was glaring furiously at the place Crowe had been standing with her little brother.

'Jack?' Ollie said.

She didn't answer, and Ollie shared concerned glances with Sol and Lily.

Ollie moved to his friend's side, and crouched in front of her.

'We'll get out of this,' he told her. 'And we'll save Errol. I promise you we will.'

Jack closed her eyes then. When she opened them again, they glistened wetly. '*How?*' she said. 'The door's sealed, and there's no way to get any kind of signal down here. Even our messaging app is useless this far out of range.'

'I know, but . . .'

'But what, Ollie? Sikes has won. You know she has. Do you see that on the wall?' Jack pointed towards the head end of the bunk, and Ollie saw a little etching in the brickwork.

'Is that . . . a bird?'

'It's an eagle. Errol made it. He must have. It's what he calls himself, remember? Which means he was locked in this cell, too, and he was down here for *days*. Don't you think he would have escaped if he could have?'

Ollie had been harbouring a glimmer of hope, but if Errol had been locked in this cell the whole time he'd been held captive, and still hadn't found a way out, what chance did Ollie and the others have of breaking free in a matter of hours? Because that was all the time they had left. If they didn't escape soon, there would be nobody to prevent the nerve agent from being released.

'There must be something we can do,' said Ollie. 'Something we're missing.'

Jack shook her head vehemently. 'There's no escape. We must be twenty metres underground. What are we going to do, *burrow* our way out?'

Ollie dropped his eyes to the floor . . . and then he raised them to the wall in front of him, and the single feature amid the ancient brickwork. He looked at Jack then, and he smiled.

'It's way too small,' said Sol, his voice echoey and distant as he peered into the air vent. 'I'm sorry, guys, but there's no chance.'

Ollie looked up at his friend, who was balancing on the frame of the bunk.

'Are you sure?' Ollie said. 'I'm smaller than you are, remember. I could probably crawl through a space you couldn't.'

'Pretty sure,' Sol answered. 'And there's no need to get personal. Just because I've put on a couple of kilos recently, doesn't mean . . . Wait.'

'What is it?' Ollie said.

'I think . . . I think I can feel something.' They'd already managed to prise off the cover of the air vent, and Sol was reaching into the cavity. He had to turn his head sideways to allow him to do so, and his cheek was pressed awkwardly against the wall. As Ollie looked at him, Sol wrinkled his nose. 'It smells awful up here. Like it did down in those tunnels.'

Ollie and Lily shared a glance, and he could tell she was thinking the same thing he was. If the air vent smelt like those tunnels had, the chances were they were connected.

'The bricks,' Sol said. 'They're loose. And the gap gets wider. Not much, but . . .' Sol extracted his arm, and jumped nimbly from the bed frame to the dusty floor. He faced the others. 'I reckon it might be big enough. *Just*. The only problem is getting through the opening. About a metre in, the shaft widens, but the gap at this end is only about the size of my head.'

'So it's no use after all,' said Lily, her face falling. 'If we can't squeeze through the opening, it hardly matters how wide the rest of the shaft is.'

'Unless we make the opening wider,' said Sol. 'Like I say, some of those bricks already feel loose. And if we can scrape away the mortar from between the rest of them, maybe we could remove enough to allow us to get through.'

'But that could take hours,' said Lily, peering up at the opening in the wall. As it was, the vent was only about twenty centimetres wide. They would need to remove two courses of brickwork at least.

'I don't see we have any other option,' said Sol. 'And it beats sitting around waiting for Maddy Sikes to declare herself Grand Poobah.'

Jack was already investigating the bed frame. 'Here,' she said. 'We can use these springs. If we uncoil the ends, we can use the wire to scrape away the mortar.'

Ollie removed his school blazer and started rolling up his sleeves. 'So what are we waiting for?' he said.

Ollie, Sol and Lily took turns working at the vent. There was only space for one of them to reach into the shaft at a time, so while one person worked, the other two sat on the bunk to keep it steady. Jack rolled anxiously back and forth across the cell, periodically checking her watch and then craning her neck to try to measure their progress.

By 3 p.m. they'd managed to widen the opening by about ten centimetres. By five, it was almost double its initial width, but still perilously small. Looking at the gap from below, it appeared hardly any bigger than it had been when they'd started. But the prime minister's speech was due to take place at 6.15 p.m., which by Ollie's reckoning meant it was now or never.

'That's it, Sol. There's no more time.'

Sol was balanced on the frame of the bunk. He looked down at him, his brow coated in dust and sweat. 'But it's not big enough. There's no way we'll be able to get through.'

Ollie looked again at the opening. 'I reckon I might be able to. If I can get a hand hold on the other side to pull myself through, and one of you pushes me from this end.'

Sol climbed down wearily from the bunk.

'If you can get through, so can I,' said Lily. She held Ollie's eye determinedly. Even now, after everything that had happened, she was clearly still angry with him. And Ollie could hardly blame her.

Sol looked up at the air vent. He drew in his breath and sucked in his stomach, as though trying to gauge whether he would make it through as well. But the answer would have been as obvious to him as it was to Ollie. He exhaled, defeated, and let his belly swell to its normal shape.

'Sol and I will stay behind,' said Jack. 'I'm not going to be much help even if I could get through, not without my chair. You and Lily are our only chance, Ollie.'

'Here,' said Sol. 'Take my phone. It's fully charged, so if you do get into the main shaft, at least you'll have a light to guide your way.'

Ollie nodded, grateful, and still ruing the fact he'd lost his own phone when he'd toppled from the cliff.

He looked at Lily. 'Heads or tails?' he said. He didn't have a coin, but Lily understood what he meant.

'Heads,' she said. 'If we get stuck in there, I don't want the last thing I see before I die to be your backside.' She started clambering on to the bunk.

'Remember, Ollie,' said Jack. 'The nerve agent is probably a liquid. Sikes said something about a vial, and it will probably be small enough to fit in the palm of your hand.'

'And what do we do when we get hold of it? Can we touch it?'

'You'll be safe while the vial remains airtight. But if the lid comes off, or the glass smashes, get out of there as fast as you can. Don't inhale the fumes, and whatever you do, don't let the liquid touch you.'

Ollie nodded. 'Got it,' he said, with more confidence than he felt. The enormity of the task ahead of them was suddenly dawning on him. Squeezing through the ventilation shaft was one thing. But assuming they managed it, escaping from the dungeons would be just the beginning.

At first Ollie didn't think he would fit. Lily had made it to the main shaft, and she'd declared it wide enough to crawl through, even if she couldn't tell yet where it led. But Ollie was struggling to squeeze through the opening.

'Grab my hand, Ollie,' said Lily.

Ollie looked for it, but was dazzled by the light from Sol's phone that she was shining back at him. 'I can't see your hand.'

Lily adjusted the torch beam. 'Here.'

Ollie felt Lily's hand latch around his wrist. Behind him, he could sense Sol braced to shove the soles of his feet.

'Ready, Sol?' Lily called. 'One, two, *three*.'

For a moment nothing happened. But then Ollie began to shift. He sucked in his breath, grimacing as the jagged brickwork scraped against his stomach.

And then he was through. It happened in a rush. One moment he was stuck fast, the next his shoulders were free, and he was able to wriggle into the main shaft.

'I'm through!' he yelled, angling his chin towards his armpit.

'Tell Errol I love him!' Jack called back.

'And tell Crowe that if he's expecting a Christmas card from me, he's going to be sorely disappointed!' added Sol.

Lily had already started forwards. Ollie followed. He could see glimpses of the shaft ahead in the glow of her torch, but mainly his view was blocked by Lily herself. Behind him, already, there was only darkness, and very quickly the relief at being freed from the tunnel opening was replaced by a fluttering, flurrying panic. Ollie had never liked confined spaces. It had taken him weeks to get used to walking around in the sewer tunnels, not to mention living in the ghost station. He would never have admitted it to anyone else, but the whole being-trapped-underground thing was another reason he was personally so desperate to find the Haven another home.

'Are you OK, Ollie?' Lily said from up ahead. 'You're breathing very fast.'

He was, Ollie realised. He focused on taking longer, deeper inhalations. It helped, a bit.

'Can you see anything up ahead?' he asked Lily.

'Nothing. Well, plenty, if by "anything" you mean an endless tunnel of blackness.' She paused. 'Sorry, that's probably not helping much, is it? I take it you're not a fan of tight spaces.'

'They're up there with mushrooms. And mutant, over-sized rat-dogs.'

Lily snorted. It was the first time in ages she'd laughed so naturally at something Ollie had said. But then she seemed to remember she was mad at him, and her laughter dwindled. In its place there came a silence, more stilted and awkward than before.

'Lily . . .' Ollie said, and he waited for Lily to cut him short, the way she had in the classroom. When she said nothing, he carried on. 'I'm sorry, Lily. Really I am. For doubting you, and for . . . for everything. I've just been worried, I guess. And kind of ashamed. For letting everyone down. For letting *you* down in particular,' he added in a rush, glad Lily couldn't see his face. 'After Dodge, and everything else, I was desperate to show you I could be leader. For you to have faith in me. But I understand why you don't.'

Lily stopped moving, and Ollie's head butted into her heels.

'What?' she said.

'I just . . . I said I'm sorry. For—'

'Not that part. The other thing. Is that what you think? That I don't have faith in you?'

'I . . . kind of. But I understand. That's what I'm saying. To be honest, I don't exactly have that much faith in myself. And I totally get why you think Flea should be leader. He's your brother, after all, and—'

'Ollie.'

'And it makes sense that you would—'

'*Ollie.*'

'What?'

'I don't think Flea should be leader.'

'You don't?'

'No! If I did I would have voted for him when we had the election.'

It took a moment for Ollie to work out the implication of what Lily had said. 'You mean . . . you voted for *me*?'

'Of course I voted for you, you idiot. And if you insist on having another – totally pointless, by the way – election, I'll vote for you again.'

'But then why . . .' Ollie shook his head in the darkness. 'If you voted for me, why have you been acting so weirdly around me?'

'I haven't been,' said Lily, and Ollie could hear her frown. 'Have I?'

'A little bit. A lot, actually,' Ollie said. 'Every time I walk into a room you find some reason to leave. And you never look at me. When I say something, or suggest something, you turn away as if you think it's a stupid idea.'

'That's not true! I don't think your ideas are stupid. Except this one, maybe.' She jiggled the light to indicate the ventilation shaft.

Ollie crawled after her in silence. Rather than feeling relieved, he was more confused than ever. He hadn't imagined it. Had he? Lily had definitely been acting strangely around him, even if Ollie had misinterpreted the reason why.

'OK, OK,' said Lily, stopping again, as though Ollie had spoken out loud. 'I admit I *may* have been acting a bit weirdly towards you. But that's *because* I voted for you. Not because I don't have faith in you.'

Ollie allowed himself a moment to try to figure that out. 'I don't get it.'

Lily sighed. 'Look. Put yourself in my shoes. Voting for you meant voting *against* my brother. I mean, he's a blockhead, but he's still the only family I have left. And he doesn't *know* I didn't vote for him. He'd probably disown me if he did. If you ask me, he'd be well within his rights.'

All at once it started to make sense. Ollie had been so focused on worrying about what people thought of *him*, he hadn't stopped to consider the dilemmas they might be wrestling with themselves.

'And it's weird for other reasons, too,' Lily went on. 'I . . . I like you, Ollie. And I think you could be the best thing that's ever happened to the Haven, at least in the time I've been there. But saying that out loud, even *thinking* it . . . Well. It just . . . it feels a bit like . . .'

'A betrayal,' Ollie said, remembering Dodge. For Ollie, stepping into Dodge's shoes had felt awkward enough. But Lily had also been his girlfriend.

Now Ollie was the one to sigh.

'Look,' said Lily, into the silence. 'Let's start again. Shall we? I'll forgive you if you'll forgive me. Deal?'

'Deal,' agreed Ollie, and his relief escaped into a grin. It occurred to him that maybe all apologies should be made in the dark. It was definitely easier talking to Lily's feet than it would have been to look her in the eye.

They resumed crawling.

'Lily . . .' Ollie said, after a moment.

'Really, Ollie, it's fine,' Lily responded. 'You don't need to apologise again. I told you, I forgive you. Let's just leave it at that.'

'No, I . . . I was going to say, what's that? Up ahead.'

Ollie had caught a glimpse of something over the top of Lily's shoulder.

Lily paused and angled the torch light. 'I think . . . I think it's a junction. And maybe . . .' She made the torch beam brighter. When she spoke again, there was a smile in her voice. 'And there's a ladder.'

At the junction, the shaft split four ways. In one of the directions the unpleasant smell was stronger, suggesting it veered off towards the access tunnels. They couldn't tell where the second channel led. Like the shaft behind them, it carried itself away into darkness. But it didn't matter, because there was also another bore leading up.

As before, Lily went first. The ladder was old and rusted, but it was solid, and after shaking out the stiffness in their legs, they scrambled up the rungs quickly.

At the top of the shaft there was a metal cover, and it lifted after a few thrusts of Lily's shoulder. When Lily shoved it to one side, daylight washed away the darkness like a flood of crystal-clear water.

Lily glanced down at Ollie, grinning, then hopped out on to solid ground. Ollie followed, drawing the fresh air deep into his lungs. As he climbed the final few rungs, he could see trees overhead, and he expected to emerge into the forest.

But when he poked his head through the opening, he barely noticed their surroundings. He saw only Lily, with her hands in the air, and the gun barrel that was levelled between his eyes.

25 ACCESS DENIED

'On your feet! Hands where I can see them!'

Ollie did as the armed police officer commanded, stumbling slightly as he stepped out of the shaft. His eyes never left the barrel of the man's assault rifle.

'*Move*,' the police officer barked. 'Over there. Beside your friend.'

Ollie sidled next to Lily, his hands raised. 'Listen, sir . . .'

'Quiet!' the officer instructed. He was edging forwards to peer down the shaft, one eye never fully leaving Ollie and Lily.

'It's just the two of us,' Lily said. 'But please, you need to listen. Something awful is going to—'

'I said, button it!' The police officer used his foot to flip the cover of the ventilation shaft closed, and swung his attention – and his weapon – back towards Ollie and Lily. For the first time, it seemed to register with him that the two of them were wearing school uniforms. 'What are you doing out here? What were you doing down *there*?'

Ollie noticed that they were indeed in the forest, but only a few metres from the tree line. The ladder in the ventilation shaft had led them up to something like a manhole, half buried in the overgrown grass. Forest Mount was directly over the police officer's shoulder, maybe fifty metres away across an open lawn. Ollie could see a flurry of activity outside the main entrance. A motorcade was parked in the drive, meaning the prime minister must already have arrived.

When would Crowe instruct Errol to release the nerve agent? Strain had said the PM's speech was to be broadcast live, as she announced the start of her re-election campaign to the nation. Knowing Maddy Sikes, she would wait until the cameras were rolling. Maybe she wouldn't be able to claim credit for the attack, but she would still want the entire world to see.

Ollie focused on the policeman. 'Look, it's a long story. And we don't have time to tell you everything. But the prime minister is in danger. There's a plot to kill her. With a Russian nerve agent. You need to get her out of there. You need to get *everyone* out.'

The police officer lowered his weapon. And then he smiled.

'How old are you?' he said. 'Thirteen? Fourteen? I've got a nephew about your age. He's got an imagination on him, too.'

'I'm not imagining things!' Ollie insisted. 'It's true, I swear it!'

The radio hanging from the police officer's jacket crackled to life. The policeman dipped his ear, and then thumbed the walkie-talkie to deliver his response.

'Roger, Sierra One. Sweep completed. All clear, sector six.'

He raised his head, and his smile set into something more serious. 'Right, you two. Let's go.'

'Go?' said Ollie. 'Go where?'

'Not inside the school, I'll tell you that for nothing. No one's getting in or out now until the PM has left the grounds. I'll find a bobby to babysit you until it's all over.'

'But there's no time for that!' said Ollie. 'Didn't you hear what I just told you?'

The police officer had tried to shepherd Ollie, and he bucked away.

'I mean it, sunshine,' the policeman growled. 'Save the stories for bedtime.' His temper visibly fraying, the policeman grabbed hold of Ollie more roughly.

'But it's not a story,' said Lily. 'Ollie's telling you the truth!'

'Don't you start, love. Come on, get moving.' This time the policeman gestured with his weapon, and Ollie and Lily had no choice but to fall into step ahead of him. Ollie fumed with frustration. They'd made it out of the dungeons, and found someone who could have warned the prime minister, but the police officer simply didn't believe them. And they were running out of time to try to convince him.

Ollie looked over at Lily. Lily looked back. She nodded.

Hoping Lily was on the same wavelength as him, Ollie spun, catching the police officer by surprise. 'Hey—' the man started to say. He didn't notice Lily spin the other way, and her foot swing towards his groin.

There was a crunching noise, and the policeman's eyes went momentarily wide. Then he toppled forwards, collapsing with an *oof* to the mulchy floor.

As Ollie looked on, wincing, a lesson from Song's karate training came back to him. *Feint first, then strike.*

Lily grabbed Ollie by the shoulder. 'Come *on*.'

With the police officer moaning on the ground, they made a dash for the edge of the forest. They broke through the tree line, and skidded to a halt on the lawn.

A helicopter was swooping in their direction. It passed low overhead, and Ollie and Lily were battered by the rush of wind stirred up by the chopper's rotor blades. The helicopter banked as it closed on the school, then started to climb as it tracked the driveway that cut through the forest. From the markings, Ollie could tell it was a police helicopter, but there were others hovering high around the periphery of the school. Those were news crews, Ollie guessed, and for an instant he could picture the scenes the cameramen up there would shortly be filming if Sikes and Crowe got their way: armed police officers storming the school, as pupils and teachers fled in panic the other way.

'How are we going to get inside the building?' said Lily. 'You heard what that policeman said. No one's allowed in or out until the PM's left.'

Ollie could see more armed police officers guarding every visible entrance into the school. Forest Mount was in lockdown. 'I . . . I'm not sure.'

'We could see if someone else will listen?' Lily suggested. 'Another police officer, maybe. Or the person in charge.'

Ollie shook his head. 'We can't risk it. We have to try to stop Crowe and Errol ourselves. If we tell someone, and they don't believe us, we could end up being "babysat", just like the policeman said. By the time they let us go, it would be too late.'

'So . . . what? We just march up to the main entrance?'

'I can't think of a better idea,' Ollie answered. 'Can you?'

They were spotted halfway across the lawn. Guns were raised in their direction, until the police officers also noticed their school uniforms.

'Keep walking,' said Lily, as the two of them did their best to brush themselves down. 'Act as if we're supposed to be here.'

She beamed as they approached the guards on the steps outside the main entrance. Ollie kept checking across his shoulder, fully expecting the policeman from the woods to suddenly come lumbering from the trees.

'Sorry we're late,' said Lily to the guards, using a tone Ollie had never heard before. She sounded posh, and she was holding herself the way the prefects did, her shoulders back and her nose in the air.

Feeling awkward, and conscious of how dishevelled they must have looked, Ollie did his best to mimic her.

'Yeah . . . I mean, yes, we were . . . er . . . playing and we lost track of time. Um, sorry.'

There were two guards outside the main door, one male, one female. Lily had attempted to walk straight past them, but the female police officer used an arm to block her path.

'Not so fast, young lady. It's authorised personnel only from now on.'

'But we *are* authorised,' Lily insisted. 'We go to school here. We're supposed to be in the assembly hall.'

'That may be, but you've missed your chance. The PM is on stage in four minutes. If you want to hear what she has to say, you'll have to hurry and find yourselves a television.'

Ollie caught Lily's eye. *Four minutes?*

'Look,' said Ollie to the policewoman. 'Couldn't you just . . . make an exception? Just this once? You could show us to our seats yourself.'

The woman scoffed. 'What do I look like to you, a bloody usher?' She turned to her colleague. 'Bloody toff schools. Honestly.'

The policeman beside her smiled snidely. Then he turned slightly to listen to the voice that had come through on his radio. 'Say again, Oscar Seven. I didn't catch that.'

But Ollie had – fragments at least. The words 'pupils' and 'impostors' and 'assault' . . . And he recognised the voice, even though it was distorted by the radio. It was the officer they'd escaped from in the forest, broadcasting what had happened to every other police unit on the grounds.

The policewoman was trying to listen to the transmission as well. But she wasn't taking her eyes off Ollie and Lily. One twitch from either of them in the wrong direction, and Ollie didn't doubt she'd have them by their collars.

Ollie looked around him frantically, but the main entrance was the only way in. All the windows around the courtyard were shut, and anyway there were more armed police officers positioned around the perimeter.

There was no help on offer inside the school, either. When Ollie peered through the open door into the entrance hall, he saw not a single face he recognised. All the pupils and teachers were presumably already in the assembly hall, as it seemed was the prime minister herself. In the lobby of the school there were only more police officers, a number of people wearing suits, and—

'Mr Ross!'

The short, greasy-looking man had his back turned. He'd been chatting to some of the other people in suits – more of the PM's assistants, Ollie assumed – but when Ollie called his name, he looked across his shoulder. His eyes narrowed suspiciously.

Ollie was leaning and waving, trying to catch Ross's attention.

'What are you doing, Ollie?' Lily hissed. 'You said we couldn't trust him!'

'We can't,' Ollie whispered back. 'But that doesn't mean we can't *use* him.'

When Ollie had called out, the policewoman had turned away from her colleague, who was still straining to hear the voice on his radio. She stood up straighter as Ross crossed the lobby towards them.

'*You*,' said Ross, focusing on Ollie. 'What are you doing out there? Why aren't you in the assembly hall with all the others?'

'You know these children, sir?' said the policewoman, her voice changing in the same way Lily's had. It was more formal all of a sudden, and Ollie guessed Ross was her superior.

'What? Yes . . . I suppose so.' Ross wrinkled his nose as he took in the state of Ollie's uniform.

'And they're authorised to be inside the school?'

'Authorised? They're pupils here. Of course they're—'

Ollie and Lily needed no further invitation. They shoved their way past the policewoman, who wobbled but made no move to stop them.

Ross whirled in confusion. 'I say! What do you think you're—?'

'Sorry!' Lily called. 'We're *really* big fans of the PM. We'd just *die* if we missed her speech!'

The two of them darted towards the doors that led into the assembly hall. Ollie looked across his shoulder as he ran. He could see Ross staring after them, his outrage showing on his face. Behind him, the policeman on the steps was gesturing frantically to his colleague, who whipped her head towards Ollie and Lily. She spoke urgently into her radio, and then both officers moved to give chase.

It seemed the message from the policeman in the woods had finally got through.

'They're coming after us, Lily!'

They'd reached the set of double doors, and as one, Ollie and Lily hauled them open . . . to be greeted by thunderous applause.

The noise shocked Ollie to a standstill.

They'd emerged into the rear of the hall, into a tangle of wires and TV equipment. No one inside the hall had seen them come in. The people operating the cameras were already busy filming, and the entire audience was on its feet, facing away from Ollie and Lily, towards the stage. Ollie could just make out Professor Strain beside the lectern. He was clapping along with everyone else, and slowly making way for the guest of honour. Crowe was nowhere to be seen – but then Ollie spotted him sidling from his chair on stage towards the exit, as though in anticipation of what was about to happen.

The prime minister herself was walking towards the lectern, one hand raised to acknowledge the applause. With all eyes on her, nobody would have noticed the boy who had appeared from the wings, eyeing Crowe nervously as he passed him, and shakily carrying a glass of water. He set it down behind the lectern for the prime minister, then slipped his hand discreetly into his blazer pocket.

Ollie knew at once what Errol was reaching for. Even the fumes would be enough, Jack had said, meaning all Errol had to do with that vial was open it. After that, there would be nothing Ollie or anyone else could do. Errol would die, the prime minister would die, and Sikes's revolution would begin.

26 STAGE FRIGHT

It was a shout from close behind him that set Ollie moving.

The two police officers from the main entrance had burst into the hall, and though the policewoman's holler was almost lost amid the applause for the prime minister, Ollie and Lily heard it clearly enough. They turned around just in time. The policewoman was nearly upon them, and would have caught them had she not tripped on a cable running from one of the television cameras. Her stumble gave Ollie and Lily precious seconds, and they started shoving their way towards the stage as fast as they could.

'Errol!' Ollie yelled. '*Don't!*'

But the applause was so loud, it was only the people standing closest who would have heard him. The hall was as packed as Ollie had ever seen it, with every seat taken, and prefects and teachers three-deep along the aisles. For Ollie it was like being in the forest again, fighting to forge a path through the trees.

'Errol!' Lily was shouting. 'Don't do it, Errol! You've been tricked!'

One or two heads spun their way, but mainly in response to Ollie and Lily trying to barge their way past. Prefects glared at them angrily, and one grabbed Ollie by the collar of his blazer. Without thinking, Ollie spun as he moved, allowing his arms to slip from the blazer sleeves, and leaving the prefect clutching an empty jacket.

Ollie raised himself on tiptoe. He caught a glimpse of the prime minister waving towards the cheering crowd, but he'd lost sight of Errol completely. Had he opened the vial? Was he even still on stage? For all Ollie knew, he and Lily were already too late, and they were heading straight into an invisible cloud of toxic fumes.

They hit a wall then: three enormous prefects standing shoulder to shoulder, and blocking the aisle completely.

Ollie looked at Lily desperately, and caught sight of the policewoman in the background. She wasn't following them, but instead was talking into her radio. She seemed to be maintaining eye contact with whoever she was speaking to, and when Ollie tracked where she was looking, he saw a man in a black suit on the steps to one side of the stage. He had a finger raised tellingly to his earpiece.

And he wasn't alone. For the first time Ollie noticed others like him: four or five plain-clothed bodyguards dotted along the aisle ahead of them. As one they started moving, clearly intent on stopping Ollie and Lily from getting any closer to the prime minister.

'What now?' said Lily, anxiously.

Ollie spun, searching for some way forwards. 'Follow me!'

With the audience still on its feet, the chairs in the main rows were empty, and Ollie jumped up on the one closest, using the seats like stepping stones until he was right in the middle of the row. The prime minister had come to the edge of the stage, he saw, and was cheerfully acknowledging the crowd. Even from half the hall away, she looked shorter in real life than Ollie had imagined her. Errol was at the lectern behind her, and Crowe was there on stage, too. He was beside the curtain, as far from the lectern as he could get without leaving the stage completely, but from the way he was glaring at Errol, it was clear something wasn't going according to plan. Errol's hand was still in his pocket, and he was staring fixedly at the glass of water, as though caught in a trance of indecision.

'Errol!' Ollie yelled, waving his arms above his head.

Errol appeared hypnotised by his predicament, oblivious to everything around him.

The applause was finally beginning to die down, and with the security guards pressing through the crowd, people were beginning to notice that something was wrong.

Everyone, that is, except Errol. As Ollie watched, he withdrew his hand from his pocket. He glanced at Crowe, who nodded impatiently, even as he started to back away. Errol turned to the lectern, and something glinted as he raised his hand.

The vial.

'Errol, *no*!'

The applause had turned into an anxious buzz, and if anything the noise in the hall got louder. Even Professor Strain appeared to have noticed something amiss. After re-taking his chair beside the other dignitaries on stage, he was on his feet again. He was casting his frown into the crowd, peering blindly against the glare of the television lights. Clearly aware of the commotion herself, the prime minister continued smiling awkwardly, no doubt conscious of the cameras at the back of the room.

Ollie had to get Errol's attention. More than that, he had to get everyone else in the room to listen, too, and start moving away from that vial before the nerve agent was released.

And so he said the first thing that came into his head. Shouted it, rather – as loudly as he could.

'BOMB!' he yelled, at the top of his voice. 'There's a bomb! Everybody out – *now*!'

There was a moment when nobody moved. Then, everybody did.

It was as though Ollie and Lily were standing on an island as the sea around them came suddenly to the boil. Chairs scraped and some of the younger children screamed. The adults in the room whirled helplessly, as they desperately tried to work out what was going on. From his position on top of the chair, Ollie could see it all. Professor Strain was on his feet behind Errol, wide-eyed and immobile, as the rest of the people on stage fled gracelessly for the wings. The bodyguards who'd been closing on Ollie and Lily were caught hopelessly out of position. The prime minister was stranded in front of the lectern, alone and utterly defenceless. And there was Errol himself, vial in hand – and eyes raised finally towards Ollie.

'Errol!' Ollie called, relief surging through him. 'Don't open it! Whatever you do, don't open that—'

Neither Ollie nor Errol saw it coming. Crowe had come rushing against the tide, and he knocked Errol from his feet. There was a glint in the camera spotlights as the vial tumbled in the air, and for a moment Ollie thought it was all over. The bottle would land, the glass would break, and the nerve agent would be released into the air.

But as Errol crumpled, Crowe spun, and he caught the vial as it fell. Ollie saw Errol crack his head on the stage floor, and the sound of the impact was enough to get Ollie moving. He and Lily began hurdling forwards, across the backs of the chairs. Lily was lighter on her feet, and managed to stay upright, as Ollie tripped awkwardly from one row to the next. Around them the panic continued, as even the teachers began fleeing for the exits.

Ollie was almost at the front now, but he didn't know what he intended to do when he got there. He just knew he had to stop Crowe from releasing that nerve agent. The PM's bodyguards were fighting the same battle Ollie was, thrashing their way towards the front of the room.

'Lily!' Ollie called. His friend had pulled further ahead, but the rows of chairs were breaking apart in the flood of pupils, and she was being forced steadily towards the aisle. 'Get to the wings!' Ollie shouted. 'The rope!'

Lily looked where Ollie was pointing. He didn't know whether or not she'd understood him, but she veered in the direction Ollie had indicated. Ollie, meanwhile, continued forwards, directly towards Crowe and that vial. He'd seen what Crowe intended to do, and with Strain in some kind of stupor, and Errol unconscious on the floor, Ollie was the only one who could stop him.

But then a hand grabbed hold of Ollie's ankle. He was caught mid leap, and he toppled into the gap between the rows of chairs. He tried to stand, ignoring the impact in his ribs, but all of a sudden there was a weight pressing down on him, pinning him to the parquet floor. One of the prime minister's bodyguards was right on top of him, his knee in the small of Ollie's back.

'Let me go!' Ollie yelled. 'It's not me you should be after!' He felt a handcuff click into place around one of his wrists, and then he was being lifted to his feet. He fought with his other hand, desperate to try to stay free. But as he flailed, he caught sight of what was happening on stage. Crowe had taken position beside the lectern. He held the vial with one hand – and the prime minister by the hair with the other.

'Crowe, don't!' Ollie cried, and when the bodyguard who'd seized hold of him tracked Ollie's gaze, he froze suddenly in his movements. The other bodyguards had seen it, too.

'Stay back!' Crowe shouted, raising the vial. 'Come any closer, and I force this down the prime minister's throat!'

Ollie sensed the bodyguards' confusion. One moment they'd been told that Ollie was the threat, the next that there was a bomb, and now the prime minister was being held hostage by a boy who'd been cleared to sit beside her on the podium.

'Do as he says!' Ollie said, when he saw the bodyguards continue to edge forwards. The front of the room was empty now, but for Ollie and Lily, the PM's security detail, and the four people on stage: Crowe and the prime minister, Errol lying on the floor, and Strain watching on haplessly.

'That vial contains a nerve agent,' Ollie said. 'All he has to do is open it!'

The bodyguards exchanged uncertain glances. Lily, meanwhile, had made it to the steps on the right-hand side of the stage, just out of Crowe's eyeline. She was creeping forwards, upwards, one centimetre at a time.

Ollie shook off the bodyguard who'd tackled him, and clambered on to a chair.

'Crowe, listen to me,' he said, holding out his hands. The handcuffs dangled uselessly from his left wrist. 'It's over. The plan failed. You don't have to do this!'

'Nothing's over,' Crowe growled. He looked over Ollie's head then, towards the back of the room. Ollie turned, and saw some of the news reporters had stayed at their posts. Those cameras were still rolling.

When Ollie turned back, Professor Strain was circling the podium, backing towards Lily on the steps. His face was a picture of panic and confusion. Beside the lectern, Errol was raising himself on to an elbow.

'Crowe, please,' said Ollie. 'Think about it. There's no way you'd be able to get away if you go through with this. You'd be sacrificing yourself, and for what? Sikes doesn't care about you. She doesn't care about *anyone*.'

Crowe rounded on him, yanking the prime minister's hair as he spun. The prime minister cried out, and Ollie saw the bodyguard closest to her twitch. 'You think I don't know that?' said Crowe to Ollie. 'She gave me up when I was a baby, didn't even acknowledge I was alive until it suited her. The truth is, I've got no one. I never have!'

Ollie saw one of the bodyguards lift a finger to his ear. Someone was communicating with him, clearly. What were they saying?

Lily meanwhile had reached the top of the stairs, as Strain stumbled past her the other way. She was still heading where Ollie had pointed, towards that rope at the side of the stage.

Ollie tried to gauge the distance between him and Crowe. There was another row of chairs directly in front of him, and then a gap between the chairs and the stage. There was no way Ollie could close the distance and make a grab for that vial before Crowe realised what was coming.

'*Why* then?' Ollie pressed. 'Why go through with it at all? Why not . . . come with us?' he went on, and he caught Lily turn to him in shock. 'There's a place,' Ollie told Crowe. 'A place for kids like you and me. A *good* place, where it doesn't matter if you're alone. We could help you, just as you could help us.'

But Crowe only sneered. 'I told you why I'm doing this,' he hissed. 'Because as much as I hate my mother, I hate my father more. *And because I've got nothing left to lose.*'

All at once the hall was filled with movement. Through the doors closest to the stage, a team of armed police officers burst in, assault rifles levelled at the lectern. The windows on the opposite side of the room exploded, showering both Strain and the prime minister's bodyguards with fragments of glass. More armed police officers surged through, flanking Crowe on both sides.

'Don't shoot!' Ollie yelled, even as Crowe raised the vial above his head.

Errol was on his knees now, roused by the commotion, and he was casting around at the scene in front of him. He saw Ollie, and the prime minister, and he saw what Crowe was holding in his hand.

'Errol, Lily,' Ollie shouted. '*Now!*'

The three of them started moving at once. Lily made a dash for the rope, as Errol lunged to catch hold of Crowe's arm. Crowe lashed out, but he was forced to let go of the prime minister. The PM collapsed, coughing, as Crowe's elbow caught Errol on his cheek.

Ollie leapt towards the stage, only just making it across the gap, and crash-landed against the lectern. The prime minister was beside him, Errol too. Crowe was looming over them, his expression caught between triumph and fury. A shadow fell as Crowe's hand did, and the vial began its arc towards the floor.

Ollie scrambled forwards, dragging Errol with one hand and the prime minister with the other, so that the three of them tipped from the edge of the stage. They landed amid the chairs in a bundle, and Ollie felt a crunch in his shoulder.

He looked up, ignoring the pain, and praying Lily had made it to that rope in time – the rope that would release the stage curtain. He saw the curtain fall as the vial did, beating the deadly nerve agent to the floor.

There was the sound of glass breaking, quickly drowned out by a shrill, ear-splitting keen of agony.

It was all hidden behind the curtain, but in his mind Ollie saw it anyway: Crowe suffering the full force of the nerve agent, and the torturous horror of his death throes.

27 POWER STRUGGLE

Ollie woke to a view of medieval grandeur. From the window of the ward in St Thomas' Hospital, he could see the Houses of Parliament glinting goldly across a sparkling River Thames. The sky was a single shade of blue, cloudless to the curve of the horizon. It was a beautiful day, as splendid and full of promise as the city itself, and Ollie knew it was time to go home.

Lily was asleep in the bed beside him. Errol was across from them, snoring gently somewhere beneath his covers. As the only children who'd been in the assembly hall when the nerve agent had been released, they'd been placed in isolation, and as such had the ward to themselves. After five days of tests and evaluations, they'd finally been given the all-clear. Ollie's shoulder had been dislocated when he'd fallen from the stage, but even that was getting better. It ached, especially at night, and he had to wear a sling, but on the whole he considered himself incredibly lucky. They all were. If it hadn't been for that curtain, and Lily releasing it in time, they would have suffered the same fate as Colton Crowe.

Ollie wished there'd been something that could have been done for Crowe, in spite of everything he was responsible for.

But apparently by the time the ambulances had arrived, Crowe was already dead.

Ollie climbed from his bed and made a start on packing his things. He didn't have much. Everything he'd been wearing or carrying in the assembly hall had been taken away from him at the scene. There was just a book that one of the nurses had given him – a copy of *Oliver Twist* by Charles Dickens – which Ollie intended to contribute to the Haven's library, and the clothes he'd been gifted from the hospital's slightly random supply.

He looked at the view again, at the building that dominated the northern riverbank. The seat of power. It seemed hard to believe that a quest to find Jack's brother had turned into a battle for the country itself. It made Ollie feel relieved and scared at the same time.

A knock at the door into the ward caused him to turn. Before he could react, the door opened, and a man almost the size of the doorway itself walked through. He wore a dark suit and a grimace, and Ollie recognised him immediately. The last time Ollie had seen him, he'd been kneeling on Ollie's back, attempting to put him in handcuffs.

The man walked straight towards the window. He looked out, around, then marched back through the ward and took up position beside the door. Then he looked at Ollie, and he smiled.

'Um,' said Ollie. 'Can I help you?'

'You might perhaps be able to help *me*,' said a voice, and through the doorway a woman appeared. She was around fifty, immaculately dressed – and shorter than she looked on TV.

As the prime minister stepped into the room, Ollie sensed his eyes widen. He felt an odd compulsion to kneel, or bow, or do *something* anyway.

Instead, he said, 'Er . . . hi.'

The prime minister smiled. Like Ollie she wore a sling. While Ollie had dislocated a shoulder, the prime minister, he'd learned, had broken her arm. And technically it was Ollie's fault.

'Leaving so soon?' said the prime minister, noticing Ollie's bag.

Ollie stepped in front of the rucksack. 'No, I . . . I just want to be ready. I'm kind of eager to get home.'

The prime minister had moved to the foot of Lily's bed. Both Lily and Errol remained fast asleep.

'And where is home exactly?' said the prime minister, her smile becoming something like a frown. 'The hospital accessed your personal details from your school records, but there seems to be some confusion. Your home address doesn't appear to exist. And the medical staff say they're having trouble contacting your parents.'

Ollie knew Jack had faked their personal details on their Forest Mount application forms. Their first names were real, but their surnames, their home addresses, their parents' names,

Ollie's date of birth, even their academic records, had all been adjusted to disguise their identities.

'My parents are . . . away,' Ollie answered. 'But my, er, aunt lives close by.'

The prime minister showed her concern. Ollie had seen similar expressions on the nurses who'd quizzed him recently. At first the medical staff had been focused on ensuring Ollie and his friends were OK, but over the past two or three days, their questioning had become more and more insistent. That was one of the reasons Ollie had decided it was time to leave.

'Well,' said the prime minister. 'I hope your aunt will take good care of you.'

'Oh, she will. She's . . . special,' Ollie said. 'More like a best friend, actually.'

The prime minister smiled warmly. 'I'm glad to hear it. And I'm glad to see you on your feet. I stopped by because . . . Well. I wanted to thank you. We're still trying to get to the bottom of what happened exactly, but there's one thing I'm certain of already. You saved my life, Ollie. And not just mine: the lives of everyone who was in that room.'

Ollie blushed. 'I didn't exactly . . . I mean, it wasn't just me. To be honest, I didn't really do anything, other than pull you from the stage. And your arm . . .'

'My arm is fine,' the prime minister insisted. 'Bones heal. As do dislocated shoulders, I'm relieved to say.' She took Ollie's good hand with hers. 'But please do not underestimate what you accomplished, Ollie. There is a fine line between modesty and allowing yourself to feel proud.' She shook Ollie's hand, looking at Ollie earnestly as she did so.

Ollie smiled at her, grateful.

'As for your friends,' the prime minister went on, 'I will certainly be thanking them, too. But for the time being I think it would be kinder to let them sleep. It's been a traumatic period. For all of us,' she added, and it occurred to Ollie that she must only just have been released from medical care herself.

The prime minister gave Ollie's hand a squeeze, and then she turned and left the room. Her bodyguard shut the door behind her, casting a wink in Ollie's direction on his way out.

Lily stirred at the sound of the closing door. 'Ollie?' she mumbled, foggily. 'What time is it?'

'It's . . . morning,' Ollie said, still gazing at the door.

Lily sat up, rubbing her eyes. 'Did I miss anything?'

Ollie smiled. 'A bit,' he answered, honestly.

What Ollie had said to the prime minister was true. He *was* eager to get home. They'd been treated well at the hospital, and Ollie had relished the chance to rest, but he missed the Haven. Not so much the ghost station itself, he would have had to admit, but his friends, Aunt Fay, even Flea . . . sort of. And he was desperate to catch up with Jack and Sol.

They'd been admitted to St Thomas' themselves, Ollie knew. After the drama in the assembly hall, Ollie had told the police about the dungeons, and his friends had been rescued – together with all the other children who'd been reported missing and held captive. Jack and Sol had filled Ollie in on all the details, shortly before slipping away from the hospital themselves. But because Ollie and the others had been in isolation, they'd only been able to communicate using a phone Jack had smuggled on to their ward, and Ollie was looking forward to seeing them in person. And Jack, he knew, was desperate to finally be reunited with her brother.

Errol was coming with them to the Haven, it had been decided. The hospital had apparently tried to contact Errol's stepfather as well, and he'd proven as elusive as the fictional parents Jack had invented for Ollie and Lily. The nurses had left messages, sent emails, even written a letter, but Errol's stepfather clearly didn't want to know. The news had wounded Errol, Ollie had seen, but at least he finally knew the truth about the man who'd claimed to care for him. And Ollie was certain Errol would fit in perfectly at the Haven, especially with his big sister there to watch over him.

After a final, surprisingly edible breakfast on the ward, Ollie, Lily and Errol stole past the nurses' station and down the stairwell around the corner from the lifts. They emerged into the hospital car park, and from there made their way to the banks of the Thames. After pausing briefly to soak in the autumn sun, they found an entrance to the sewers close to Westminster Bridge, and were soon splashing a path towards the Haven. Ollie would never have thought he'd be so glad to be surrounded by the stench of sewage.

When they finally reached the entrance to the ghost station, Ollie found himself feeling suddenly uncertain. He'd been so focused on getting back home, he hadn't paused to wonder what sort of welcome there'd be in store for him. When he'd departed on the mission to Forest Mount, at least half the Haven had turned against him, and Flea was primed to take over from Ollie as leader, subject to the election Ollie had promised him. Had Flea been campaigning in Ollie's absence, Ollie wondered? Would *anyone* still welcome him home?

Yet when the secret door clicked open, and Ollie and the others entered the main hall, all his worries receded. Lily had messaged to say they were on their way, and it was as though the entire Haven community had gathered to wait for them. As Ollie led his companions into the ghost station, the packed hall erupted into spontaneous applause. Ollie saw Song, and Erik, and Keya, and Imani, and Jack, and Sol, and all the other children he counted as his friends, all whooping and whistling and clapping their hands.

After all the time Ollie had spent at Forest Mount, amid the stuffy halls and musty corridors, and the poisonous atmosphere that Crowe – and even Strain – had allowed to spread, it was like being whisked aloft on a gust of fresh air. Or, like waking from a dream, and emerging blinking into a world that was at once familiar and safe.

The biggest cheer was reserved for Errol. When the younger boy stepped from behind Ollie, the applause surged to a new level, as though someone had dialled the volume up to maximum. Errol flushed, and looked behind him, as though expecting the prime minister herself to have appeared at his shoulder, and that just made the Haven kids roar even louder.

Sol had moved forwards to shake Ollie's hand. 'The video,' he explained, leaning close so Ollie would hear him. 'The camera footage of what happened in the assembly hall. Everyone's watched it. All we see of you is the back of your head, and Lily's not even in shot, but Errol is there front and centre. That moment when he leaps up and grabs Crowe's hand . . .' Sol shook his head in wonder. 'It was like watching England score a penalty in the World Cup.'

Ollie beamed back at him, then turned and started applauding Errol himself. As he did so, there was a sudden commotion, and the crowd that had gathered around Errol began to part. Ollie watched, trying to work out what was happening – and saw Jack appear from amid the press of people.

'Errol!'

She rolled forwards, and Errol turned. He was already beaming, but when he saw Jack, his smile split his face from ear to ear. He threw himself at his sister, clasping her as though he would never let go. Jack hugged him back. With her eyes screwed tight and her chin pressed against her brother's shoulder, Ollie had never seen her looking so happy.

She met Ollie's eye, and the two of them exchanged grins.

After a moment the applause died down, to be replaced by excited chatter, and a hand on Ollie's shoulder pulled him round.

'Welcome back, PJ. I hope you're ready for another fight.'

Inwardly Ollie sighed, but he wasn't surprised, and the euphoria of their homecoming did something to offset his sudden weariness. 'Hello, Flea. It's good to see you back on your feet.'

Flea nodded at Ollie's sling. 'What did you do, scrape your elbow?'

Ollie gave a snort. 'Something like that.'

Flea sneered knowingly. 'Now about that election,' he said. 'I hope you don't think you're wriggling out of it just because you fluked another win.'

'Ollie didn't fluke anything, Fleabag, and you know it.' Sol and the rest of the investigations team were gathering round. 'You saw the video, you know what happened,' Sol went on.

'And you know what Ollie and the others have been through. At least give him a chance to walk through the door.'

'It's fine, Sol,' said Ollie. 'I gave Flea my word. We'll have the election, just as I—'

'No.'

All eyes turned towards Lily.

'I've been thinking,' she said. 'And what I've decided is, neither of you should be leader.'

Ollie stared at her in surprise. Flea looked as shocked as Ollie was.

'What are you saying, sis? Don't tell me *you* want to be leader?'

'Well . . . Yes, actually.'

This time Flea looked at Ollie, incredulous.

'But not just me,' said Lily. '*All* of us. We should form a council. A *democracy*. If we need to decide on something, we take a vote. Among the investigations team if it's something to do with a mission. And if it affects everyone at the Haven, we open it wider. One person, one vote. And majority rules.'

Ollie was already grinning. Flea opened his mouth to argue, but no sound came out.

'We'll need a chairperson, of course,' Lily pressed, taking advantage of her brother's silence. 'And my vote is for Ollie. Sorry, Fletcher,' she added. 'You're my brother, and I love you, kind of, but everybody has their strengths. And yours are more . . . physical.'

Flea managed to look pleased and offended at the same time.

'Seconded,' said Sol. 'Ollie for chairperson. Anyone else?'

He cast around, as Jack, Song and Erik all raised their hands. Flea made to protest, but at the show of unanimity around him, he seemed to realise there was nothing he could say. He folded his arms in a huff.

'That's settled then,' said Lily. 'And that's the way it's going to be, until a majority vote elects a new chairperson. And in the meantime, all the important decisions are shared.' She looked at Ollie as she spoke. 'It's not fair that one person should carry all the responsibility. And it's not right that power should be in a single pair of hands. That's why with Dodge, it . . .' Her voice wavered, and she took a breath. 'That's why it went wrong before,' she said.

To Ollie it looked as though she meant to say something more, but she clearly didn't trust herself. And by Ollie's reckoning, she'd already said what they needed to hear.

Ollie nodded at her, and Lily, eyes glistening, nodded back.

'Ollie?' It was Keya. 'Sorry to interrupt, but . . . Well. Welcome back, first of all.' She gave Ollie a hug, and Ollie noticed her glance afterwards at Lily. The two girls smiled at each other awkwardly. 'Also,' Keya said, 'Aunt Fay wants to see you. She said you had a visitor. She asked if you could come and find her once you'd said your hellos.'

'Sure, but . . . a visitor?' said Ollie. '*Here?*'

Keya shrugged. With another quick glance at Lily, she moved out of Ollie's way.

Ollie started to move off. Then he turned back towards his friends. 'This sounds as if it might be council business. Wouldn't you say?'

28 UNEXPECTED QUARTERS

As the investigations team walked together to find Aunt Fay, Lily fell in at Ollie's shoulder.

'About what you said to Crowe in the assembly hall . . .' she said. 'Would you really have let him in? To the Haven, I mean. Even after everything he did?'

Ollie had been pondering the same thing himself. During the time they'd spent in St Thomas' – the nights in particular – he'd found himself pondering a lot of things.

'I don't think it would have been possible,' Ollie answered. 'The police would have wanted to deal with him first.'

'But you wanted to save him?' Lily pressed. 'You *would* have let him in, if you could have?'

'If I could have . . . yes,' said Ollie.

'*Why?*'

'Honestly? Because I felt sorry for him. You heard what he said about his parents, about how he had nothing left to live for. He didn't *choose* to be the way he was. Or, I don't know. Maybe he did, but only because he couldn't see another way. And that's what the Haven is all about, isn't it? Saving kids – from themselves sometimes, if that's what it takes.'

Lily frowned at the floor. 'I guess,' she conceded. 'But I'm still not sure I would have voted in favour.'

Ollie sighed. 'To be honest, I'm not sure either. I mean, I know how I would have voted, but I'm not convinced it would have been the right decision.'

There was a small sub-chamber just off the main hall, too awkwardly shaped to be used for sleeping quarters, and Keya had told them they would find Aunt Fay there. Aunt Fay had been using the space to try to grow things – with limited success. Some of the children had designed and installed some stackable soil trays, as well as a system of LED lighting, but it remained a long way from Aunt Fay's rooftop garden at the old Haven. Whenever Ollie thought about that garden, and the love Aunt Fay had put into nurturing the plants there, he felt a fresh wave of sadness. He'd made a promise to himself that, wherever they ended up after the ghost station, he'd make sure there was space for Aunt Fay to begin again.

'Aunt Fay? Are you in here?'

Ollie winced at the sudden brightness as he led the others into the room. When his eyes adjusted, he stopped short, and felt his friends collide clumsily behind him.

'*You?*' he blurted.

Aunt Fay was sitting at a little table she normally used for tending to her plants. The surface was clear now, but for a pot of tea. Seated across from her, on a metal stool just like Aunt Fay's, was Mr Ross.

Ross rose as Ollie and the others appeared through the archway.

'Ollie Turner,' he said. 'Or should I say *Chambers*? It's a pleasure to finally meet you. Properly, I mean.' He stepped and offered out his hand. Ollie didn't take it, and Ross let his hand drop. He chuckled, and it was a sly, slippery sound. But for the first time that Ollie had witnessed, Ross was smiling, and his smile completely changed his face. Before he'd seemed shrewd and calculating, but that smile made him appear more . . . innocent.

'I told you he didn't trust me,' he said, still chuckling, and tipping his chin towards his shoulder.

Aunt Fay rose from her seat. 'Ollie? This is Montgomery Ross. Monty, to his friends.'

Ross shifted uncomfortably. 'Come now, Felicity. I haven't gone by that name in thirty years.'

Monty? *Felicity?* It took Ollie a moment to recall that Felicity was Aunt Fay's real name. Felicity Fagin. But how did Ross know that? How did he know Aunt Fay at *all*?

'Who else has joined us?' said Aunt Fay, brightly, lifting her unseeing gaze over Ollie's shoulder. 'Lily, is that you? And Fletcher?'

'We're all here, Aunt Fay,' said Jack. 'All the members of the investigations team.'

'The council,' Erik corrected her, which caused Aunt Fay to frown for a moment – and then to smile.

'The council,' she echoed, and she nodded approvingly. 'Well, children, Monty – Montgomery, rather – was once in exactly the position you are. He was a member of the Haven before you were even born.'

Ollie glanced at the others – at Jack, Sol and Lily in particular – and from their expressions they were clearly as surprised as he was.

'Felicity and I have kept in touch over the years,' Ross explained. 'She told me all about you, Ollie. That's why I was so surprised to see you at Forest Mount. I tried to talk to you a couple of times, but you always seemed to . . . slip away.'

'I . . . I thought you were part of it,' Ollie said. 'The plan, the attempt on the prime minister's life . . .'

Ross suddenly turned serious. 'And that's partly why I came here, Ollie. The prime minister thanked you personally, I believe, but she doesn't know who you really are, nor where any of you come from. And you can relax, by the way: your secret is safe.' He twitched a smile at the murmurs of relief. 'But as I *did* know where to find you,' he went on, 'I felt it my duty to reiterate the PM's appreciation. The *country's* appreciation, in fact, for everything you did.'

This time when he offered his hand, Ollie took it. He watched as Ross shook hands with each of Ollie's friends in turn.

'I also want to reassure you all that the culprits have been rounded up,' Ross said. 'It is over. Truly.'

Ollie exhaled in relief. That was what had been bothering him most during the time he'd spent in the hospital. The fear that Sikes might have escaped justice yet again. 'You mean . . .' he started to say, and Ross nodded reassuringly.

'I mean, everyone at the school has been interviewed, the plan has been exposed, and Professor Strain is now safely behind bars.'

'Wait,' said Ollie. '*Professor Strain?*'

'That's right,' said Ross, proudly.

'But Strain didn't do this. It was Maddy Sikes. It was Sikes all along. Strain was just the fall guy. A cover story!'

Ross jerked his chin in surprise. 'Maddy Sikes? The businesswoman? Ms Sikes was killed in the terrorist attacks last summer. I hardly think—'

'She wasn't killed,' Ollie insisted. 'And those weren't terrorist attacks. That was all Sikes as well!'

Ross showed his incredulity.

'Monty,' said Aunt Fay, 'I would urge you to listen to what Ollie has to say.'

'But Felicity,' Ross responded. He smiled, maddeningly. 'We have testimony. *Everyone* at the school verified that they were working for Strain. And he has a history, you know. A proven record of fostering dissent. And links to the Russian government, which as we all know—'

'You're wrong,' Ollie told him, simply. 'If you pin this on Strain, you'll be doing exactly what Sikes planned. And she'll try again. She won't stop until she gets what she wants.'

Ross's patience was clearly wearing thin. 'And what exactly *does* she want, young man? This . . . this *dead* woman. Who nobody but you has made the slightest suggestion was involved?'

'She wants it all,' Ollie responded. 'Money, power – Sikes wants everything she can get her hands on. And she'll kill anyone who stands in her way.'

This time Ross laughed out loud.

'Ollie,' said Jack. 'The school . . .'

'Right,' said Ollie, nodding his head. 'Sikes *owns* Forest Mount. She told us. All you have to do is . . .'

But Ross was shaking his head. 'Forest Mount was owned by a charity. A *bogus* charity, it turns out, set up by Strain himself. Which is the other reason I'm here, as it happens.'

Ollie looked at Jack. 'She covered her tracks,' he said. 'She's like . . . like a ghost.'

'Look,' said Ross. His jacket was on his stool, and he picked it up. 'Clearly this is a lot to digest. I came here to thank you, which I have done, and also to reassure you – although it seems in that regard I have been less successful. There was something else I was intending to tell you, but . . . Well. Perhaps it would be better if you heard that part from Felicity.'

Ollie could only shake his head dumbly. He was right. He'd known he should be afraid, and he was *right*. Sikes had got away after all.

'Do you know,' said Ross, evidently recovering some of his good humour, 'I was one of those who found this place.' He cast around, his eyes taking in the arched antechamber of the ghost station. 'I helped clear it, kit it out. We called it . . . what was it? The lifeboat. No, the *life raft*. That was it. Some of my friends at the Haven had doubts it would ever be used, but it seems it was worth the effort after all.' He smiled nostalgically, but his smile faded when he noticed the way Ollie and the others were looking at him.

He coughed. 'Well. I think I can probably find my own way out. Felicity,' he said, nodding. 'Ollie,' he added, more uncertainly, and he nodded to the others as well.

They cleared a path for him, and watched as Ross took his leave.

When he was gone, Ollie turned to Aunt Fay.

'She still has the book, Aunt Fay. Maddy Sikes does. Crowe's black book, the one containing everybody's secrets. She could still *use* it.'

Aunt Fay's features had clouded. She didn't say anything, but she reached out and touched Ollie's cheek.

'Why didn't he believe what Ollie was saying?' said Jack. 'Why didn't he listen?'

Aunt Fay sighed. 'Monty is a good man. And he has done a lot over the years for the Haven, not least in keeping our secret safe. But some people, when they grow up . . . their perspective changes. They stop . . . imagining. They decide to view the world based only on the evidence before their eyes.' She smiled, sadly. 'Which is wise, I would say, in most instances. It is a *safe* path, but also a narrow one.'

'Would he have believed us earlier?' Ollie asked. 'If we'd gone to him when we suspected Strain, do you think he would have listened then? Could we have stopped the attack completely, before it even began?'

Aunt Fay turned to him. 'What do you think, Ollie?'

'I think . . . I think he would have asked for evidence. Which we didn't have. Nothing conclusive, anyway.'

Aunt Fay bobbed her head. 'I think you are right. And if it's any consolation, it seems to me that you did everything you could. All of you. And this time, fortunately, it was enough.'

Almost, Ollie thought to himself, his mind on Sikes again. *It was almost enough. But not quite.*

'What was the other thing?' said Sol.

Aunt Fay turned to the sound of his voice. 'The other thing?'

'Right,' said Song. 'Ross said you had something else to tell us.'

Aunt Fay's face suddenly brightened. 'Ah yes!' She reached with her arms, gathering Ollie and the others in close. 'Monty, bless him, has found us a home.'

'A home?' Jack echoed.

'That was the reason I was in touch with him in the first place,' explained Aunt Fay. 'As I said, Monty has always been one of the Haven's dearest friends. I told him of our troubles, how the old Haven had been destroyed, and I asked him if there was anything he could do to help. There wasn't – until now.'

'So . . . where is it?' said Flea. '*What* is it?'

'I believe some of you know it already,' said Aunt Fay. 'Monty did his best to describe it to me, and I have to say it sounds just perfect. He said it sat high on a hill, not far from the centre of the city, but well removed from sight. It is well equipped, Monty said, with more than enough space for us all. And there is a garden,' she added, turning to Ollie. 'More than a garden, in fact. An entire woodland just waiting to be nurtured.'

'You don't mean . . .' said Lily.

'*Forest Mount*,' said Ollie, and smiles of bemusement flickered around the group.

'But how is that possible?' said Jack. '*Maddy Sikes* owns Forest Mount. Doesn't she?'

'Not any more,' said Aunt Fay. 'The charity she set up, apparently to cover her tracks, has been disbanded, and its assets seized by the government, which means the school itself has been closed. Monty isn't a powerful man, but he has influence enough. And once Forest Mount has been thoroughly decontaminated, which he estimates should be done within the month, he will see to it that it is also condemned. To all intents and purposes, anyway. As far as anyone who is looking will see, the building will be empty, sitting there waiting to be sold. Which Monty will personally ensure never happens.'

Ollie looked around at his friends. The delight was written on their faces. The relief, as well, that they would finally be able to escape the ghost station. And Aunt Fay was right: Forest Mount was perfect. Or it would be, once the atmosphere there had been allowed to air.

'You did it, Aunt Fay,' said Lily, squeezing the old woman tightly.

Aunt Fay laughed as though she'd been tickled. 'No, Lily. *You* did it. All of you, together. We had some help, in the end, but I think we were due a bit of luck. Wouldn't you say?'

Ollie remembered something Aunt Fay had told him when they'd been talking in the tunnels, just before he'd set off on the mission to Forest Mount. *Keep faith in yourself*, she'd said. *If you manage to do that, solutions often present themselves from the most unexpected of quarters.*

As the others celebrated, Ollie removed himself slightly from the group. Allow yourself to feel proud, the prime minister had told him, and he *was* proud. Of his friends, of what they had achieved, and of everything the Haven stood for. But the fight wasn't over, Ollie knew – not while Maddy Sikes was still out there. Maybe the Haven had won the battle, but Sikes wouldn't give up without a war.

READ ON –
OLLIE'S ADVENTURES
CONTINUE IN ...

THE HAVEN
DEADFALL

There wasn't much time.

Lily had only bought herself a twenty-minute window, meaning she had approximately six minutes left before the opportunity was lost. Either she found a way to hack the electronic lock on her prison cell door, or she would remain trapped in this godforsaken pit – perhaps forever.

The problem was, on top of the time she'd wasted simply trying to access the door's control unit, she couldn't be sure which circuit would release the lock, and which would fuse the door permanently shut. And there was the danger she would electrocute herself before she had a chance to find out, simply by touching the exposed circuitry.

Realising she was sweating – from the nerves as much as from the sweltering heat inside the prison cell – Lily turned her attention back to the control board.

Top circuit or bottom? Which would open the door, and which would seal it shut? It was fifty-fifty. Lily had a small piece of exposed wire in her hand, which she'd swiped from the prison workshop earlier that day, and she raised it nervously to the circuit board. Top or bottom? Heads or tails? In her mind she flipped a coin, and watched as it landed on . . .

Tails.

She moved the wire towards the bottom loop on the circuit board, meaning to bridge the metal solder and create a short circuit – but at the last moment she changed her mind and chose the top loop instead, for no other reason than her instinct telling her to do so. She flinched, expecting a shock, but there was nothing more than a light tingle, like pins and needles, spreading from her fingertips into her palm. There was a fizz as the circuit board fried itself, followed by a decisive-sounding *click*.

The door remained resolutely shut.

Lily cursed. Rather than freeing herself, she'd trapped herself inside. There would be no escape now. So much for her plan. She hadn't even got as far as the corridor outside her cell – and this was supposed to be the easy part!

All she could do now was sit and wait for the guards who'd been stationed in the corridor to come back, at which point there would be a full search of the entire cell block. When they found the damage to the control panel in Lily's cell, there was no telling what they would do to her. Beat her, torture her, kill her? Anything was possible, because this wasn't an ordinary prison, and the normal rules didn't apply. Lily had been here less than a fortnight – twelve days, according to the notches she'd marked on her cell wall – but already she'd witnessed first-hand how brutal the prison staff could be.

She swore again, and beat her hand against the door. She shut her eyes, furious with herself – and when she opened them again, she saw the door had slid slightly ajar. Casting off her surprise, Lily hooked her fingers around the door and tried to pull it open further. It was like trying to prise apart the doors on an elevator, but at least the lock had been disabled. She'd chosen the right circuit after all! The click she'd heard had obviously been the catch disengaging. It hadn't occurred to her that, to open the door, she would have to try to move it manually.

Using all her strength, Lily tugged at the door until there was gap wide enough for her to squeeze through. She poked her head out first, fully expecting to turn and see Warden Bricknell, a sneer on her craggy face. Either the warden or one of the guards, who as well as truncheons carried electric cattle prods.

But there was no one.

Lily slipped into the corridor and paused just long enough to try to gauge how much time she had until the guards returned. It was a matter of seconds now, surely. Lily could hear the commotion in the recreation area, which was only two corners away. The fire she'd set as a distraction would probably already have been extinguished, though with any luck the smoke would be lingering.

But even as she listened, Lily could hear the guards' voices getting louder, meaning they were on their way back.

It was time to go.

PHOTO © JUSTINE STODDARD

SIMON LELIC IS A WRITER OF CRIME AND THRILLER NOVELS FOR ADULTS – WINNER OF THE BETTY TRASK AWARD, SHORTLISTED FOR THE CWA DAGGER AWARDS AND THE GALAXY NATIONAL BOOK AWARDS.

HE LIVES IN BRIGHTON WITH HIS WIFE AND THREE CHILDREN. OTHER THAN HIS FAMILY, READING IS HIS BIGGEST PASSION. HE ALSO HOLDS A BLACK BELT IN KARATE, IN WHICH HE TRAINS DAILY.

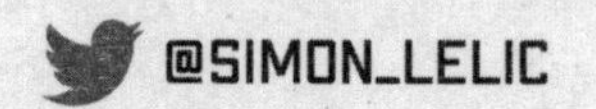